Time was running out and one last chance was all he had...

Channing brushed by the receptionist without saying hello and headed to his office. The hearing in court that morning had been a routine matter. He had filed several evidentiary motions in a burglary case, hoping to prevent the jury from hearing of his client's prior felony convictions when the case came to trial in two weeks. The judge had agreed to suppress the evidence as long as his client wouldn't testify that he had a clean record or a good reputation in the community. His client congratulated him and invited him to lunch as they left the courtroom, but Channing declined.

His mind was on other matters. In less than two weeks the lottery ticket would expire, but he would have at least one good chance to find it. In three days Susan would be at her lawyer's office in Culpeper for depositions. Channing had arranged to have Billy wait outside the law office, watching for Susan to leave the building when the business was concluded. Billy would follow her wherever she went. Channing had not told Billy about the books, fearing that he might inspect them and find the ticket. If he did, he would surely steal it.

Channing instructed Billy to call him as soon as he knew where Susan had been staying. Channing would take it from there. If the books were not at Susan's hideout, he would have to resort to more dangerous tactics. He or Billy would threaten her and use whatever force was necessary to make her talk.

"In this gripping, clever novel, reminiscent of Scott Smith's bestseller, *A Simple Plan*, the author takes what begins as a reasonable path to riches and shows the many ways a sure thing quickly can devolve into uncontrolled chaos. Attorney Channing Booker lives and works in Charlottesville, Virginia, where he spends most of his free time betting on various sporting events and cheating on his wife, Susan. Channing has lost most of his money on bad bets, until one day he buys a lottery ticket at Wally's Quick Mart and finds he's just won $241 million. You'd think he'd be overjoyed, but Channing is such a sleazebag that he's annoyed that he's going to have to split it with his wife, who he is planning to divorce. He decides to entrust the ticket to one of his drinking buddies, Sully Pendleton, and have him cash it in and then secretly turn the money over to Channing after his divorce is finalized. After all, what could go wrong with that plan? Obviously, everything. But the author's genius is in eschewing the obvious plot arc and supplying readers with all the many other things that could possibly go wrong, most of them completely unexpected. Threaded within the plot twists are other stories of secondary characters, some hapless, some heroic, that in the end knit together to create a terrific, satisfying read." ~ Amazon Breakthrough Novel Award Contest

"I know it is a reviewer's cliché, but *The Ticket* is a page turner. Once I began reading, I couldn't put it down until I learned the fate of 2, 6, 9, 17, 55, 12. Economists are not great forecasters, but I predict that readers of Shackelford's first novel will demand that he supply more titles in the future." ~ Kenneth G. Elzinga: aka Marshall Jevons, author of the Henry Spearman mystery novels and Mystery Writers of America Edgar judge for the Best Mystery Novel of the Year

"The hunt for the lost lottery ticket is exciting, dangerous, and fun. Fred Shackelford juggles a cast of characters who are resourceful, driven, complex, potentially lethal, and always entertaining. The villain, Channing Booker—the name is a great pun—is both amusing and frightening in his evil ways. The author works insights about the law into the quick moving plot, and he keeps readers tense about impending dangers. For fans of thrillers and of legal novels, Fred

Shackelford artfully marries both genres in this superb début." ~ John Jebb, author of *True Crime: Virginia*

"*The Ticket* takes you into the mind of a true sleazebag. Channing Booker wins a jackpot lottery ticket one day and loses it the next. This blunder sets off a captivating chase, keeping the reader guessing at every turn. Fred Shackelford, the author and a keen legal mind himself, weaves obstacles throughout, confronting his protagonist with colorful characters who thwart Channing's progress and confound his oily maneuvers. Channing is a jerk, no doubt; so why do we keep hoping he'll win? Maybe, we want a sequel! Beware! The cunning suspense herein will disrupt your sleep. A breathless read!" ~ Janet Martin, author of *The Christmas Swap*

"Fans of the film and TV series *Fargo* will relish the wicked plot twists Shackelford concocts in this winning thriller. Sleazy Charlottesville, Va., attorney Channing Booker, a compulsive gambler whose addiction has devastated his assets, gets a chance at a new start when he wins more than $200 million in the state lottery. With his marriage to his wife, Susan, unraveling, Channing plots to keep what her share of the winnings would be from her. He intends to give the winning ticket to a friend who would cash it in and give the bulk of the jackpot back to him after the divorce is finalized. He conceals the ticket in one of Susan's books, but he's later horrified to find that the book, Susan, and all the rest of her possessions have vanished from their home. That development sets up a delicious cat-and-mouse story line, as Susan attempts to begin a new life away from Channing, who becomes increasingly desperate to find her and the book before the 180-day deadline for coming forward with the lottery ticket expires. Shackelford makes the most of his intriguing premise." ~ *Publishers Weekly*

In addition to winning honorable mention for the Eric Hoffer Award, *The Ticket* was a finalist for the National Indie Excellence Awards, a finalist for both the Clue Award and the Mystery & Mayhem Award from Chanticleer Book Reviews, and a quarterfinalist in the Amazon Breakthrough Novel Award Contest.

ACKNOWLEDGEMENTS

Everyone in my family helped me in some way as I wrote *The Ticket* and searched for a publisher. Many others provided helpful advice, proofreading assistance, or general encouragement. If any flaws remain in the book, in spite of their best efforts, those mistakes are mine alone. In addition to my family, I gratefully acknowledge the assistance of Alden Bigelow, Gale Burns, Janet Martin Carmichael, Ken Elzinga, Hugh Gildea, Lucy Ivey, John Jebb, Jim Jones, Noël King, Barney Mazursky, Bill McPherson, Brad Pettit, Al and Pam Trigger, and Gail Wiley.

THE TICKET

Fred Shackelford

A Black Opal Books Publication

GENRE: CRIME THRILLER/SUSPENSE/MYSTERY

THE TICKET
Copyright © 2016 by Fred Shackelford
Cover Design by Jackson Cover Designs
Author photo by Michael Bailey
All cover art copyright © 2016
All Rights Reserved
Print ISBN: 978-1-644370-09-4

Mega Millions logo is used on the cover with permission from the Georgia Lottery Corporation.

First Publication: DECEMBER 2016

Published by Black Opal Books **http://www.blackopalbooks.com**

DEDICATION

The Ticket is dedicated to the members of my family, all of whom supported me as I wrote my first novel. Thank you so much for your advice, patience, and love. In addition, I dedicate *The Ticket* to three of my former teachers. Clarence W. Chambers and John A. Stillwell, who are now deceased, taught me English at Woodberry Forest School, and Kenneth G. Elzinga taught me economics at the University of Virginia. These gentlemen were inspiring and dedicated educators, and their legacy extends well beyond the confines of their classrooms.

CHAPTER 1

Channing Booker's hand trembled as he held the slip of paper. Bleary-eyed from a Friday night of drinking and revelry, he wasn't sure if what he saw was real. In the darkness of his study, he stared at the Virginia Lottery's website in the pale glow of a smartphone screen. Slowly he read the six winning Mega Millions numbers one more time. He had been playing the lottery for at least a decade but had little to show for it—until now.

Glancing back and forth between the winning numbers on his smartphone and a row of digits on the slip of paper, he confirmed that his ticket was a winner. Tonight's projected jackpot was $239 million, but with a flurry of last-minute ticket buying it may have inched up another million or so.

Knowing he had beaten odds of 303 million to one, Channing hoped his luck would hold when the final results were announced. Surely no one deserved a windfall more than he did, and he pondered the injustice that would befall him if someone else held a lucky ticket. His elation began to ebb as he considered the possibility that he might have to share his jackpot with another player. It ebbed even further as he realized that his new fortune, in whatever amount, would have to be divided between him and the woman who was sleeping upstairs.

Channing began to contemplate the radical changes that his sudden stroke of luck would bring. He was almost certain that Susan's lawyer would be filing divorce papers soon, and until tonight he had dreaded the monetary implications of being single again. His few remaining assets would be snatched away by an irate wife, a greedy divorce lawyer, and a hostile judge. *But they can only take what they can find.*

He would wait until the divorce was final before cashing in the ticket, speeding the litigation along with magnanimous concessions and generous settlement offers. At least they would seem generous coming from a man whose apparent wealth had dwindled. Without children, there would be no protracted fight over custody or child support. He could wrap up the whole sorry process in a couple of months, grab his lottery winnings, reclaim his Mercedes, and retire with his favorite girlfriend to an island in the Caribbean.

As he leaned back on the couch, his pulse rate gradually returned to normal, and the shock of seeing the winning numbers on his ticket subsided. Minutes passed as he reveled in his vision of a carefree future. The house was silent, except for the gentle purr of Tony, the resident Siamese cat, who was curled up in a ball at the other end of the couch. Unfazed by the silent drama that was unfolding before him, Tony watched placidly as his master stared at the ceiling. A sliver of moonlight peeked through the curtains and cast faint shadows around the room. Channing set the winning ticket on the small mahogany table at the end of the couch and gazed at it for several minutes.

His thoughts turned to the practical implications of his plan. He knew that when he cashed in the lottery ticket his win would be a matter of public record. Virginia's lottery rules required jackpot winners to appear at a press conference, shake hands with an official, and accept an oversized replica of a check. Although he had no expertise in family law, he suspected that Susan's lawyer could reopen the divorce case and seize much of his new fortune. His precarious legal position called for a more sophisticated plan to preserve the money until it could be secretly deposited in an offshore bank account.

He assumed that he could count on help from one of his drinking buddies, Sully Pendleton. A local attorney who practiced out of a small office downtown, Sully was Channing's closest confidant. The two of them had collaborated on a commercial fraud case some years ago, and a friendship developed and grew over time. In addition to drinking and pursuing women, they shared an interest in professional football and often attended Carolina Panthers games together.

In fact, Channing was planning to leave with Sully the following Sunday morning to see the Panthers play the Falcons. On the way to the game he would ask Sully to safeguard the ticket until his divorce was final, and then wait a decent interval before cashing it in, as if

Sully were the lucky winner. Sully could take a percentage off the top, plus enough to pay the taxes that would accrue, and then quietly wire the balance to an account that Channing would open at a bank in the Cayman Islands.

Channing hoped his friend would accept a share of eight to ten percent for his trouble, but if he wanted more, the additional expense would be worth it. A matter of this delicacy required the sensitivity and discretion that only Sully could bring to the task.

Having spent years perfecting the art of calculating odds, point spreads, and payoffs, Channing was able to do the math in his head. Taking the lump sum payout would reduce the $239 million pot by about half. Federal and state income taxes, which would be assessed to Sully, would eat up a portion of the balance. He guessed that Sully's fee, plus a deduction for taxes, might siphon off about forty-five percent. Assuming there was only one winning ticket, Channing would be left with roughly $66 million. He was confident that this would buy a nice piece of real estate where he could park his Mercedes and girlfriend du jour, even at the inflated prices that prevailed in the Caymans.

Although he thought he could trust Sully, it occurred to Channing that his friend might develop amnesia and claim the ticket as his own. Perhaps in Sully's mind a lottery jackpot would be fair compensation for the loss of Channing's friendship. Channing would need some insurance in case the plan went awry—some proof that Sully was simply holding his ticket for safekeeping.

On the shelves behind the couch was a row of rare books that Susan had collected over the years. Channing picked up the ticket and carefully placed it on one of the shelves, letting it rest upright against a row of rare, limited edition Charles Dickens novels. He quietly slipped into an adjoining room and groped in a closet until he found a camera, thinking that its picture quality would be superior to what his smartphone could produce. He returned and pointed the lens at the ticket, leaning over the couch until he was about a foot away from it. The flash blinded him for a moment, but as he looked at the camera's display screen he could see that the image was clear. All the numbers on the ticket were in sharp focus, and now he could prove that the ticket was his, without having to sign his name on the back.

He set the camera in the mahogany table's open drawer and eased it shut. Picking up the winning ticket, he pulled one of the Dickens novels from the shelf. Its ornate leather jacket protected a fragile binding, and the title was printed in elaborate gold lettering. He opened the back cover and slipped the ticket behind the jacket, pushing it all the way in for a snug fit. He turned the book over in his hands and read its title several times until he was certain he would remember it. Placing the book back in position, he turned around and silently crept upstairs to the bedroom.

Susan was under the covers, facing away from him and apparently in a deep sleep. He slipped into bed without disturbing her, smiling as he thought about his incredible luck. He had often dreamed of winning a lottery jackpot, but, in the past, the big money had always gone to some undeserving factory worker or senior citizen. He decided to delay his celebration, as he had already arranged a date with a recent acquaintance, Melissa Sorensen, for tomorrow's Baltimore Ravens game. It was a Saturday game near the end of the season, and he recalled that the Ravens were favored by six points over the Bengals.

As Channing drifted off to sleep, Susan opened her eyes and glanced at her bedside clock. It was one-thirty-five a.m.

Channing woke up six hours later and crawled slowly out of bed. Susan was still curled up under a thick blanket, her head buried in a pillow. Showering and dressing quickly, he headed downstairs to check the latest point spreads.

Walking with a newfound swagger to his Volvo, he nestled into the driver's seat. He brushed the palm of his right hand across the fabric upholstery that covered the passenger seat. Soon he would be sitting on fine leather seats, the kind he had grown accustomed to before a creditor repossessed his Mercedes. With an air of satisfaction, he started the engine.

As the car headed down the driveway, Susan sat up in bed. She reached for the phone and placed the call that would change her life forever.

CHAPTER 2

Channing drove effortlessly through the streets of Charlottesville, which were nearly empty in the early hours of the morning. Ordinarily, on football game days, his attention was focused on injury reports and playoff implications, but today his mind was swirling with thoughts of his winning lottery ticket.

It was probably safe to leave the ticket at home through the weekend. There was only a slight chance that Susan would decide to read the particular book he had chosen as a hiding place, and even lower odds that she would peek inside the back jacket. First thing Monday morning, he would stash the ticket in a safe deposit box.

He would need to do some basic research to carry out his plan. He had already mastered every detail as to lottery odds, jackpot amounts, and purchase options. But he never had occasion to consider the implications of actually winning a jackpot. He doubted that the lottery's website would give advice on how to win $239 million without telling your wife.

Channing knew his scheme would more likely remain secret if he personally researched lottery procedures, technicalities of divorce law, and other issues, but the thought of doing this work himself was repugnant. A senior partner of his standing and tenure shouldn't compromise his dignity. This was a job for his law firm's newest associate, Winston DeHart.

Winston was single, seemed to have few friends, and kept a remarkably low profile at the firm. He rarely said a word to anyone and spent most of his time burrowing into law review articles and running Westlaw searches on the computer in his office. Fresh out of law school, Winston willingly carried out even the most monotonous research assignments. Channing would tell him the work was for a client who wanted to remain anonymous. He could trust Winston to keep quiet.

Channing's thoughts returned to traffic as he sped up to get through a yellow light. Heading north to pick up Melissa, he passed an array of car dealerships on both sides of Seminole Trail. He ignored the fleets of Hondas, Chevys, and Toyotas that were on display for the common folks, but slowed down as he approached a lot that was graced with a full selection of more appropriate vehicles. He smiled as he cruised past a dozen Porsches and a row of Mercedes coupes that gleamed in the early morning sunlight. He made a mental note to stop by and take a test drive on Monday, after the ticket was safely tucked away in a bank vault.

Melissa waved at him from the door of her condo as he guided his Volvo into a parking space nearby. Channing had met Melissa, a friend of one of the firm's secretaries, a few weeks ago when she stopped by for advice about a speeding ticket. Spotting her in the waiting room, he struck up a conversation and invited her to discuss the case over lunch. Usually one of the junior associates handled routine speeding cases, but Melissa was much prettier than a routine client, and, after a pleasant lunch, Channing decided the matter required his personal attention. He had explained that since she knew one of the secretaries, he would represent her himself, as a professional courtesy.

Traffic was light as they reached the outskirts of the city and drove toward Baltimore. "I don't know much about pro football," Melissa confessed.

"I'll explain the basics," Channing replied, stealing a glance at her legs as he outlined the rules of the game.

Melissa asked a few questions and then tuned the radio to a jazz station and chatted casually about a variety of topics. She carried most of the conversation herself, as Channing's thoughts kept returning to the details of his scheme. He couldn't wait to get through the game, head back to Charlottesville, drop off his date, and find out how many winning tickets there were.

The ride to Baltimore was uneventful, but traffic was brutal as they approached the Ravens' stadium. As his car inched forward in a long line of vehicles, Channing daydreamed of revving up a new Porsche and zipping along an open road in the Caymans. He could see the sparkling turquoise waters of the Caribbean Sea off to his right, with the reflection of a setting sun dancing on their surface. He could smell a hint of salt in the ocean air, tinged with the fragrant aroma of a nearby grove of mango and coconut trees. He could hear the powerful purr of his engine and the rush of wind swirling through his hair. He could feel the force of acceleration as he rounded a curve and surged ahead on a straight stretch of smooth, narrow pavement. Fields of lush grass, dotted with hyacinths and palm trees, were a colorful blur as he flew past them in his coupe.

"Hey, Channing, turn in here," Melissa instructed, drawing him back to reality.

He entered the parking lot, following behind a green pickup truck laden with coolers, a charcoal grill, a portable TV, and an assortment of other game-day necessities. The scent of overcooked hot dogs wafted through the lot as raucous rap music blared from a large van full of scruffy teenagers. As they approached the stadium entrances, Channing noticed a special reserved lot next to a private entrance. Observing the collection of Jaguars, stretch limos, and luxury SUVs, he chuckled at the thought of parking there after collecting his lottery funds.

They settled into their seats and surveyed the players warming up on the field below. Channing checked the lottery's website again on his smartphone, but there was no information about the Mega Millions drawing, other than the list of winning numbers. "I'll get us some hot dogs and popcorn," he volunteered.

"Thanks. I'll hold your binoculars while you're gone."

On the way to the concession stand he detoured into a men's room, squeezing through the crowd until he spied a newspaper on the floor near an open stall. He peeled it off the floor, trying to ignore the footprints and tobacco stains on its sports pages.

Closing the stall door, he sat down and flipped through to the metro section, searching for a lottery update. Seeing nothing about last night's drawing, he assumed the announcement came after press time and would not appear until a later edition was printed. He threw the paper down in disgust and left the bathroom.

As the game progressed, both teams concentrated on a ground game to grind out yardage in a methodical fashion. Late in the fourth quarter, the crowd came alive when a hulking lineman picked off a batted pass and headed toward the goal line, lurching forward like a rambling beer truck. On the next play a fullback crashed into the end zone, allowing the Ravens to escape with a three-point win.

Although the home team failed to cover the point spread, costing Channing $500, he didn't mind losing what was now just chump change.

The drive back to Charlottesville tested Channing's patience as he went through the motions of idle conversation and listened to several more hours of radio jazz. He never suggested listening to news, knowing that any reaction he might have to hearing lottery reports could compromise the secrecy of his plan. He dropped Melissa off and promised to keep in touch. Driving across town, he listened to several different radio stations but heard nothing about the lottery.

Pulling into his driveway, he noticed that Susan's car was gone but assumed she was shopping or at a movie. The lights on the front porch illuminated some unusual tire tracks and footprints in the grass near the house and along the edges of the walkway, which he guessed were left by friends who must have visited Susan earlier in the day. He opened the door and stepped into the front hall, completely unprepared for what awaited him.

CHAPTER 3

From his vantage point near the front entrance, Channing saw that rugs and most of the furniture on the first floor had disappeared, including all of the tables, chairs, and lamps that Susan owned before their marriage. He quickly spied the note that Susan had left on the only table that remained in the front hall. Scribbled on a piece of scrap paper, her message was short and to the point. *Channing, don't try to find me. I will contact you later. Susan.*

Tossing the note aside, Channing raced into the study and stared in disbelief at the disaster in front of him. Strictly speaking, the disaster was what he *didn't* see there. For the most part, the missing furniture was of no concern to Channing. Susan's absence, by itself, was no big deal either. But when he glanced across the empty room, his worst fear was confirmed. The bookshelves were nearly bare. Only a handful of legal treatises were left behind. Susan's entire collection of books, including her set of rare Dickens novels, had vanished.

On the verge of becoming unhinged, Channing ran throughout the house, searching aimlessly for any clue to the fate of his winning ticket. Grabbing a flashlight, he dashed out into the night and scoured the front lawn, hoping that somehow the ticket had escaped before the books were loaded into a moving van. In desperation, he crawled under a row of ornate boxwood, emerging minutes later with nothing to show for his effort except grass stains and grime on his clothes. As midnight approached, he finally gave up, staggered upstairs, and flopped onto the bed. Susan had slipped away without leaving a trace, taking the lottery ticket with her.

When Channing opened his eyes the next morning, Tony's face covered his entire field of vision. The cat's wet tongue licked his forehead, reminding him that it was time to put out another can of liver bits for breakfast. Channing lay motionless as he watched the minutes advance toward nine a.m. on the bedside clock. He was still in the clothes he had worn to the Ravens game the day before. Most of the sweat had dried from his rumpled shirt, but it still had an uncomfortable damp feeling and clung to his body.

The bed and a small table were the only pieces of furniture that remained in the room. Outside the bedroom, the hall was empty and its walls were bare, except for a photo of Tony and a formal portrait taken on the day he and Susan were married.

He had no idea what to do next. Brushing Tony aside, Channing rolled over and stared at the ceiling, hoping for inspiration as he struggled to get a grip on his new reality. It was possible that Susan had discovered the ticket and decided to flee with it, but this seemed unlikely. It would have taken too long to get a moving crew to the house with just a few hours' notice. Even if she tried to cash in the ticket, he could claim a substantial share of the jackpot as long as the two were still married. Of course, she might get a friend to cash it in and funnel the money to her under the table, but Channing doubted she was smart enough to try that. The marriage had been falling apart for years, so the most plausible explanation was that Susan had arranged ahead of time to move away when he was out of town. He had told her several weeks ago that he would be at the Ravens game with a client, so she had time to plan her escape.

He decided that Susan had the ticket, wherever she was, but probably didn't know she had it. Unless the ticket had fallen out of its hiding place, somewhere in the country a moving van was hauling the most valuable bookmark in the world. It was likely that Susan would file for divorce soon, so he needed to delay the proceedings at all costs until he could track down the ticket.

Tony's stomach growled as he began to scratch Channing's leg, escalating his demand for breakfast. "All right, calm down, boy," Channing mumbled as he stroked the cat's fur. "Let's see what's in the kitchen."

Relieved that Susan had left the refrigerator's contents behind, Channing found a bagel and cream cheese for himself and poured a bowl of milk for Tony. As the cat lapped it up, Channing walked to the front door and retrieved the morning newspaper. He spotted the lottery article and studied it carefully.

As the owner of the only winning ticket, he had 180 days to find it and cash it in at lottery headquarters. The ticket would expire and become worthless unless he could find it by next June.

His investigation began as soon as he took a shower and got dressed. There were two houses near enough to be visible from the front lawn. Although he had rarely bothered to speak to his neighbors, Channing approached the first house and knocked on the door. He was able to recall the owners' names before it opened.

"Hi, Greg," he said, leaning forward to shake Greg McDermott's hand. "Channing Booker from next door. We met a couple of years ago at your Christmas party."

Greg's puzzled expression began to fade a bit as he appeared to remember their first meeting. Channing had breezed through on his way to another party, downed generous quantities of spiked eggnog and shrimp, chatted briefly, and then disappeared.

Greg stepped out onto the porch instead of inviting Channing inside. "Oh, yes. Good to see you again," he replied, smiling weakly. "Can I help you with something?"

Channing hesitated, unsure of how much to disclose. "Well, this is somewhat awkward," Channing began, as Greg nodded in agreement. "It seems that my wife has moved out without telling me where she went. We've been having a little friction in our marriage. I was just wondering if she might have said anything to you or Dora about her plans."

Greg inched forward, gently closing the door behind him. "Oh, that's a tough break. Awfully sorry to hear it. I wish I could help, but I haven't seen her recently. She never told me anything about moving." Greg paused and studied the bricks at his feet, wondering what to do next. "I could check with Dora and see if she knows anything," he offered.

Channing sensed that Greg was telling the truth, and he was as uneasy as Greg about their encounter. Seeing no reason to prolong his visit, he remained where he was. "Okay, that would be great. I can just wait here so I don't disturb her."

Appearing relieved, Greg retreated into the house, leaving the door ajar. Channing overheard a short conversation inside as Greg reminded his wife who Channing was and then explained the situation. Dora followed Greg to the door and stepped outside.

"I'm sorry to hear the news about Susan," she said, apparently with genuine disappointment. She and Susan were not particularly close, but the two had sometimes gone to plays or movies together when Channing was away. She was aware that Channing treated his wife poorly, although Susan had been discreet and kept most of the unpleasant details to herself. She had covered her tracks well. "I saw a moving van in the yard yesterday and called Susan on the phone to see what was up. She told me she was moving some furniture to your summer home."

Actually, the cottage on the Outer Banks no longer belonged to the Bookers. A bank had foreclosed on it several months earlier, but Dora would not have known that unless Susan told her. Channing looked directly at Dora, trying to decide whether to believe her, but he saw only a puzzled look as he continued to stare. He finally spoke before the silence became unbearably awkward. "Are you sure that's what she said?"

"That's what she told me," Dora replied curtly.

Desperate for any tidbit of information, Channing asked if she knew what moving company Susan had hired. Dora shook her head. "I saw the van in the street, but I didn't take a close look at it."

Channing pressed further. "Did you notice what color the moving van was?"

Dora's demeanor turned from cool to downright icy. "It was a dark color, maybe brown, but I really didn't pay attention to it." She paused and, with just a hint of sarcasm, added, "I forgot to jot down the license number."

Deciding to shift his investigation to the other neighbors, Channing began to retreat. "Well, thanks. Good talking with you again. Maybe we can get together sometime—have a barbecue or something."

Dora glanced at the bare trees around the yard and the gray sky above. "Let's wait for warmer weather. They say it's going to be a long winter."

At the next house there was no answer at the door, and no lights were on inside, so Channing headed home. Grabbing a phone book in the kitchen, he carried it to his car, flipped to the movers' section in the yellow pages, and placed the book on the passenger seat. He spent the rest of the day racing around the city, frantically searching for brown moving vans.

CHAPTER 4

Susan turned off the ignition, leaned her head back, and closed her eyes. Her plan of escape was working perfectly, but she could not relax. By now Channing had returned home to discover she was gone. She had prepared for several weeks and taken every precaution imaginable to cover her tracks. She had expected to feel a sense of satisfaction and relief. Instead, she was overcome with conflicting and disturbing emotions.

In the first hours after she drove away from home, following the moving van as it headed toward West Virginia, she was gripped by fear. She imagined that Channing had arrived moments after she left and was following her. She had cringed whenever a Volvo appeared in her rearview mirror.

There was no way to be sure what Channing's reaction would be. She hoped he would be glad that she was gone. The marriage had been a charade for months, and he might welcome his freedom and leave it at that. As much as she wanted to believe this, she couldn't. Susan knew Channing would be furious that she left without warning. He would soon discover that she made sizeable withdrawals from their bank accounts to fund her getaway. His temper had gotten out of control when gambling losses mounted, and his behavior became erratic as his drug use increased. He had physically abused her several times in recent weeks. She knew he would be enraged when she filed for divorce, as this would threaten whatever money he had left. On the other hand, if she were dead, Channing would collect a million dollars on her life insurance policy. She had discovered a pistol in his closet not long ago and was convinced he would come after her.

Mixed with her fear was a profound sense of anger and sadness.

She had looked forward to a happy life as the wife of a successful attorney in a charming, hospitable community. She had tried hard to build a marriage that would last and had hoped to start a family with Channing. Instead, he had frittered away their investments, isolated her emotionally, and humiliated her by chasing women all over town. Now she was forced to leave her friends behind and go underground, facing an uncertain future with few resources at hand.

She opened her eyes and stared at the neon vacancy sign a short distance from where she was parked. The motel was a simple, rustic structure that was devoid of any charm or style. Its cinderblock walls were covered with chipped and peeling paint. The parking lot was dimly lit, with bits of loose paper and trash scattered about. Susan hesitated before getting out of the car and considered searching for a more suitable motel, but she was exhausted from driving and worrying. Carrying her suitcase, she trudged to the office to register. An elderly clerk who had been dozing behind the counter roused himself and greeted her. "Evening, Miss."

"Hi. I'd like a room for the night." She laid some large bills on the counter and signed the registry as Susan Katz, inventing an address and scribbling it illegibly below the name.

The clerk counted out some change and handed her a receipt and key card. "Checkout's at noon. I'll be here until six if you need anything. Have a good evening."

Susan yawned as she passed a row of doors along the front of the motel until she found her room. She turned and looked nervously around the parking lot, then slipped the card into the slot. She locked the door behind her, pulled the curtains together, and collapsed on the bed. She watched as midnight came and went on the bedside clock. Although her mind and body were worn out, she couldn't sleep. She brushed her teeth and turned off the light then crawled under the covers and watched TV for more than an hour before finally dozing off. She slept fitfully and woke up several times during the night. Around four a.m., her body finally succumbed to exhaustion.

She fell into a deep sleep and began to dream. In her subconscious mind, a car turned slowly into the motel's parking lot. The headlights were off, and, in the cold darkness, the driver appeared only as a shadow behind the wheel. He eased the car forward until it was closer to the light at the office door and then pulled a crumpled piece of paper from his shirt pocket. Squinting as he read, he confirmed that the name on the paper matched the sign at the entrance. He spotted Susan's Volkswagen parked in front of room twenty-three and then circled around the side of the motel, taking care not to rev the motor and wake up the night clerk or guests.

The car stopped at the far corner of the lot behind the motel, hidden from view by a pair of trash dumpsters under the spreading branches of an oak tree. The driver sat motionless inside the car for several minutes, scanning the lot and keeping alert for any sound or sign of activity. Satisfied that no one was awake, he pulled a dark ski mask over his head and quietly slipped out of the car. In the side pocket of his dark overcoat he touched a pistol with his gloved hand, making sure that its silencer was attached. Creeping along the side of the building and hugging the wall, he paused at the corner to survey the front parking lot.

Seeing no movement, he walked softly toward the office door, pausing to glance through the window. By the faint glow of a night light and an illuminated aquarium, he recognized the shape of the clerk's body, asleep in a chair.

He touched the door and lightly pressed against it to see if it was locked. It began to open and he pushed farther. Suddenly a buzzer sounded. The clerk's arm flinched, and he opened his eyes. Before the clerk could react, the masked figure flung the door open and burst inside. He leaped across the room, pulled out his gun, and slammed it against the clerk's head. The blow knocked the man out of the chair and sent him sprawling on the floor, where he moaned briefly before lapsing into unconsciousness. Blood began to seep from a gash over one ear, dripping onto the floor.

The intruder went behind the counter and rummaged through drawers until he found a master key card. Noticing a panel of light switches on the wall, he turned off the ones marked "exterior" and "vacancy."

He pushed the door open a crack and peered outside. Seeing no movement and hearing only the sound of distant traffic, he slipped out into the darkness, wincing when the door buzzer signaled his departure. Staying close to the front wall of the building, he moved quietly along the row of numbered doors. In the dim light he couldn't read the numbers, but he paused several times to feel the raised metal digits that were just below the peephole on each door. When he felt the number twenty-three, he stopped and gently pressed his ear against the cold metal, listening for any indication of activity inside. After a few minutes, he was satisfied that Susan must be asleep. He carefully inserted the card, applied slight pressure against the door, and discovered that no deadbolt lock was in place. He ran a finger along the door's edge until he touched a small security chain that was attached on the back. He took several large steps backward and slid the pistol from his pocket, clutching it tightly in his right hand. As Susan's nightmare approached its climax, the intruder's identity was revealed. Suddenly Channing rushed forward and slammed his body against the door. The chain snapped with a sharp pop as the door flew open.

Susan awoke with a start and sat bolt upright in bed. A rush of adrenalin coursed through her body, accelerating her heartbeat. Dazed and confused, she struggled to throw off the covers and waved her arms wildly in the direction of the bedside lamp, knocking it onto the floor. Crawling to the edge of the bed, she stretched her arms out and swept them along the side of the bed until she felt the lampshade. Short of breath and gripped by fear, she quickly located the light switch and pressed it. She rolled back to the middle of the bed and glanced about the room in a state of panic.

Except for the lamp and a corner of the bedspread dragging on the floor, everything was where it had been when she fell asleep. The door was shut and securely chained. The TV was still on at a low volume. The curtains were drawn, and Susan's clothes were draped over a chair in one corner. She pulled the covers around her and lay still, waiting until the shock of her nightmare gradually faded and her pulse and breathing returned to normal. The dream seemed so real, and she was disgusted that Channing dominated her mind even while she slept. She stared at the TV for a long time before reaching down to pick up the lamp. Curling up under a twisted mass of sheets, she finally went back to sleep just as dawn began to break.

Several hours later she awoke to the sound of knocking at her door. A maid's voice asked if she wanted her room cleaned. Exhausted and groggy from a nearly sleepless night, Susan closed her eyes and mumbled a grumpy "come back later."

"Okay, honey. Checkout's at noon."

She struggled to set the bedside alarm clock for eleven-fifteen and then drifted in and out of consciousness until its obnoxious beeping forced her to wake up. She pressed the snooze button several times, unable to muster the strength to get up. Tired and worried, she stared at the ceiling before finally crawling out of bed. Splashing cold water on her face, she peered into the reddish, puffy eyes that were reflected in the mirror. She went through the motions of a shower, stuffed clothes into her suitcase and shuffled out of the room.

A cold wind greeted her as she walked to the office to check out. The gray sky matched her mood. She had planned to drive to Mount Vernon, Illinois, by nightfall, but she was running late and felt as if she hadn't slept at all. She dragged her suitcase and herself to the car and tumbled into the driver's seat. Leaning her head against the back of the seat, she closed her eyes. After a long pause she started the car and headed out to the Interstate.

As the hours passed on the highway, she barely noticed the beauty of the rolling West Virginia mountains around her. She tried to think positively about the future but was consumed by doubt, fear, and uncertainty. Occasionally, she checked her rearview mirror, half expecting to see Channing's Volvo gaining ground on her. Traffic was light, and she was often alone on a monotonous journey that seemed to drain her energy with each passing mile.

After several hours, her restless stomach reminded her that she had missed breakfast and lunch. Turning off at the next exit, she spent ten minutes searching for fast food. Finding a gas station with a small market attached, Susan filled her tank and picked up a tuna sandwich and a huge cup of coffee. Seeing no chairs in the cramped store, she walked back to the car and got in.

A breeze stirred leaves and trash around the car as she pulled her coat tightly around her and began eating the sandwich. She chewed slowly, leaning back against the headrest and closing her eyes for long periods at a time. The clouds had dissipated, and gradually the car warmed a bit under a bright winter sun. The coffee did little to revive her spirits or lessen her fatigue. Although she was behind schedule, she realized she had to catch a nap before it would be safe to drive back to the Interstate.

Following signs to the nearest town, she drove around aimlessly before spotting a library with a one-hour parking space out front. She pulled into it at an awkward angle until her front wheel bumped against the curb. She slowly ascended a staircase that led to the front door and opened it. Except for a middle-aged woman at the checkout desk and two old men reading newspapers in an alcove, there was no one inside. She drifted down a corridor that was lined with stacks of old magazines, emerging in a carpeted reading room, where she slumped into a soft armchair. In a short time she was asleep.

Eventually one of the men in the newspaper alcove finished reading and ambled to the front entrance. As he left, his cane banged loudly against the door. The sound reverberated through the corridor and into the reading room, waking Susan. She rubbed her eyes and looked down at her watch. She wasn't sure how long she had been asleep, but it was five-twenty, and she was far behind schedule.

Reaching into her coat pocket, she was relieved to find that a thick envelope was still there.

She paused briefly to collect her thoughts, and then hurried outside. She hopped into the car and drove quickly toward the Interstate, never noticing the parking ticket that was tucked under the windshield wiper blade on the passenger side. She reached for the coffee cup in its holder and forced herself to drink a few gulps of stale, cold brew. She decided to drive as far as she could go until around midnight and then look for a motel.

She watched the sun sink behind distant mountains as she drove westward. The highway stretched through valleys and wound among steep hills that seemed endless. Her thoughts drifted back to the day that she first met Channing, and she reflected on a relationship that began with such promise and ended so miserably.

She was a secretary in the Dean's Office at Temple University's Law School in Philadelphia when Channing was a third-year student. He had stopped by the office one Friday afternoon to get the dean's permission to drop a class, and she was drawn to him from the moment they met in the reception area. Tall, muscular and ruggedly handsome, he exuded self-confidence and didn't appear as brash or stuffy as most of the law students who breezed through the office.

They had talked for a few minutes before he asked her to dinner, and they spent most of that evening at Chez Alphonse, a posh French restaurant on the east side of the city. They sipped from glasses of fine Bordeaux wine as the gentle rhythm of light jazz wafted over them in a private corner with dim lighting.

The night was magical, and they had dated regularly until Channing graduated. He had planned to travel around Europe with several classmates before beginning work at a small law firm in Central Virginia, but the trip was transformed into a honeymoon after he asked her to marry him.

In the early days of his career at Dunlap & Cranston, Channing represented small-time offenders and everyday miscreants, ranging from shoplifters and drunk drivers to pickpockets and loan sharks. As the months drifted by, Channing and Susan's relationship began to drift as well. Susan combined extensive volunteer work for several charities with frequent trips to the public library and small downtown bookstores. Often she went alone. She did her best to create a happy home environment, but Channing was frequently away while Susan coped with long evenings at home by herself. He ran through a litany of excuses for his absences, covering everything from trips to the local law library to meetings with clients. Susan wanted to believe him, but several times she drove to his office to surprise him with a dinner invitation, only to find that the building was locked and dark. Sometimes when he came home she smelled cigarette smoke on his clothes, a telltale sign that he had stopped at a bar or party after work.

She recalled one night when she dropped by the office unannounced, finding the front door open and letting herself in. After searching for several minutes, she found Channing alone with his "client," a shapely young blonde woman in a short skirt and rumpled blouse. Channing looked disheveled but explained that he and his defendant had spent hours preparing for trial, and he was exhausted. After a quick introduction, Channing explained that his client was just leaving, which at that point was true. The blonde woman fled through the main lobby, forgetting to take her coat.

After a few years of practice at the firm, Channing began to defend murder suspects and other high-profile criminals. He racked up an impressive string of acquittals, much to the chagrin of the Commonwealth's Attorney and a substantial portion of the general public. Notorious white-collar criminals sought his counsel and paid him handsomely, often in cash. Channing acquired the material trappings of a wildly successful practice: an impressive mansion in the best part of town, a small fleet of expensive sports cars, three vacation homes, and a substantial investment portfolio.

The couple's marriage continued to deteriorate as Channing developed an obsession with gambling. Over time, his friendly wagering in the office football and basketball pools evolved into a host of other activities: horseracing, Internet betting, lottery games, and trips to Atlantic City or Las Vegas. Added to the mix were a series of paramours who gladly accepted a greater share of Channing's attention and largesse. When Channing added physical abuse of Susan to his repertoire of gambling, heavy drinking, and sporadic cocaine use, the formula for an eventual divorce was complete.

Early in his career, Channing had a flawless track record in the courtroom, but his success faded as his appetite for gambling and women increased. More of his time was consumed in reading horse racing tips and studying football spread sheets. Casino trips cut into his billable hour ledger and diverted thousands of dollars from his bank accounts. Several evenings each week, Channing was lured away from the office by young women who helped him enjoy long nights on the town. As his gambling losses mounted and his best clients abandoned him, Channing's financial reserves withered. IRA and pension accounts were depleted, vacation homes were sold, and the last sports car was traded in for a low-end Volvo sedan. Channing had reached the point of financial desperation shortly before Susan left him.

Susan's thoughts returned to the present as her car drifted near the shoulder on a gentle curve in the highway. She eased the car back toward the yellow reflectors that dotted the center of the road and stretched ahead into the night. Struggling to keep her eyes open, she gradually slipped into a dreamlike state as the car sped through the darkness.

Out of nowhere a young deer darted onto the highway about 100 yards ahead. It froze in the glare of her headlights. As the car hurtled forward, Susan vaguely recognized the stationary form in the road. An instant later she realized the horror of her situation and jerked the steering wheel to the left, but it was too late. At the last second the animal leaped forward, just as the bumper smashed into its side, instantly crushing its ribs and sending it flying off onto the shoulder. The car shuddered and skidded wildly across the pavement. Airbags deployed with an explosive sound that drowned out Susan's scream. The car slammed violently into a guardrail, flipped over it and disappeared into the darkness below.

CHAPTER 5

Lee Barnett dropped his bulky duffel bag and flopped into a seat in the terminal at the Charlottesville-Albemarle Airport. His arms dangled loosely over the armrests, and his chest heaved as he paused to catch his breath. The walk from the rental car office to the terminal had sapped his strength, and beads of sweat gathered on his forehead and began to soak through his orange and blue UVA football jersey. A wide leather belt with a Fraternal Order of Police logo on its buckle anchored a pair of baggy shorts with large pockets that reached just below his knees. The left pants leg concealed a large oblong scar just above his kneecap. His thick mustache was framed by several days' growth of beard stubble. His shaggy, medium-length black hair drooped haphazardly, contributing to his disheveled appearance.

As time wore on, his breathing eventually became less labored, and he gathered enough strength to lean down and unzip the bag at his feet. He thought about how much easier it would be to travel with a conventional suitcase on rollers. The heavy sack that he lugged was a testament to his determination to regain the mobility he had lost in a split second a year earlier. He had struggled to regain arm strength that withered away during a nine-week stay in a hospital bed.

In his prime, he had been a star linebacker on an undefeated high school football team in his hometown of Barnwell, South Carolina. He was a fierce competitor with blazing speed, who wreaked havoc on receivers and running backs who strayed anywhere near him. His coach, the legendary Pat Tricoh, dubbed him with the nickname "Basher Barnett." Lee was a small-town hero with a bright future. He won a football scholarship to the University of Virginia and started every game during his four years on the Cavalier squad. Unfortunately, during his college years the UVA team as a whole could not match Lee's intensity, and the Cavaliers were the perennial cellar dwellers in the Atlantic Coast Conference. Scouts from the NFL avoided the team like the plague, never noticing the talent that qualified Lee for a spot on a professional roster.

Returning to Barnwell after graduating from Virginia, Lee ran for sheriff and was elected by a comfortable margin. His office occupied a nondescript building next door to the courthouse and across from a Texaco station. Outside was a bulletin board full of foreclosure notices, divorce petitions, wanted posters, and other documents that few people ever bothered to read. Inside was a small lobby with a table full of old issues of *Field and Stream*, *Sports Illustrated*, *Shotgun News*, and a plethora of other magazines. The walls in Lee's office were plastered with faded black-and-white photos dating back to the 1920s, featuring former mayors, water board members, game wardens, and other dignitaries.

The surface of Lee's desk was piled high with papers, ammo boxes, cigars, and candy wrappers. Boxes were scattered around the room, overflowing with old newspapers, tools, scrapbooks, and whatever else Lee had collected over the years but couldn't bring himself to throw away.

Often Lee had little to do except sort through the mail, drink coffee, and stroll around town, shooting the breeze with the citizens of Barnwell. After a few years the thought of patrolling the sleepy town of 5,200 for another term was less than inspiring. Lee and his wife moved across the state to Charleston, a medium-sized city on the coast, where they settled into an old waterfront residence.

Lee had worked as a detective with the Charleston Police Department until his life fell apart one night while he and Andrea were out for a walk. As they had approached an antique store that evening, a shadowy figure suddenly emerged from its entrance, clutching a pair of silver candlesticks in one hand and a pistol in the other. Lee instinctively pushed Andrea away as he reached for his own gun, but the burglar's first bullet was already on its way. It ripped into Lee's left thigh, just over his knee, sending a wave of pain throughout his body. The second shot missed Lee but hit Andrea, causing massive damage as it penetrated her abdomen.

He got off one errant shot as he fell to the sidewalk, his leg buckling from the impact of the bullet that shattered his femur. As his torso twisted to the left on its way down to the sidewalk, a third bullet pierced a weak seam in his protective vest, penetrating lung tissue and lodging near his spine. His body collapsed, and he lost consciousness as the burglar raced away and disappeared into the night.

Eight of his fellow detectives scoured the crime scene and worked relentlessly for weeks to identify the attacker, but he had worn gloves and left no fingerprints.

The only witness was a restaurant waiter who heard the shots and looked through a window while crouching behind a table, seeing only an elusive figure in black clothes fleeing the area. A week later, Lee lay near death in a hospital bed as Andrea was buried.

The bullet in his thigh had hit an artery, resulting in critical blood loss that required multiple transfusions. Another bullet that rested near his backbone was wedged precariously inside a bundle of nerves, where it was too risky to attempt removal.

After nine weeks of treatment, Lee emerged from the hospital and began the long, slow process of recovery. He would be permanently short of breath and would walk with a noticeable limp for the rest of his life.

His doctor warned that strenuous exercise could cause the bullet to shift position and produce debilitating back pain.

The criminal investigation continued but gradually tapered off when no leads developed. Officially the case remained open, but after a few months with no results, Lee realized that the assailant would never be captured. The police chief personally arranged for a generous disability package and allowed him to keep his security clearance and gun.

Now Lee spent much of his time rehabilitating his injured body as best he could. He also read and logged many hours at his computer, studying with online courses, exploring the Internet and trading collectibles on eBay. With so much free time on his hands, he accommodated his passion for sports by acquiring season tickets to football, basketball, soccer, and lacrosse games at his alma mater in Charlottesville.

As he sat in the airport terminal, waiting to return to Charleston after another UVA football weekend, Lee pulled a newspaper from his duffel bag. After studying the sports section and reading each article about the game, he quickly glanced over the rest of the paper. A brief news article caught his eye and he skimmed through it.

Local Store Sells Winning Lottery Ticket

A single lucky ticket that won the jackpot in Friday night's Mega Millions lotto drawing was sold at Wally's Quick Mart in Charlottesville, according to Virginia Lottery spokeswoman Michelle Kyle. "The winning ticket is worth just over $241 million in thirty annual installments, or a lump sum value of $124.6 million if the winner chooses the cash option. The winning numbers were 2, 6, 9, 17, 55, and 12 for the Mega Ball. As the retail seller of the prize-winning ticket, Wally's Quick Mart will receive a bonus payment of $25,000," Kyle said. She added that the winner has 180 days to claim the prize. If no winner steps forward by then, the jackpot is forfeited and the money will be rolled over into the next drawing.

Walter Pennington, who has owned and operated the small convenience store on Blenheim Avenue since 1981, said yesterday he is thrilled to play a part in Charlottesville's first jackpot sale. "A few of my customers have come close over the years, and one of my regulars won $100,000 three years ago, but I never thought I'd sell a jackpot ticket," Pennington said. "I can't wait to find out who won."

Lee looked again at the winning numbers and noticed a familiar pattern. Three numbers matched the month, day, and year of his birth: September 17, 1955. *An amazing coincidence*, he thought, wishing he had picked up some tickets when he flew into town on Friday afternoon. *I coulda been a contender*, he told himself. Glancing at his watch, he saw that his flight would leave in twenty minutes. Getting up slowly, he tucked the newspaper into his bag and headed for the boarding gate.

CHAPTER 6

Joe Davidson climbed down from the moving van's cab and stepped onto the moist pavement. He stretched his legs and surveyed the small parking lot, seeing only a tan minivan with "Earl's U-Store-It" painted on its side. His assistant, Tyson Gregory, walked around the front of the cab and joined him.

"Where the hell is she?" Joe asked. "She said she'd meet us here at two. What time is it now?"

Tyson glanced at his watch. "I've got two-forty-five. Maybe she's still on Eastern Time. I think the time changed at the Illinois line."

"Yeah, it did, but I'm not gonna waste any more time. She said the owner would know where to unload. Let's get going before it starts raining again."

They went inside the small office and found Earl Aarlex sprawled on a couch, watching a soap opera on TV. The office was about the size of a modest camping trailer, with only one window. A gray metal desk sat in one corner, next to a filing cabinet. The walls were covered with fake wood paneling, which was warped in several spots.

Beside the desk, a wall calendar featured a revealing shot of a buxom redhead in a skimpy bikini, with an advertisement for an auto parts store. The smell of cigarettes and chewing gum hung in the air.

Earl sat up as the two approached. "No sign of her, eh? She hasn't called since about a week ago, but she mailed a deposit check, so I can go ahead and open up her unit for you. I'll let you use number six because it's near the front."

After the truck was in place, Earl fumbled with a heavy collection of keys until he found the one he wanted. He unlocked the door and rolled it up, then lit a cigarette and leaned against the trailer to watch the men unload it. They struggled with various pieces of heavy furniture, packing them tightly into the low, musty space. Next came dozens of boxes, including several that were crammed full of Susan's favorite books. They stacked them beside the furniture, unaware that one of the boxes contained a priceless lottery ticket, tucked inside a Charles Dickens novel.

"I can't figure out why she's not here," Joe grunted, as he shoved the last box into place. "She was in such a hurry to get this stuff out of her house, and she said we had to get here today. She was behind us a long way on 64."

"Last time I saw her was back in West Virginia late Saturday night," Tyson answered. "I figured she'd catch up with us before we got here."

"Me, too, but it's not my problem, and I'm not hanging around here in the middle of nowhere. She paid us in advance, so we might as well get going."

"Sounds good. I'll drive the first leg. It's a long way back to Harrisonburg. Let's try to make it to Roseville for dinner."

Earl secured the door and closed the gate, snapping a padlock into place as he watched the moving van rumble out of the lot and head down the road to Interstate 64. He ambled back to the office and settled onto the couch, waiting for closing time.

Around midmorning the next day he heard the low growl of an engine as a truck lurched into the driveway outside the office. Peering through a layer of dust that coated the window, he watched as a long yellow moving van rolled across the lot. A tall, bearded man in blue jeans and a frayed wool jacket hopped out of the cab and walked to the office door.

Earl recognized Miguel Buello, the owner of a moving company in Mt. Vernon, a small Illinois town just a few miles away. "What's up, Miguel?"

"Not much. Got a lady who wants me to clear out some stuff in storage here." Pulling a slip of paper from his shirt pocket, he glanced at the name scribbled on it. "Susan Finley. She said she'd meet me here at eleven. Wants all her things moved out."

Earl frowned and sat down at his desk. He sorted through several stacks of invoices, envelopes and other records that were spread out in no particular order. "Finley. Let's see. Oh, yeah, here it is." He held up an original and one copy of a storage agreement and double checked the name and date. He looked up, puzzled. "I've never met her, but she must be one strange woman. Her stuff just came in yesterday, and now she wants to move it out?"

"I don't know her, either. She called me a couple of weeks ago and set this up. Sent me a cashier's check, even though I told her I'd take a personal check or credit card. She told me to keep everything confidential."

"Well, this sure is weird. I wondered why she only paid the minimum deposit. I thought she'd show up yesterday and sign the contract. I don't like to open up a unit without paperwork, but her check was good so I did it."

"Has she called recently?"

"Last time was a day or two ago, I think." Earl looked again at the unsigned contract. "She gave me a cell phone number." He reached for his phone and punched in the numbers. "No answer."

"Okay. Scotty's in the truck. I'll tell him to come in and we'll wait till eleven-thirty. If she's not here by then I guess we'll load up. Maybe she'll get here before we're ready to leave."

Two hours later, Scotty removed the last box from storage unit six and handed it to Miguel, who pushed it back into the trailer and packed it with the others. Hopping down from the back of the truck, he turned to Scotty and told him to tie off the load and meet him out front. He headed back to the office, checking the parking lot before going inside. "We've got a long trip ahead of us, Earl. Good seeing you again. If the lady calls, tell her I have her stuff and ask her to call me. She's got my number."

Earl stood at the door and watched the truck disappear down the road, heading west.

CHAPTER 7

Channing hunched over his desk, perusing an article in *The Daily Progress*, Charlottesville's morning newspaper. It was a follow-up to the initial lottery story, but with little new information about the winning ticket. The report noted that five days had passed since last Friday's drawing, but no one had claimed the jackpot. The winner had 175 days left before the ticket expired. There were a few quotes from Wally Pennington, who said that business had been brisk at his store all week, with hordes of regular and new customers crowding into the place to buy lottery tickets, beer, and other items. On Saturday, a few folks had rummaged through the trashcan outside the front entrance, hoping the winner had accidentally tossed the ticket in with some used play slips on the way out to the parking lot. Wally declined to speculate about the winner's identity and said he planned to spend his $25,000 bonus check on a fishing vacation in Colorado, after the rush of new business tapered off.

Wally's trashcan was perhaps the only place in the country where the ticket could not be, Channing thought, as he folded the newspaper and leaned back in his leather chair. He gazed about his office while his thoughts wandered. The room was spacious, as would be expected for a partner at Dunlap & Cranston. His massive oak desk, complete with elaborate designs carved into the wood along the edges under its top, dominated the room. Running the length of one wall was a set of bookshelves that stretched from the hardwood floor up to the ceiling. Each shelf contained a row of books that were identical except for the sequential numbers on their spines.

Channing rarely pulled a volume from its shelf, partly because young associates performed most of the legal research that was required at the firm. The main reason the books were untouched, though, was that most attorneys no longer read law books. Cases and statutes were available on computer databases, where their text could be searched electronically. Nevertheless, Channing knew that his clients expected a law office to be stocked with an ample supply of books, so he bought a collection from a prison library that had upgraded to computer terminals.

Along the wall opposite the bookshelves was a handsome display case, filled with mementos that had accumulated during his career as a lawyer. There was a copy of a Virginia Supreme Court brief he had written soon after arriving in town. There was a gavel that Channing received after serving briefly as a substitute judge in General District Court, filling in for the regular judge while he recovered from eye surgery.

On another wall was an array of framed diplomas, photographs, and certificates. The certificates attested to Channing's status as a member of the bar in the courts of the Commonwealth of Virginia and the federal courts in the Eastern and Western Districts, and as a duly qualified Notary Public. A tall window behind Channing's desk, framed by floor-length curtains in an elegant fabric, overlooked the Albemarle County Courthouse and a nearby park.

Channing stared at various piles of correspondence and files on his desk, completely unmotivated to delve into any legal work. He was eager to stay focused on the search for Susan and the lottery ticket, but wasn't sure what his strategy should be. He looked up when he heard a soft knock on his door.

"Come in," he barked. Winston slowly opened the door and peered inside, then shuffled toward Channing's desk, clutching a yellow legal pad at his side. Halfway into the room, he stopped when Channing held up his hand and pointed to the door. "Close it," he demanded.

Winston quickly slipped back to the door and gently shut it. Settling into a leather chair in front of Channing's desk, he pulled a pen from his shirt pocket and held it above the yellow pad that was balanced precariously on his thigh, poised to jot down Channing's marching orders. "I have a very important assignment that will require the utmost confidentiality and discretion," Channing said gravely. Winston paused, tapping his pen against the legal pad without writing.

"Is it too confidential for me to take notes?"

"Well, keep it to a bare minimum, and lock any notes in your desk when you're not working on this."

"Yes, sir, absolutely. How do you want me to bill my time?"

"For now, count your time on the Tyler murder case. Send your time records to me instead of your secretary, and I'll take it from there."

"Okay. Will this be all right with Mr. Dunlap?"

"Don't worry about him. Now, I mentioned that this is a highly confidential matter. I need you to report only to me directly, and don't discuss this in any way with Dunlap or anyone else in the firm. Not even with your secretary. Do you have a roommate or girlfriend?"

Winston flinched and looked down at his legal pad, scribbling nothing in particular as he wondered what he was getting himself into. "Not at the moment. I've been pretty busy here at the firm and haven't had much free time for dating."

"Good. Well, ah, what I mean is, the partners and I appreciate all of your hard work. Just don't talk about this project with anyone. If you write anything for me to see, don't print a hard copy. Just email it to me at my home email address, then delete the file and the email from your computer. Don't keep a paper file. Keep all your notes on your computer, and encrypt the files."

"Uh, well, what if I need to discuss this with Mr. Tyler?"

Channing couldn't resist smiling. "You won't need to talk to him. Your time will be billed to the murder case temporarily, but this research is for another client. Actually, it's a potential client. Someone has contacted me in connection with the recent lottery jackpot. I'll be meeting with him soon to see if I can convince him to give us his business. He'll be needing lots of tax advice, estate planning, and who knows what else when he cashes in the ticket. I want some basic background information before I give him a sales pitch. That's where you come in. The jackpot was about $241 million, with a cash payout of $124.6 million. I need to know how much federal and state income taxes would be owed on that amount—"

"Which state?" Winston interrupted.

"Virginia. I also need to know how much gift tax would be due if he gives some of it to a friend."

"How much?"

"Let's say ten percent for now."

"A friend, not a relative?"

"Right."

"Must be a pretty good friend," Winston remarked. "Wish I knew him."

"Don't we all? Now, I also need to know if his wife would have any claim on the money if he cashes the ticket in after he gets divorced."

"Okay. Anything else?"

Channing hesitated for a moment, but couldn't think of any other questions. "I think that'll be enough for now. I may need more research later, though. And remember, nobody hears a word about this."

As soon as Winston left, Channing exited the building and walked to his car. Easing out into the street, he headed downtown for an appointment with Derwood Hodges.

In happier times, Channing had been one of Derwood's best clients. As his wealth had increased, Channing relied on Derwood to manage and invest it. A string of abbreviations under his name ran the length of Derwood's business card, proclaiming his status as a CLU, ChFC and other acronyms that Channing never attempted to decipher. At one time, Channing's portfolio of assets, balance sheets and other records occupied an entire drawer in one of Derwood's filing cabinets. In recent years, as Channing's fiscal affairs declined, his bulging account files in Derwood's office became considerably lighter and thinner.

Settling into a plush chair in front of Derwood's desk, Channing accepted a cup of coffee from a secretary, admiring her figure as she left the room and closed the door. He sipped the dark liquid and savored its delicate taste, enjoying a calm moment before Derwood began delivering the bad news. Like a schoolboy expecting to receive a failing report card, he waited for Derwood to speak.

Dressed in a light gray suit, with a red power tie secured to a starched white shirt by a gold collar pin, Derwood sat straight in his chair, resting both arms on top of his desk. A crisply folded white handkerchief was expertly positioned in his breast pocket, and his jet-black hair was closely cropped and perfectly combed.

He opened a large envelope, extracted a report, and ceremoniously placed it on the desk. Slowly turning its pages, he studied graphs and columns of figures in silence. A large college ring bobbed up and down as he tapped his fingers lightly on the desk. As he turned the last page and closed the report, he leaned back in his chair and clenched his jaw. A grave expression crept across his face, and he stared at Channing with a penetrating look. "There's not much here to work with, Channing. We sold the Bahamas property last year. The pension account is down to about $100,000, and the IRA is at rock bottom—about thirty-five grand. We borrowed $85,000 from the pension six months ago, and it has to be repaid with interest." He paused, hoping to find a delicate way to ask about the borrowed funds. "I gather that money is not available at this time?"

"Not at the moment."

"I see. Okay. Now, most of the mutual funds were liquidated last summer." Derwood paused again. "I take it that the proceeds have been disbursed?"

"Yeah, I spent the money," Channing replied with a smirk. Ordinarily, Derwood's financial report would have been devastating, but Channing was confident he would find the lottery ticket before Susan discovered it.

Derwood turned a page in his folder and continued. "There's one mutual fund left. As of today it's worth about $48,000, more or less."

"Probably less," Channing joked.

Derwood tried to hide his irritation. Channing had frittered away one of his most valuable accounts, and his commissions and service fees had declined along with Channing's fortune. "Yes, perhaps," he replied, forcing a smile. "Well, then, there's $12,400 in your checking account, and about $80,000 in savings."

"Are you sure?" Channing said, leaning forward.

"Those are the balances from the most recent statements," Derwood replied tartly. He fumbled through the loose documents in the back of his folder, pulled out last month's statements, and pushed them across the desk in front of Channing.

"Actually, Susan took out $5,000 from checking and half of the savings on Saturday," Channing replied. "I closed the accounts when I found out yesterday and put the money in a new checking account. Here's the account number for the file," he said, pulling a receipt from his coat pocket and tossing it on the desk.

"Fine. Moving along then, there are a few utility stocks left. They've taken a real beating in the market this year. As of this morning, they're trading at around $2.50 a share, and you're down to 8,000 shares." Derwood turned another page and started to speak when Channing cut him off.

"I need about twenty grand to tide me over for a couple of weeks. How fast can you sell the stock?"

Taken aback, Derwood dropped the folder and looked at Channing. He was surprised that Channing seemed so unconcerned about his financial collapse. "If you sell at that price, you'll be jumping out of the basement window. It makes no sense. The only thing you'll get is a capital loss, which you don't need now that your income has dropped."

"Well, what else can we liquidate?"

"All I see here is some equity in your house and a whole life policy."

Channing smiled. "What's the cash value on the policy?"

Derwood leafed through his report until he found the figure. "Thirty-two thousand, plus or minus."

"Good. Cash it out and wire the balance to my new account."

"But what about Susan? She's the beneficiary. Are you sure it's okay?"

"No problem. I'll tell her about it later," Channing answered. He swallowed the rest of his coffee and set the cup on Derwood's desk as he stood up. "Gotta run. Good talking with you again." He shook hands quickly and exited the office, leaving Derwood with a blank look on his face.

As he headed back across town, Channing glanced at his fuel gauge and saw that the tank was almost empty. Cutting through a side street, he arrived at the parking lot in front of Wally's Quick Mart. A white banner with large red letters was stretched across a window at the front of the store, announcing that the winning Mega Millions ticket had been sold there. He filled his tank and then went inside the store. A small bell jingled as he pushed through the front door and approached the counter, passing racks of chips and munchies, batteries and miscellaneous wares.

Wally was sitting behind the counter, reading a newspaper and puffing a cigarette. His wrinkled wool plaid shirt hung loosely over a large beer gut, with a coffee stain on one sleeve. A faded Budweiser cap rested at an angle atop his large head. "Chan, my man, what's goin' down?"

"Not too much, Wally. How's business here? I've been reading all about you in the papers. Any idea who won the big prize?"

"All I know is it wasn't me. Nobody's stepped up yet, as far as I know. It shoulda been you, with all the tickets you've bought here. Say, where ya been hiding? Haven't seen you since the drawing."

"Yeah, I've been meaning to come by. Susan left me, and I've been busy trying to deal with that."

"Oh, man. Sorry to hear it. Have you heard anything from her?"

"Nothing yet."

"If there's anything I can do, let me know. I'm real sorry."

"Thanks, Wally. I'll be okay. Here's money for some scratch tickets."

"See you next time, buddy."

CHAPTER 8

Lee slowly opened his eyes and gazed at the television across the room. Gradually he began to recognize the figures on the screen. Highlights of last night's Knicks-Pistons basketball game flashed before him. He had dozed off at some point during halftime of a football game that ended several hours earlier. He sat motionless as the night drifted on, carrying his mind with it as he reclined in an overstuffed armchair. The colorful images that flickered on the screen faded in and out of his consciousness, dancing in a fog of drowsiness that slowly lifted.

He found the remote resting in his lap and turned off the TV. The house was quiet except for the faint ticking of the antique clock on the mantle over the fireplace to his right. Looking past the TV and through the window in front of him, Lee could see the glimmer of several distant lights from watercraft moored in Charleston Harbor. Glancing up at the clock, he saw that it was almost two-thirty.

Time meant little to him now that he was retired and living alone. With few commitments to tie him down, Lee often slept late in the morning and sometimes napped off and on during the day.

He frequently stayed up at all hours of the night, watching movies, reading and exploring the Internet.

A bowl of potato chips and a partially filled Dr. Pepper can were within reach on the end table next to his chair. As he munched on a mouthful of chips, he picked up his laptop computer and checked a few sports scores before logging onto eBay. In recent months he had become fascinated with searching for bargain items that were up for auction. He had watched in amazement as people sold goods ranging from an "autographed photo of Jesus" to used oyster cans. He also saw more practical items for sale and regularly bid on them.

Lee had become a collector of sorts, amassing an assortment of old coins, movie memorabilia, books, and miscellaneous trinkets. He told himself he was merely investing and would sell the items at a profit someday, but so far his treasures had simply piled up around the house. Boxes of sale items, some unopened, were scattered throughout the place. He checked the status of his bids and then pushed the laptop aside, settling back for a few more hours of sleep.

☙☙☙

Sylvia Ricketts paced nervously across her kitchen floor, wondering why she hadn't heard from Susan. When they had talked a week ago, Susan promised to call after she got on the road. Sylvia had tried Susan's cell number several times in recent days, but there was never an answer.

The voice mail was deactivated, but that was not a surprise because Susan would have been avoiding any calls from Channing. Perhaps Susan had her phone off to prevent tracking or to stop any calls that might leave an electronic trail. Still, Susan should have contacted her by now.

Susan had told her that nobody else knew of her plan to leave Channing. She wanted to prevent Channing from pressuring other friends or family for information. It was risky to try Susan's home number, but there was nowhere else to call. It was about nine-thirty a.m. in Virginia, so Channing was probably at work. Out of an abundance of caution, she decided to drive to Aberdeen and use a public phone, just in case the call could be traced.

The drive took about thirty minutes, as she drove gingerly over a fresh coating of snow that made the road treacherous. White plains stretched for miles in all directions, with a few trees poking through the snow here and there. The route was narrow because large chunks of ice and slush had accumulated on each side of the pavement, freezing where the snowplows had deposited them. The road was essentially a deep trench that sliced through the countryside on the way to town.

She chose a phone in a hotel lobby and dialed the number, unsure of what she would say if someone other than Susan answered. The phone rang six times before the answering machine picked up. Sylvia hung up immediately.

cʒcʒ

Winston finished typing some notes and then carried his laptop down the hall. Ordinarily he would have jotted a few figures on a yellow legal pad or printed a short memo, but Channing had insisted that he keep nothing in hard copy. The whole affair seemed rather odd, but Winston was used to dealing with several of the more eccentric personalities at the firm. Channing seemed preoccupied as Winston stepped into his office. He looked up from his desk and pointed to the door, and Winston closed it quietly. He scooted a chair up close to the desk and started to set the laptop on its edge, but saw Channing's scowl in time to pull it back and rest it on his knees.

"I've got a short report on those questions you asked, but I wasn't sure if you wanted me to print it out for you."

"For now you can just tell me, and I'll pass it on to the client."

"Yes, sir. First, I checked the income tax rates. Assuming the client takes the lump-sum option, the gross payout is $124.6 million. Obviously he'd be in the highest tax bracket, so the federal rate would be about thirty-seven percent and the state would be around six percent. I didn't do an exact calculation to account for the lower brackets, but after taxes he'd have roughly $71 million. Now, you asked what would happen if he gave ten percent of it to a friend. This is a bit complicated because the tax rates have been changing, but for now there's a lifetime exclusion credit for roughly the first eleven million. Do you know if he has made gifts in previous years?"

"No, he hasn't."

"Okay, then he could take the full credit, so if he gives less than eleven million he can avoid the gift tax. If he gives more, the tax rate is forty percent. The donor owes the tax, so—"

Channing interrupted. "Just give me the bottom line."

"Yes, sir. Your client would end up with about $71 million."

Channing's face turned a bright crimson color as he slammed his fist down on the desk. "That's outrageous! I can't believe that's all there is!"

Winston stared in disbelief. "Excuse me?"

Channing paused until he regained his composure. "Well, I've always believed that a good lawyer puts himself in his client's shoes. I'm just speaking metaphorically. My client will be very disappointed that he gets only $71 million after winning a $241 million jackpot." Channing knew that his "client's" disappointment would be far more extreme than Winston could possibly imagine. Under his plan, Sully would not be donating ten percent of the take—he would be keeping ten percent and "giving" ninety percent back to Channing. The gift tax would apply to the entire ninety percent, taking an enormous bite out of his winnings.

Channing scratched some figures on a note pad. Starting with $71 million, he subtracted ten percent for Sully's handling fee, which left about $64 million. He subtracted another eleven million for the gift tax exemption, and then calculated forty percent of $53 million to find that the gift tax would be about $21 million. He subtracted the tax from $64 million and stared at the number in disbelief. After all was said and done, Channing's $241 million jackpot would dwindle to about $43 million before he got his hands on it.

Resting both elbows on his desk, he buried his face in his hands and took several deep breaths. Ten percent for Sully now seemed far too generous, but if he cut Sully's share too much the plan might unravel. Sully might balk at handing any money over and simply disappear with the whole $71 million. He would have to keep Sully in the dark until he could come up with a better idea.

Winston looked at Channing's face and saw nothing but pain and frustration. He had no idea what thoughts were churning in Channing's head, and was not particularly eager to find out. Whatever the problem was, Winston assumed it was his fault, or it would be as soon as Channing figured out how to blame it on him. He cleared his throat and decided to speak before Channing's face got any redder. "Actually, your client might be able to avoid some of the taxes if he chooses the lottery's annual payout option, and I'm sure we could think of some creative strategies to reduce the tax burden. If you want me to take a look at his recent tax returns, I could get a better idea of what we're working with."

"Uh, let's hold off on that for now. I'm sure he wants to take the lump sum, and his tax returns are confidential. What did you find out about the divorce angle? What happens if he cashes in the ticket after he gets divorced?"

"Yes. Well, that's complicated. Generally the court will equitably distribute all marital property—"

"This isn't marital property. He won the lottery on his own. It's his money, right?"

"Unfortunately for your client, it's probably going to count as marital property unless they were separated or divorced before he won the jackpot."

"Even if he doesn't cash in the ticket until after they're divorced?"

"Right."

"That really sucks!"

"You mean, for your client?"

Channing loosened his tie and sighed. "Yeah. I mean, it's no big deal for me, of course. I'm just thinking of him." He stared out the window and watched as traffic flowed along the streets below. Turning back toward Winston, he glanced at the door to be sure it was still closed, and then leaned forward. He looked straight into Winston's eyes and spoke in a low voice. "I doubt it would ever come to this, but I want to ask you a hypothetical question. What happens if he gives the ticket to somebody else and lets him cash it in as his own, then takes the money back after he gets divorced?"

Winston squirmed and his eyes widened. The conversation had taken an ominous turn, and his mind was suddenly filled with memories of an ethics seminar he had attended a few months ago. It was also filled with visions of grand juries, indictments, disbarment proceedings, and a host of other unpleasant thoughts. Researching tax law was painful enough, but now he feared he was being drawn into dangerous territory. He made a halfhearted attempt to deflect the question. "Well, I believe the tax consequences would remain the same. The rates and figures that I mentioned would still apply."

The dodge was unsuccessful. Channing shook his head and pressed further. "I gathered that. What I mean is, would there be any criminal liability or effect on the divorce?"

Winston's tie felt like a noose around his neck. He coughed and tried to ignore the dryness in his throat. He decided to stall for time, hoping he could find an excuse to avoid further work on the matter. It was a long shot, but maybe another partner would pull him off this case to deal with something else, perhaps an antitrust or bankruptcy case that nobody else wanted to touch.

"I think I'll need to conduct some more research. This question goes beyond what I looked at before. My gut feeling is that failing to disclose the ticket in a divorce case might constitute fraud on the court. You might have to warn the client not to do it."

Channing rolled his eyes and smirked. "I'll be sure to tell him not to do anything unethical. Take a look at this and get back to me. And remember, this is a very sensitive matter that requires the utmost confidentiality."

"Certainly, Mr. Booker. I'll see if I can find a case where something like this has happened before." Winston scooped up his laptop and exited as quickly as he could without giving the appearance of sprinting.

⁂

The Volkswagen lay on its side with the roof pushed tightly against the trunk of a scraggly pine tree. The force of the impact had shattered the safety glass in the windshield, rear window and two side windows. The roof sagged several inches inward but had not collapsed entirely. The fuel line had ruptured, allowing gas to leak out onto the rocky soil and run down the hillside, leaving a strong odor all around the vehicle. Farther up the slope was a swath of broken saplings and underbrush that had been ripped from the ground as the car tumbled and slid down the hill. About one hundred feet above, a section of twisted guardrail was bent outward and hung low to the shoulder.

Inside the car, a small suitcase in the back seat had split open when it flew against the roof, and clothes were strewn throughout the interior. It was midafternoon, and the temperature had hovered in the forties since the sun came up. Susan's limp body tilted against the driver's door, resting on a deflated side airbag. Her head lay on a sheet of crumpled safety glass that was pressed against the ground. The shoulder strap and seat belt were intact and held her coat snugly around her.

Her breathing was shallow, as if she were sleeping. Gradually she drifted back to consciousness and opened her eyes, feeling a burning sensation in her left leg. Instinctively she flinched and tried to move, which sent a sharp pain all the way to her ankle. Her leg throbbed with pain but would not budge. She clenched her teeth and began to feel the stiffness in her neck. As more of her senses awakened she became aware of a dull aching throughout her body. The smell of gas triggered a wave of fear as she worried that her car might explode. Her body began to shiver.

Stretching her right arm as far as possible, she was able to reach some clothes that were scattered nearby. She wrapped a pair of pants around her neck and pulled other clothes over her chest, hoping to ward off the cold air. Despite the soreness in her neck, she managed to tilt her head forward and look down at her left leg. She could see the side frame of the car buckled inward, and the dashboard had been wrenched toward the floor, trapping her leg. She could move it slightly in several directions and thought she might be able to free it if she could pull her body upward while bending her knee.

Reaching down to unbuckle her seat belt, she discovered that it was jammed. She struggled with it several times during the afternoon but couldn't release it. She realized that the force of her body movements during the accident had bent the metal tab and locked it in place. After several attempts to bite through the shoulder belt and rip it apart, she had no more energy and gave up. She was trapped.

CHAPTER 9

Boswell Dunlap squinted to get a closer look at a printed copy of one of Winston's Westlaw research trails. With meticulous care, he jotted some notes on a yellow legal pad. The trail was a computer-generated record of every case and statute that Winston had looked at during a recent online research session. The heading "Tyler" appeared at the top, and Boz knew the Tyler case was the firm's most important ongoing criminal matter.

What puzzled him was the nature of the documents Winston had reviewed. Many of the cases involved suits against the Internal Revenue Service, and most of the statutes were from the federal tax code. The Tyler case involved a fatal shooting that arose out of a cocaine transaction, and it had nothing to do with tax law.

Boz had pulled this research trail from one of the thick folders that were spread out on every available surface in his office. Each day his secretary printed them out and piled them neatly on a credenza that ran along the wall behind his desk. Any other attorney in the firm would have simply reviewed the trails online, but Boz was a novice with computers. He had barely mastered the concept of email and could do little else in cyberspace.

He had joined the firm thirty-four years earlier and had quickly established himself as a man with no apparent legal skills. He reeled off a string of losses in general district court before the partners decided to minimize damage to the firm by cutting him off from contact with clients and judges. Had he not been the son of a founding partner, he would have been put out on the street within a few months. Since he could not be fired, the partners placed him in charge of ordering supplies, monitoring the progress of new associates and clerical personnel, and performing menial tasks that were beneath the other lawyers. Any normal self-respecting employee would have resigned, but there was nowhere else for Boz to go.

He kept voluminous files and papers strewn about his office to give the appearance of activity, but in reality he had no significant function in the firm. He spent his days doing mindless busy work, convincing himself that he was contributing valuable support to the firm. His single pleasure was riding herd on new attorneys. During the first two years of every new recruit's tenure, Boz reviewed each of their cases and offered incessant unsolicited advice on how they could be more productive. A master of micromanagement, Boz terrorized new associates until they gained enough confidence to ignore him. Some of the senior associates nicknamed him "the weasel," but in truth the comparison was unfair to the genuine animal.

Perusing Winston's records, Boz sensed that a scandal was afoot, and he saw an opportunity to prove his importance to the firm's other partners. If he could catch an associate billing time improperly, or using company resources for personal business, he would expose the corruption and vindicate his reputation, such as it was.

As he pored over the research trail, he recalled something unusual from reviewing Winston's time records. He rose from his chair and hunted among stacks of paper until he found several records of meetings between Winston and Channing. The nature and timing of these conferences were curious. They occurred during a period when the Tyler case was inactive, and Winston rarely worked on criminal matters. There were also some gaps in the records.

His first impulse was to fire off an email to Winston, demanding to know why he was billing time for tax research in a murder case, and why he was meeting with Channing. However, he didn't want to give Winston time to think of a cover story to explain the discrepancies.

The next morning Winston found a note from Boz on his chair. *I have some questions about administrative matters. Let's discuss it at ten.*

Disgusted, Winston tore the note into bits and tossed them into his trashcan. A message from Boz was never a good thing. Whether it was to feel a sense of power, or simply because he was a meddlesome pest, Boz never congratulated the associates for a job well done.

Instead, he seized every opportunity to find some perceived flaw in their work, and he relished each chance to point it out to them, usually in the form of a note or email.

Most of his fellow worker bees adopted a rope-a-dope strategy when meeting with Boz. While Boz berated them and expounded at length about the need to follow procedures, the hapless associates simply looked down at their legal pads and scribbled meaningless notes, occasionally nodding as if they were paying attention to Boz's ranting. Often they were so incensed after a tongue lashing that they threw in the towel and went out drinking for the rest of the day, blowing off steam as constructively as they could. Winston was tempted to skip the meeting with Boz and proceed straight to drinking, but he needed the job.

He found Boz leaning over his desk, seemingly engrossed in a mound of papers and folders. Boz hoped to convey the impression that he was furiously working on developing bold new strategies for the firm, or was wrestling with a complex legal problem that only a senior partner could hope to master. Boz had no idea that everyone in the firm knew he served no useful purpose and was literally shuffling papers all day long.

Winston settled uncomfortably into a hard-backed chair and glanced about the office as he waited for Boz to complete his charade. The walls were as bland as the personality of the man who occupied the office. Only two pictures were hanging—generic, unimpressive prints of old English foxhunting scenes. They were the kind of works that could be picked up for a few dollars at most yard sales. Like a schoolboy sitting in the principal's office, Winston wondered what was in store for him.

Boz slowly pulled off his reading glasses and pushed a stack of papers aside. He rubbed his forehead and sighed, as if recovering from a major intellectual challenge. He opened a drawer and pulled out a file, placing it in the space he had just cleared on his desk. After grunting a perfunctory "good morning," he sprung the question, hoping to catch Winston off guard. "I see you've been doing tax research and billing it on the Tyler murder case. I also see some conferences with Channing and some gaps in your time records. What's this all about?"

Winston knew immediately that this would not be another routine lecture about office paperwork. Completely unprepared for this line of inquiry, Winston was at a loss about what he should say.

Channing had been adamant about keeping the research confidential.

Stalling for time and inspiration, Winston gave a puzzled look. He leaned back in his chair and stroked his chin, glancing briefly at the ceiling. "Well, Mr. Dunlap, I've been working on a variety of matters lately. It may be that I got some billing records mixed together. Maybe I can sort through my time sheets and clear up any confusion. I know you're busy, so if it would be more convenient for you, I could drop by this afternoon after I get this straightened out."

Sensing that he had Winston on the ropes, Boz was not about to let the round expire without landing some more punches. "I'd like to clear this up right away. I've got some monthly reports to generate, and they have to get to accounting on time. What kind of murder trial involves tax work?"

Winston tried to appear cooperative but felt like he was melting into his chair and running out of options. He was not a good liar, but knew he would have to make something up for now and find a way to fix it later. "I'm trying to recall that work. Was it a while ago or something more recent?"

"Within the past week. Surely you haven't forgotten it already."

Winston forced a smile and tapped his pen several times against his legal pad. "Oh, yes, of course. It slipped my mind because it was sort of an outside project. I was thinking I might write an article for one of the bar journals about possible changes in the tax code. I figured the firm could get some referral work or at least some publicity. I wanted to do some background research before I mentioned the idea to one of the partners. I think what must have happened was that I forgot to put my personal time code on the billing records. I can go back and fix that in an hour or two and bring you updated time sheets. Sorry for the error."

Boz tried to read Winston's face and body language to see if he was telling the truth. He glared at the flustered associate without speaking, waiting to see if Winston would crumble under the pressure and say something to incriminate himself. Winston prayed that his story would hold up long enough for him to sneak into Channing's office and seek cover. He assumed that the less he said now, the better.

Boz ratcheted up the pressure. "You say you wanted to do some research before discussing it with a partner. So what were the conferences with Channing about?"

Hoping to avoid an all-out panic attack, Winston knew his only chance was to backtrack. "Well, I should clarify what I meant. I didn't want to talk substance with a partner before I did some research to get a feel for the subject matter. I didn't want to waste their time with elementary questions about tax law, but I thought it would be good to discuss the idea in general terms with a partner. I had the impression that Mr. Booker knows a lot about getting publicity for the firm, so I thought he might give me some advice."

Boz slumped in his chair. This sounded like a complete load of crap, but Winston was catching a second wind and was able to think fast enough to cover his tracks, at least temporarily. This was his story and he was sticking with it.

"I see." In a last attempt to trap his prey, Boz reached for his phone and dialed Channing's extension, switching on the speaker button.

Channing's booming voice echoed off the mostly bare walls in Boz's office. "Yeah, who is it?"

"Hi, Channing. Boz here. I've got Winston in my office. We're discussing that project he's been talking with you about." There was a long silence at the other end of the line. "Channing, are you there?"

When Channing spoke again, the swagger in his tone had vanished, and he mumbled softly, a hint of fear in his voice. "What project is that?" he squeaked.

Winston knew he had to act quickly. Leaning forward, he spoke loudly into the speaker phone. "I told Mr. Dunlap that I had asked you about whether I should write a tax article for the bar journal." Boz swiveled his chair abruptly away from the phone and glared at Winston, who immediately looked down at his legal pad and began writing feverishly.

Regaining his composure and sounding profoundly irritated, Channing replied quickly. "Oh, yeah, that project. I wanted to help the kid out. Look, Boz, I'm very busy. I suggest you find something else to do, and let Winston get back to work."

Boz was no match for Channing, and both of them knew it. So did Winston, who breathed a sigh of relief that the crisis had been averted, at least for the moment. Boz retreated with a whimper. "Right. Sorry to bother you. I just wanted to keep the time records straight."

"Great work, Boz," Channing replied, with all the sarcasm he could muster.

Boz tossed the folder back into his desk drawer, like a poker player throwing his cards on the table to fold. He scowled at Winston, hating to lose face in front of a lowly associate. "Well, be sure to get those time sheets corrected and back to me this afternoon. That's all for now."

"Yes, sir. I'll get right on it."

"And I'll be looking forward to reading that tax article."

CHAPTER 10

As Winston left Boz's office, he could barely contain his disgust and contempt for the man who had pushed him into a corner and forced him to lie. Although he had escaped any immediate harm, he knew Boz would be watching him like a hawk in the next few weeks, eager to expose the slightest infraction. Boz could hold a grudge indefinitely, and Winston would be under the microscope for the foreseeable future. Adding insult to injury, now he would have to write a stupid tax article to confirm his cover story. Knowing that he needed to contain the fallout from what had just happened, Winston headed straight to Channing's office. As he entered and closed the door behind him, he never noticed Boz following at a distance.

"Okay, what the hell happened?" Channing barked.

"I wish I knew. Mr. Dunlap called me in this morning and gave me the third degree. I thought it would be a routine lecture about some paperwork screw-up, but he's been tracking my research and wanted to know why I was doing tax work and billing it to the Tyler file. I had to make up some bogus story to keep the research under wraps. I don't think he bought it."

"Damn it. I didn't think he'd notice what you've been up to. Well, you did the right thing just now. Hold up on further work for a few days until I figure out how to handle the situation."

"What about the tax article? Should I write something up for a bar journal so my story will hold up?"

"I guess so, but keep it short and sweet. Nothing fancy."

In the corridor outside Channing's office, just beside the door, Boz had pulled a volume from a long shelf of Virginia Law Reviews and pretended to leaf through an article. He leaned his head as close to the door as possible without making it obvious that he was trying to eavesdrop on the conversation inside. He couldn't hear every word, but he got the gist of what was going on. Some kind of conspiracy was afoot, and he would get to the bottom of it. He knew he lacked the courage or prestige to confront Channing directly. He would have to build his case quietly and, if he found a smoking gun, he could take the matter up with the other partners and emerge as a hero.

Hearing a chair squeak inside Channing's office, Boz knew Winston was getting up to leave. He quickly shoved the book back on the shelf and hustled down the hall to his office, where he would plot his next move.

As Winston began the unwelcome task of throwing together a tax article, Channing left his office on a different mission. He drove to a rough neighborhood near the outskirts of the city, arriving at Billy's Pawn Shop. He looked around carefully before stepping out of the car, making sure nobody with a knife in his hand was loitering nearby. Two teenagers with dyed green hair and black leather jackets were out front admiring a motorcycle, but they seemed relatively harmless.

He stepped quickly into the shop and saw Billy Scaggs standing behind a glass display case, reading a true crime magazine. A heavy smell of cigar smoke permeated the room. The walls were lined with guitars, boom boxes, TV sets, and bicycles. Several locked display cases were filled with pistols, watches, cameras, and jewelry. Three security cameras were suspended from the ceiling in strategic locations. A space heater blew hot air across the bare wooden floor. Behind Billy was a large one-way mirror beside a door that led to the back office.

Billy looked up and smiled, flashing a gold tooth. He wore one earring, and portions of several tattoos were visible on his forearms below rolled-up sleeves. His jet-black hair was greasy and thinning on top, and was pulled back into a short ponytail that hung over the collar of a faded yellow shirt. A thick goatee covered a deep scar on his chin, where a beer bottle had been crushed against his face long ago in a barroom fight. The skin under his eyes was puffy and wrinkled, evidence of years of hard living.

Channing pointed to the office door, and Billy followed him inside and shut it behind them. The room was dimly lit, with one window beside a rear entrance. Thick iron bars covered the window, the same kind that ran across the front of the building. A bare wooden table stood in the center of the office, its surface covered with coffee stains, cigarette burns, and nicks where chips of wood had been scraped away.

A naked light bulb hung from a long cord over the table. Billy lit a cigarette as the two men sat down.

The pawn shop was open three days a week and was run by Billy and his brother Royce. It was not clear how the brothers spent their time when the shop was closed. The police suspected they were involved in drug trafficking or money laundering, but had never been able to prove it. On three occasions Channing had successfully defended Billy in criminal court, once for fraud and twice on assault charges.

"Need some more stuff?" Billy asked.

"Thanks, but not this time. I need your help with some fieldwork. My wife ran off, and I'll pay good money to find her."

"Why bother? Let her go. I know you've got a lot better girls than her."

"I don't want her back. I just need to find her so I can settle a score."

"You want me to take care of the whole thing or just find her?"

"No, no. If you find her, back off and call me. Don't make any contact. I don't want her to know you found her. I'll take care of it from there."

"What kind of money are we talking about?"

"How about $500 a day and a $10,000 bonus if you find her?"

"The bonus sounds okay, but $600 a day plus expenses sounds better."

Channing frowned but didn't hesitate. "All right. Let's go for a week and see what you come up with. Don't call me at the office." Channing pulled a pen and business card from his shirt pocket and set the card on the table. He crossed out the office number and wrote his home and cell phone numbers on the back, then pushed it across the table.

Billy glanced at the card and then spoke. "What do you have to get me started?"

"Hardly anything. She left last Saturday." Channing placed an index card on the table. "Here's her parents' address in Northern Virginia. I doubt she's there, but check it out. She drove a dark blue Volkswagen Passat. Here's the license number. She took a lot of furniture in a moving van. I don't know what company she used, but the van may have been brown. Here's a recent photo, but she might have changed her hair color by now."

Billy took a long puff on his cigarette, turned his head up and blew a trail of smoke toward the ceiling. "That's all you got? Man, I'm not a magician. I'll take a look around, but this ain't much to go on."

"Yeah, tell me something I don't know. She was pretty slick about it. Really covered her tracks." Channing pulled a fat envelope from his coat pocket and set it on the table in front of him.

Billy smiled. "Hey, your credit's good, man. A check's fine."

"Let's keep it simple and use cash, like regular business," Channing answered, opening the envelope and counting out forty-two $100 bills.

"You're the boss, Channing. You sure you don't need me to handle the whole job?"

"Billy, just find her and don't get anywhere close. Don't do anything else. Just tell me where she is and leave it at that."

"Okay, whatever. Just trying to help."

"Good deal. Keep me posted." Channing stood up, peered through the one-way mirror to see if the coast was clear, then hurried back through the shop and drove away.

CHAPTER 11

Susan's body ached and felt numb all over. During the long afternoon she had discovered a patch of clotted blood in her hair, and her head was gripped by an increasing level of pain. She faded in and out of consciousness. Her only water bottle was now empty, except for a thin sliver of ice. Her mouth was dry, and she sensed that she had little time left.

It was pitch black around her, except for lights of vehicles that occasionally passed in the distance along the highway up above. She tried to turn on the headlights to signal passing motorists, but her car's electrical system was dead. Frigid winter air surrounded her, passing easily through the shattered windows. Her breath turned to fog as she shivered uncontrollably. Having no idea how long she had been trapped, she knew she could not hold out much longer against hunger, thirst, and freezing temperatures.

Her eyes followed the path of several cars as they moved along the road in the distance. Their lights emerged from around a bend and remained steady for about forty-five seconds as they approached the guardrail above her, flickering several times as they passed behind trees that grew on the slopes below the road.

At some point, she thought of checking the glove compartment, which was just within reach of her right hand. The only useful items in it were some crackers, which she ate quickly, and a flashlight. The plastic cover of the flashlight was cracked, but the bulb was intact and the batteries still had some life in them. Her only hope of being found was the chance that someone on the highway might see the flashlight blinking. Struggling against the pain and stiffness in her legs, she gripped her right leg in her hands and pulled it toward her until her foot slipped past the dashboard. She rested it there for a few minutes while she rubbed it and tried to ease its cramping and stiffness. Mustering all of her remaining strength, she suddenly kicked her foot forward, directly into the windshield. The pressure was just strong enough to knock a small hole in the fractured glass.

Wincing in pain, she pulled her leg back and heard it drop to the floor with a gentle thump. She closed her eyes and waited, hoping that in time some semblance of energy would return. She gripped the flashlight, pointed its beam forward, and held it against her chest as she slipped into unconsciousness.

තිංග

Boz parked his car three blocks away from the office, turned off the headlights and sat still as his eyes darted about, watching for any signs of movement on the streets around him. All of the office windows were dark. He glanced at the illuminated face of his watch and noted the time was eleven-forty-five. To be absolutely certain the building was empty, he pulled an office telephone directory from his pocket and began calling each number on his cell phone. He ran through the entire list without getting any response. He had prepared a lame excuse in case someone answered—he would say he couldn't find his wallet and ask them to check his office to see if he had dropped it there. He knew from his regular review of time records that attorneys in the firm rarely worked past eleven at night, although he wasn't sure the place would be empty. He had no personal experience with activity at the firm after hours, as he left every day promptly at five.

Slipping his hands into leather gloves, he held a flashlight in one hand and his briefcase in the other, and then got out of his car. Looking over his shoulder and seeing no movement nearby, he eased inside the building, turned off the burglar alarm, and locked the door. Guided only by his flashlight, he carefully made his way to Winston's office.

Once inside, he closed the door and opened his briefcase. With his smartphone he took several photos of the office. If he moved any furniture or papers, he could review the pictures later to be sure everything was left in its proper place.

He shined the flashlight around the room several times, looking for an inconspicuous place to hide a bug. He moved toward a set of bookshelves near Winston's desk and ran his fingers along the inside of a flange above the bottom shelf, finding just enough space to attach the device.

Directing the light inside his briefcase, Boz located the first bug and lifted it out. It was a thin strip about an inch long, disguised as an air freshener. Inside the strip was a sophisticated miniature transmitter with a range of about 300 yards, more than enough to reach his office. He peeled off an ultra-thin layer of material from the back of the strip, exposing an adhesive substance. Holding the bug gingerly in one hand, he reached under the bookshelf flange to press it into place. It was a tedious process because with gloves on he could not easily manipulate the device. Satisfied that it was snugly in position, he stood up and swept the light around the room. Everything was in place, so he opened the door and stepped into the corridor.

He turned off the flashlight and stood perfectly still for more than a minute. Light from street lamps and nearby buildings cast faint, eerie shadows into the corridor around him. He felt a sudden urge to run out of the building and abandon his risky surveillance plan, but the feeling passed quickly as he listened for the sound of anyone else in the building. Hearing nothing but his own breathing, he switched his flashlight on again and pointed it down at the floor. He crept toward Channing's office, pausing before stepping inside.

He walked softly over to Channing's large display case. Its underside was recessed several inches above the thick wooden edges that supported the glass top. Boz gently pressed the second bug into place on the bottom of the display case, up close to the edge. Silently he retraced his steps to the building's rear entrance, reset the alarm, and locked the door. He walked briskly down the street to his car and hopped in. Glancing at his watch, he saw that the entire operation took just twenty-five minutes.

છ૭ળ૭

Alvin Colquitt reached into his pocket for a candy bar and ripped the wrapper open with his teeth. He ate the chocolate in several large bites and washed it down with the last gulps of Coke that remained in a can on the seat beside him. He hoped the caffeine would keep him alert for at least another hour. If not, he would turn the driving over to his son Ted, who was sleeping on the seat to his right.

They were still more than fifty miles from home and it was

already close to twelve-thirty a.m. They had hunted all day in the woods of West Virginia, having no luck until late in the afternoon. In the back of their white pickup truck were three large coolers full of deer meat. Hours earlier, Ted had spotted a six-point buck moving across a ridge. He brought it down with a single shot at a range of eighty yards, firing before the animal disappeared behind a row of trees. It took nearly two hours to dress the carcass, cut the meat into chunks, and carry them out of the woods to the truck. They had stopped at a convenience store to buy sandwiches for the ride home and ice for their coolers.

As a light snow began to fall, Alvin eased off on the gas pedal, knowing that the road would soon become slick. He switched on the windshield wipers and watched them sweep aside the first flakes of snow. As he followed one of the wipers with his eyes, something in the distance caught his attention. Beyond the edge of the road and to the right of the shoulder, he noticed a faint blinking light. Directly ahead in his lane of travel, he also saw the taillights of a car. Judging from the position of the blinking light in relation to the car, he knew the light was coming from the slope beside the highway, in an area where no house could be standing. He slowed down and pulled onto the shoulder, shaking Ted to wake him up.

"What are you doing?" Ted responded in a groggy and irritable voice. "Are we home yet?"

"Look over there. You see that light down the hill? Somebody must be down there."

Ted peered into the darkness and saw something, but was unimpressed. "Well, they can stay there. Anybody who's hiking this time of night deserves to freeze their ass. We need to get home."

"Ted, we have to check this out. There's a flashlight under the seat. Get it out." Just then he saw the bent guardrail up ahead. The light was no longer flashing, but he knew that something was in the darkness down below. He drifted forward and stopped just short of the guardrail before switching on his emergency flashers. He took the flashlight from Ted and stepped over the guardrail, shining the beam down the hill. The light followed a path of brush that had been mashed down until it revealed a brief glimpse of a car, which was already coated with a thin layer of fresh snow. He scrambled back to the truck, flipped the seat forward and pulled a rope from behind it. Handing the flashlight to Ted, he tied one end of the rope around the door hinge and carried it to the edge of the hill.

"Okay, Ted. Keep the light shining just ahead of me as I go down there. If I need you to come down, I'll yell."

"I'll be right here. Be careful down there."

Alvin pulled a pair of gloves from his pocket, put them on, and then started down the slope. The snow was thick in the air as he approached the car. He was able to open the passenger door, but the force of gravity slammed it shut as soon as he let go of it. He tied the rope around the door handle and shouted to Ted to pull. With the door open, he leaned forward and looked inside. Ted struggled to hold the rope and keep the flashlight pointed at the car, but as the beam bounced back and forth Alvin could see a woman slumped over in the driver's seat.

He called to her, and she turned her head slightly at the sound of his voice. He smelled a faint hint of gasoline in the air as he reached inside and slipped the flashlight out of her hand.

"My leg's jammed," she said in a soft, shivering voice.

Alvin shined the light on the seat belt and saw that the metal tab was bent. He wedged the flashlight into the back of the passenger seat to keep it pointed toward the woman and then leaned into the vehicle as far as he could. He shoved with all his strength against the tab, forcing it to straighten just enough to pull it free from its receptacle.

As snowflakes landed on her face, she gained a bit of energy. She whispered "thank you" and then motioned toward her left leg. "It's caught in there, but I can move it a little."

"All right. Reach toward me and I'll try to pull you in my direction."

She raised her right arm and extended it out. Alvin grabbed the arm with both hands and tugged on it as she pushed her right leg against the floor. She gritted her teeth as pain shot through her left leg when it began to slip free. Clutching the man's coat in both hands, she helped him pull her toward the open door.

He lifted her out and gently set her on the ground while he untied the rope from the car door. Wrapping the rope around his waist, he leaned down until his face was just above her head as she lay on the ground. "There's no way you can walk on that leg. This will probably hurt, but I'll have to carry you over my shoulder. Hold onto my coat as best you can."

She nodded. Alvin gathered her in his arms and lifted her onto his right shoulder, with her legs dangling across his chest. He wrapped his right arm around the back of her knees and grabbed the rope, then shouted to Ted to pull on it. Holding his left arm out to keep his balance, Alvin gradually climbed up the hill. His feet slipped several times, causing her to moan in pain. By the time he reached the highway she had lost consciousness. The two men placed her in the middle of the seat, and Ted quickly untied the rope and threw it in the truck bed. He jumped into the cab as Alvin started the engine and then headed down the highway.

Ted held his hand under her nose and felt her shallow breath against his cold fingers. "She's got a pulse and she's breathing, but we need to get her to a hospital. She may have been down there for several days."

"I think there's a hospital about fifty miles away. Hang on and I'll go as fast as I can, but I have to be careful not to skid off the road."

Ted put his arms around the woman and held her as the truck headed through a thickening snowfall on the way to Charleston. He checked her pulse every few minutes. As they reached the outskirts of the city, he turned to Alvin. "I think she's gone."

CHAPTER 12

Dropping several quarters into the paper box, Lee reached inside and retrieved a copy of *The Daily Progress*. He was back in Charlottesville for another weekend of UVA sports. He had chosen a place about eight blocks from the soccer field, deliberately passing up a room in a closer hotel. Walking to the game would help him strengthen his legs. Recovery from the bullet wounds had been slow, but he was determined to keep pushing himself. He knew he would never fully recover because part of his lung was missing, but he would do his best with what he had to work with. He ambled inside the hotel and recognized the clerk from earlier visits.

Handing him a key card, the man complimented Lee on his recovery. "You're walking a little stronger every time I see you. Keep it up and you'll be running wind sprints before long."

Lee laughed loudly and handed his credit card across the counter. "I'm working on it. I guess I'll have to leave you a big tip when I check out."

He found his room and stretched out on the bed, waiting for his breathing to slow down. Stuffing some pillows behind his back, he sat up and reached into the bag for the morning paper. He studied the sports page at length and then took a quick look at the front page and local news section. He was about to put the paper away when he noticed a short paragraph entitled "Lottery Update." The winner of last week's jackpot had 172 days left to claim the prize, it said. Wally Pennington was quoted, saying he doubted that any of his regular players had won. He knew those customers personally, and none of them had said anything to him about winning. He guessed it was someone who had been passing through town, or an occasional player who had jumped on the bandwagon during the buying frenzy that led up to the drawing. He would have to wait like everyone else to see who turned in the ticket. "All I know is that I didn't win it," he added.

"Me either," Lee said to himself as he closed his eyes for a nap before the game.

Two hours later, he awoke and began to gear up for the soccer match. He folded the sports page, tucked it into a pocket, and left the hotel for a leisurely trek to Klöckner Stadium. Along the way, many fans scurried past him, eager to arrive early for good seats. Lee watched them hustle around him and longed for the days when he could have sprinted all the way to the stadium without breaking a sweat. He kept up a measured, steady pace, occasionally feeling pain in his injured knee but pressing ahead with a determined spirit. He saw couples and families with young kids running back and forth, and thought of the family life that had been stolen from him by some miserable punk in Charleston.

In the months that passed after Andrea's murder, loneliness had often been his only companion. Occasionally he visited the bars in Charlottesville and back home, but most women he met there were too young to take any interest in someone his age. He hoped he would find another soul mate someday, but as time wore on his hope was fading.

Lee recognized the ticket collector as he passed through the stadium entrance, exchanging a quick greeting as the surging crowd carried him along like driftwood on an ocean wave. He had slept too long to take time for lunch at the quaint restaurant across from the hotel, so he stocked up on hot dogs, pretzels and a huge souvenir cup of Dr. Pepper at a concession stand.

At first, the game was not as exciting as Lee hoped it would be. There was no score after eighteen minutes, and then the Cavaliers made some adjustments to help penetrate Duke's defensive formation.

After that, the home team put on a scoring clinic, leading by as much as four goals during the second half.

A rookie center forward scored the first goal of his college career, and then added two more before the game ended with Virginia holding a comfortable lead.

As the crowd thinned out, Lee remained in his seat and enjoyed the afternoon air. He had no schedule to keep, and no urgent business. When the stands were nearly empty he began his descent to ground level, climbing gingerly down the steps to avoid putting too much pressure on his knee.

With no particular destination in mind, Lee drove around the city for about an hour to kill time. Recalling the lottery story from the morning paper, he decided to visit the store that sold the jackpot ticket.

The place was almost deserted when he arrived. Wally had left his post behind the counter and was tidying up some misplaced merchandise on a display rack. Lee noticed the nametag on Wally's shirt and recognized him as the owner who was quoted in the newspaper. With a broad smile he greeted Wally and extended his hand. "I'm in town for a visit and saw your name in the paper this morning. I figured if I shook your hand, some of your luck might rub off on me."

Wally gripped Lee's hand and welcomed him to the store. "Well, I can't guarantee anything, but thanks for stopping by. The lottery thing was great for business, but to be honest it got too hectic for me. I'm glad the pace has slowed down now. I'm hoping to take a fishing trip out west sometime, but I'll wait for warmer weather before I go out there."

"That's a good idea. I did some fly fishing in Wyoming one summer, back about fifteen years ago. I think it was in June, and conditions were just perfect that time of year."

Wally's eyes brightened, and the two men had a friendly conversation in the middle of the store, exchanging fishing stories. Eventually the conversation turned back to the lottery win, and Lee asked if Wally had heard any rumors about who might have won.

"I really don't have a clue about it," Wally said. "Well, I have a clue, but it's not much to go on."

Intrigued, Lee pumped Wally for details. Motioning for Lee to follow him, Wally strolled back to the counter. A stack of music CDs sat near the end of the counter, next to a boom box. Nearby was a green plastic case with an unlabeled DVD inside. Wally held it up and showed it to Lee.

"I saved my surveillance camera photos from the week of the drawing. When the winner comes forward I'll check this disc to see if I can spot him. I thought it would be fun to see a picture of him buying the ticket. I also figured a guy that rich might pay me something to have it as a souvenir."

Lee glanced above the counter and saw a security camera pointing down at the cash register and lottery ticket dispenser. "What a great idea! I never would have thought of something like that." He paused and then asked a question. "You say a rich guy might pay for the picture. I'm just curious—do you think it was a guy and not a woman?"

Wally laughed and shrugged his shoulders. "Who knows? If it's a woman, maybe she's single and wants a man in her life!"

Lee let out a laugh that echoed off the walls. "Wouldn't that be great?! If she's interested in a guy from South Carolina, give me a call."

Wally smiled. "Sure, buddy, but only if she turns me down first. I have to look out for number one. It's fun to think about it, but the winner's probably some old geezer from California who'll never set foot in my store again."

"I hope you can sell the photo anyway." Lee reached in his pocket and extracted a $10 bill, handing it across the counter. "Well, I better let you get back to work, but while I'm here I might as well buy a ticket just for luck."

Wally pressed a button on the lottery machine and handed Lee a slip with several rows of numbers on it. "You never know. Good luck."

CHAPTER 13

Annie Louise stared out of her window in Saint Albert Hospital, watching as a flurry of snowflakes drifted silently past the thick plate glass, nearing the end of their gentle descent. Across the street in a public park, a shimmering blanket of snow continued to thicken as the storm showed no sign of weakening. It had snowed intermittently for more than two days, dumping more than twenty inches across most of West Virginia. The streets were virtually deserted, except for an occasional snowplow or emergency vehicle. The sidewalks were invisible, buried under the heavy accumulation, and the few hardy souls who dared to venture outside were forced to walk in the street, directly in front of the hospital.

For several days Annie had the luxury of being the only occupant in the room, until a second patient was brought in two nights before at around three a.m. The new patient had been quiet for the most part, sleeping much of the time. Occasionally she would open her eyes and shift about in bed or mumble a few words, most of which were unintelligible.

Annie lived in a dilapidated mobile home, one of several dozen that were crowded onto a lot at Rudy's Trailer Court. She worked sporadically at several odd jobs, sometimes as a waitress at various fast food joints. Over the years she had bounced in and out of a series of relationships but had not managed to hang onto any of the men in her life. The last one lived in her trailer for three months before running off with a Walmart cashier.

Annie had finished her shift at a pizza restaurant around noon last Saturday. She started drinking early that afternoon and drained the last ounce from a bottle of apple wine before heading into town to stock up on essentials before the snowstorm hit. As she emerged from a liquor store and stepped onto a treacherous patch of ice, her feet shot out from under her and sent her sprawling onto the sidewalk. A brown paper bag stuffed with a large bottle of bourbon flew out of her hand and landed with a loud crunch a few feet ahead of her. She gripped her right leg and felt a searing pain in her ankle, which had fractured like the glass bottle in her bag. She watched as bourbon leaked out of the soggy bag and spread into a small puddle on the ice.

A surgeon inserted several metal pins to stabilize the bones in her ankle and covered it with a heavy cast that was thick and uncomfortable.

Annie watched as nurses and doctors slipped in and out of the room from time to time to check on the new patient. They took her pulse, monitored her heartbeat and occasionally shined a small light in her eyes, then scribbled notes on a clipboard that was tucked into a slot at the end of her bed. Sometimes they glanced across the room and nodded at Annie, but rarely said a word.

When the patient eventually opened her eyes, she lay still for a long time without showing any reaction to her surroundings. She felt little sensation in her body at first, but gradually realized that many of her muscles were sore and stiff. There was a slight burning feeling in her right hand, and she wondered if her fuzzy thinking was an indication of a dull headache or just too much sleep. Her eyes moved slowly along the bedrails and down to her hand, which was buried in a mass of white bandages. She could see a thin streak of discolored skin around the edge of the wrapping, which stretched as she slowly extended her fingers. The motion aggravated the nerves on the surface of her skin, and it felt as if someone had rubbed a wire brush across the back of her hand.

She noticed a plastic tube that ran from under a patch of gauze that was taped to her left arm. She felt her starched sheets with her left hand and held the plastic wristband up to her face to read it. She understood that she was in a hospital bed but had no memory of arriving there.

The last moment she could recall was the flash of a deer in front of her car, followed immediately by the roar of inflating airbags. *It's probably better that I don't remember anything after that*, she thought. At least she was alive and all in one piece. She turned her head gently to one side and noticed her roommate a few feet away, staring out the window as the snow continued to fall. Susan could think of nothing to say.

Eventually Annie turned her head away from the window and glanced at her roommate. "Well, you're still alive, honey. My name's Annie."

Susan managed a weak smile before introducing herself. "Susan—Susan Booker." She paused. "I mean Susan Finley," she whispered. "How long have I been here?"

"A couple days. You've been out of it most of the time."

"Yeah, I guess so."

"What happened, sweetie?" Annie asked.

"I thought maybe you could tell me. Don't remember much. I think I was in a car wreck somewhere."

Annie smiled. "Your doctor's real quiet. He ain't told me nothing."

Susan brushed her left hand against her head and felt the small knots on a row of stitches. "I must have hit my head and blacked out."

"You've definitely been out of it. That's for sure."

Their conversation continued until they were interrupted by the arrival of Susan's doctor. He was a young, earnest fellow with tired eyes and a rumpled white lab coat. He had been on duty for three straight shifts, covering for other physicians who lived at a distance from the hospital and couldn't get through the snow.

The doctor wore a haggard expression but brightened a bit when he saw that Susan was finally awake and relatively alert. Ordinarily, he would have made small talk for a moment or two, but today he had neither the time nor the mood for it. "Hi, I'm Dr. Bogert. You're at Saint Albert Hospital. You were in an automobile accident. Do you remember anything that happened?"

Susan started to extend her right hand but pulled it back when she remembered it was covered with bandages. "Not really. I think I hit a deer, but that's about it."

"Do you remember your name?"

"Susan Finley."

"Hmm." He reached for the clipboard at the end of the bed and glanced at the top page before turning back to her. "We have you listed as Susan Booker."

She decided it wasn't worth a long explanation. "Oh, right. Finley's my maiden name. Sorry."

"No problem." He held up two fingers and asked how many she saw.

"I see all of them—both of them," she replied.

"That's good. I'd like you to follow my finger with your eyes," he said, waving his index finger back and forth across her field of vision as she watched its movement.

"Excellent. Now I'll check your pulse." He reached across to her left wrist and gently pressed two fingers against an artery as he looked down at his watch and counted thirty seconds. "Very good." He flipped through several sheets on the clipboard and scanned them quickly. Pulling a pen from the front pocket of his lab coat, he scribbled some notes and check marks on one page. Susan studied his face intently as he reviewed her chart, trying to read his expression for a sign of her condition. His face revealed no hint of emotion until he looked up and saw her eyes focused on his. He smiled briefly, and then set the clipboard down. "Susan, you're very lucky. Your vital signs are essentially normal. Blood tests are within acceptable limits. You had some slight cerebral swelling when you were brought in, but it cleared up nicely. I believe you had a concussion, but your latest MRI and neurological tests are unremarkable. There was a scalp wound that we cleaned and sutured. The stitches will dissolve in about two weeks. Unfortunately it'll take some time for your hair to grow back."

Susan breathed a sigh of relief. "I guess I'll try a shorter hairstyle."

"The tissue on your right hand sustained some damage, but we caught it well short of frostbite. You'll have some pain or discomfort for a week or so, and we'll give you medication for that. The discoloration should clear up over time. The only other concern is some facial abrasions, probably from contact with the air bag. One may leave a slight scar. We'll have to wait and see, but there's a chance that all of them will resolve nicely, with no scarring at all. I don't see any internal injury as of now, but I'd like to keep you here for observation for several days. Do you have any questions?"

"So basically I'm going to be fine?"

"I'd say your prognosis is excellent. You were lucky."

"How did I get here after the accident? I don't remember being rescued."

"That's not unusual with a concussion injury." Dr. Bogert picked up the clipboard again and turned to the initial intake page. "The admission form says two men brought you in, but their names aren't in the records. That's all the information I have."

"Thanks, I feel much better after talking with you. The only other question I can think of right now is when can I eat something?"

"I'll tell the nurse to bring you some dinner. We won't need to feed you with the IV any more so she can disconnect it." He slipped the clipboard back into place and said goodbye, then headed out the door and disappeared down the corridor to continue his rounds.

Susan glanced over at Annie, who had been following the conversation from the beginning. "Looks like I'll be out of here soon. That's a relief."

"Yeah, you look much better than when you came in here."

"The doctor looks tired, but he seems to know his stuff."

"Yeah, I think you can trust Bogert."

"I guess I'll have to. I don't have much choice." Susan looked across the room at the window beside Annie's bed and watched the falling snow. She was pleased to know her injuries were only temporary, but she remained uneasy about her circumstances. She wondered if her accident had been reported to the police or written up in the local paper.

She was convinced that Channing would try to hunt her down and retaliate for her surprise departure, for her large withdrawals from their bank accounts, and for removing much of the furniture from the house. Channing had been abusive enough before she left, and it was a safe bet that he was furious now, even to the point of behaving irrationally.

She could only imagine what Sylvia must be thinking out in South Dakota. With no word from Susan, would she panic and call Channing and blow her cover? Did the movers deliver their load according to plan? What happened to the money she withdrew from the bank? Had the hospital contacted Channing? Questions swirled through her mind like the snowflakes outside the window.

"So where are you from?" Annie asked, trying to keep the conversation going.

"Charlottesville, Virginia."

"Never heard of it."

"It's in the central part of the state. A great place, but I had to get out of there. My husband's been cheating on me for a long time, he's into drugs, and he's gambled away most of our money. He started slapping me around, and I was afraid it would get worse."

"Sounds like some of the men I've known, honey. Well, except for the gambling. My men never had much money to lose."

"Yeah, it got to be more than I could handle."

"I'm real sorry. You think you'll go back someday?"

"No chance. I moved out one day while he was away. He doesn't know where I am. At least I hope he doesn't. I need to keep moving to be safe."

"Well, right now you won't get far with that snow out there. I heard a lot of them hospital workers still can't get in here. So what's next? Where you goin' when you get out of here?"

Susan had been careful to keep her plan quiet so far, but she was sure Annie and Channing would never meet. Annie seemed sympathetic and harmless, so Susan decided it was safe to share some details with her. "I've got a college friend out west. I'm heading out to Aberdeen, South Dakota to stay with her until I figure out what to do next. I don't know where I'll end up after I get a divorce and things calm down."

"Aberdeen. Ain't that some kind of cow? I heard about Aberdeen Angus steaks over at a diner I used to work at."

"I don't know. I really don't know much about Aberdeen, but I know it's a hell of a long way from Charlottesville, so I'm pretty sure—" Susan paused for a second, feeling a sudden sense of paranoia. Maybe she shouldn't give out so much information. Maybe it would be better not to mention Channing's name. Who knows, maybe someday he'd offer a reward to find her, and it was at least possible that Annie could hear about it. As if to explain her sudden pause, she cleared her throat. "Excuse me. Pretty sure he won't find me," she continued.

"Well, if he's as worthless as the men I know, he won't try to find you," Annie replied. Her advice came with an air of authority. Susan sensed that she was an expert on the subject, a woman who had endured the worst that men could offer.

"I hope you're right, but I don't want to hang around long enough to find out." Her voice trailed off as a nurse entered the room, carrying a plastic tray with her dinner.

Like Dr. Bogert, she looked exhausted after working extra shifts during the snowstorm. She set the tray down next to Susan, pushed a button to elevate one end of the bed, and helped adjust the pillows behind her back to prop her up. She said a perfunctory greeting and disconnected the IV tube before disappearing as quickly as she had come in, leaving Susan to eat her first meal in several days.

Annie decided not to bother her while she ate, and turned her attention to a game show on TV. Their conversation resumed after she finished eating, but a short time later Susan drifted off to sleep.

When she awoke the next morning, most of the clouds outside were gone, giving way to bright sunshine and rising temperatures. She turned to look outside, gazing at the park across the street. She could see deep drifts that spread out like giant waves on an ocean of white snow. Icicles that hung from the streetlights and the rooftops nearby had started to melt, dripping water onto the ground below. A convoy of snowplows was clearing the streets, and pedestrians were moving about as the city began to resume its normal activity.

Susan rubbed her eyes and took several deep breaths. She felt no pain in her chest, and the fuzzy sensation in her head had subsided for the most part. There was still some stiffness in her legs and a little tenderness under the bandage on her right hand, but she felt much better. Annie's TV was off and she was still asleep. Susan found the call button that was attached to her bedrail and signaled for the duty nurse, who appeared a few minutes later with a breakfast tray. She greeted Susan with a smile, a sign that she had just started her shift after missing several workdays because of the snow. The nurse checked her vital signs and recorded the results in the chart before tucking it back in place at the end of the bed.

"Your signs are looking good, Susan," she chirped.

"Thanks, I'm feeling much better. Is there any chance I could check out later today? I need to get on the road as soon as I can."

"We'll have to see what Dr. Nokes says. I understand you were in a pretty nasty accident, and you need to be careful that you don't leave before you're really up to it." She patted Susan's arm and slipped out of the room.

Susan gobbled up her scrambled eggs and bacon, and then found a magazine in the bedside table drawer and read it until she got tired and settled back for a nap.

A few hours later, a gentle squeeze on her arm awoke her. She slowly gathered herself into a comfortable position as her eyes began to focus on the man who stood beside her bed. "Simon Nokes, Ms. Booker," he announced as he extended a hand. She brushed the magazine off her lap and held out her hand to shake his.

"I guess I better use this hand until the other one heals. Susan Finley. I go by my maiden name now."

"I see. Nice to meet you, Susan." He studied the chart that was clutched in one hand as he checked her pulse with the other one. He jotted some numbers on the chart and then set it down before taking her right hand. He gently unwrapped the bandage and lightly touched the back of her hand. The skin was dull red in color and sensitive, but the slight pressure from his finger was only mildly uncomfortable. "Does that hurt?" he asked.

"It's not too bad. It doesn't seem as tender as it was yesterday."

"Excellent. You're making great progress." He reached into one pocket of his lab coat and produced a tube of ointment that he expertly applied to her skin, then pulled a fresh bandage from another pocket and carefully wrapped it around her hand. He asked her to turn her head toward him as he examined the stitches before scribbling more notes on the chart. He flipped through each page of her records until he reached the last one, pausing to read it carefully. He glanced up at Susan and then back at the page. After a few moments he set the clipboard down on the bed and spoke. "Well, I've read Dr. Bogert's report and looked at the lab tests. You're improving rapidly and I think you'll have a full recovery. I'd like to keep you here another day or two for observation, and then you should be ready for discharge. How does that sound?"

Feeling rested and optimistic about her condition, Susan was eager to leave. She assumed that Channing was still searching for her, and Sylvia must be going crazy worrying about her. She could only imagine how high the hospital bill was at the moment, and she would have to pay it in cash. Filing an insurance claim would leave a paper trail for Channing to follow. "Doctor, I'm really feeling pretty good. I've been traveling and I'm way overdue. I'd like to leave this afternoon if at all possible."

He frowned and shoved a hand in his pocket as he rubbed his chin with the other one. "I don't recommend it, but you'll probably be okay if you take it easy and promise to call immediately if you feel any unusual symptoms." He hesitated a moment and then continued, leaning forward and speaking in a low voice. "It's not really my concern, but the intake sheet says you were carrying almost $45,000 in cash and checks when you were brought in. Are you sure you're ready to go? Is there anything I can help you with?"

Susan wanted to accept his offer and unload her problems on him. It would be a relief to confide in someone and ask for help. But she resisted the temptation, believing it was best to stick with the plan that she and Sylvia had crafted so carefully. She had probably told Annie too much already, and her plan's success depended on secrecy. "I appreciate the offer, but I'll be fine. I've got some personal business to take care of. I promise I'll be careful, and I'll call if there's any problem."

He looked at his watch and then back at Susan. "If you insist, I'll sign a release order, but I strongly advise against leaving today. It's going to be getting dark in just a few hours, and I'd hate to see you out on the road tonight."

Susan had to agree. She wasn't eager to drive right away, and it would take some time to rent a car. By the time she got on the road it would be almost sundown, and she certainly wasn't going to drive all night. It would be easier to spend one more night in the hospital than to find a motel. "Okay, you've convinced me. I'll wait until tomorrow morning."

Nokes gave her left hand a gentle squeeze and smiled. "Great. I wish you good luck. I'll be off duty in the morning, but Dr. Bogert will be back, and the nurses will help check you out." He gestured toward a locker in the corner of the room. "Your clothes are in there. Your wallet is in a safe at the business office on the main floor. You'll have to sign a receipt for it when you check out with the bursar. They'll give you some pain medication to take with you in case you need it, with instructions and our contact information."

CHAPTER 14

Scotty Warfield dropped his cigarette butt in the ash tray and arched his back, pressing it against the cheap vinyl surface of his seat. His back and neck felt as stiff as the seat, but he decided to keep driving since they were in the home stretch. The cab was cluttered with napkins, crumpled hamburger wrappers, empty aluminum cans and other trash that had accumulated from truck stops and fast food joints along the way. The floor was damp and slimy from the mud and snow they had tracked in at each stop. The side windows were streaked with a grimy film that remained after dirty snow had melted, and the edges of the windshield were covered with slush kicked up from the pavement by passing vehicles.

On Scotty's right, Miguel Buello dozed under an old Army surplus blanket, resting his head and shoulder against the door. Both men wore shirts that were rumpled and stained. They had packed only a few extra clothes, expecting to be on the road for just a couple of days each way. Heavy snow and ice storms in Missouri and Iowa had slowed their progress, forcing them to spend several extra nights in small towns along their route.

The drive had been unbelievably monotonous—hundreds of miles across the flat, snow-covered plains of the Midwest. During the trip, the numbing sameness of the countryside was broken only by the occasional appearance of a barn, grain silo or herd of cattle. Visibility was poor much of the way, as frozen precipitation constantly pelted their windshield. The defroster had been running at full blast most of the time, drowning out the radio with an obnoxious humming sound. Several times they had tried to call Susan, but never got an answer.

As he passed a road sign with Aberdeen listed at the top, Scotty leaned forward and checked the GPS to measure their progress. They were approaching Aberdeen from the east, and their destination was about twenty-five miles beyond the town. Checking his watch, he decided there was enough time to stop for lunch.

He gently tapped Miguel's leg and waited for a response. After a few moments Miguel opened his eyes and slowly shifted his weight away from the door. He yawned and rubbed a hand on the back of his neck, turning his head from side to side to ease the stiffness in his muscles. "Where are we?" he asked in a groggy voice.

"We're just a few miles from Aberdeen. The drop's about twenty-five miles after that, and it's almost noon, so let's find someplace in town and eat before we go on."

Miguel lifted the blanket off his lap and left it in a heap between them. He looked at the open fields ahead, which were brilliantly white now that the clouds had parted and allowed the sun to appear. Waving a finger at the clouds, he sighed. "It's about time it cleared up. I'm sick of snow and ice and all the crap we came through." He touched the window glass with the palm of his hand and held it there for a few seconds. "Still pretty cold out there. Man, that snow is bright." He pulled a pair of sunglasses from the glove compartment and put them on.

As the truck approached the outskirts of Aberdeen, its tires glided over long patches of packed snow on the highway, which muffled their sound. There was little traffic in evidence, and few signs of other activity, as they headed down what appeared to be the primary street in the town. They saw a short, stocky man emerge from a barber shop and walk briskly down the sidewalk. His breath froze in the air as he exhaled, puffing like a smokestack.

Scotty glanced up at the icicles that hung from overhead power lines as he guided the truck through the middle of town. They came to a small shopping center with a McDonald's restaurant. Two crows that had been scavenging for crumbs on the pavement flew away as the truck approached. Scotty eased it into an open space next to a huge mound of snow that remained after the parking lot had been cleared.

As they walked across the pavement toward the restaurant, Miguel reached into his shirt pocket and realized he had left his pack of cigarettes in the cab. He turned to retrace his steps, but stopped in his tracks when he saw the back of the truck. Scotty whirled around as he heard a string of four-letter words and saw Miguel staring at the base of the two large doors at the rear of the cargo bay. The padlock that usually secured the doors was missing. There were several deep scratches around the latch, evidence that someone had wrestled with a bolt cutter to break the lock.

The weather was dark and nasty when they had started out that morning, and they had hopped into the cab without checking the rear doors. Fearing the worst, they turned the latch and pulled one door open. Several boxes were torn apart, and it was obvious that some were missing. Packing paper was strewn about haphazardly, tossed aside as the thief had searched through the boxes for items that were both valuable and easy to carry. Apparently this was not a professional burglary because most of the cargo was still intact. They guessed that whoever stole the items probably took only as much as they could cram into a single vehicle.

Scotty surveyed the mess while Miguel walked to the cab and returned with his cigarettes and a roll of thick packing tape. They began collecting the scattered wrapping materials and placing loose items back in boxes, taping them shut as each one was filled. Scotty noticed one box that was turned on its side, half full of old books. A few leather-bound volumes were spread around the floor nearby. He quickly packed them back into the box, glancing at their titles as he stuffed them in. "We got some Chaucer and Dickens here, and some guy named Voltaire," he muttered. "What a weird name. Who reads junk like this?" he asked rhetorically.

"Who cares? Just so we don't get caught. Maybe she won't notice," Miguel replied.

"I don't know. It looks like they took some of these books. The box ain't full now," Scotty said, as he dropped the last one in and covered it with wads of crumpled paper.

Miguel taped the last box shut and the two hustled into the restaurant to get lunch. They glanced back at the truck several times while they waited in line to order. When their food was ready they chose a table near a front window so they could keep an eye on the truck. They quickly gobbled down their hamburgers and fries. Miguel puffed on a cigarette, flicking the ashes into a cheap plastic ash tray. "Did you see a hardware store anywhere? We'll need a better lock for the truck."

"No, but don't sweat it. The truck's empty on the way back, and we're already late. Plus I want to get out of this dump," Scotty answered. "Let's get going. You can drive the rest of the way."

As they reached the truck, Scotty checked the rear door latch again to make sure it was closed all the way. They climbed up into the cab, rumbled out of the parking lot and followed signs to Route 281. Scotty stretched out his legs as far as the cab would allow and studied the notes he had scribbled when Susan called two weeks earlier to give directions. When he saw a sign pointing to Westport, he told Miguel what he was waiting to hear. "We're close now—less than five more miles. Look for a big red mailbox that's shaped like a bird house, with 'The Haven' written on it."

Miguel rolled the window down and tossed his cigarette out. "I hope she won't open any boxes while we're there."

They drove the rest of the way in silence. Approaching the entrance to Sylvia's farm, Miguel slowed down and carefully turned the truck into her driveway, watching in the side mirror to be sure the van didn't scrape against the mailbox. The truck shifted slightly as its wheels dropped off the pavement onto the gravel surface of the driveway, which was almost a half mile long. It was lined on both sides with a row of tall evergreen trees. Behind the trees was a solid board fence, painted black, tall enough to keep horses in their fields. A thin strip of snow ran along the tops of each board like a layer of white icing on a chocolate cake. The truck bounced up and down as it rolled through potholes that were filled with melting slush.

In the paddock to their left, a circular riding ring sat empty. A small shed nearby was filled with barrels, poles and assorted equipment that would return to the ring when warm weather arrived in a few months.

Beyond the ring and farther down the driveway, a long metal structure was set back away from the fence. There were two wide doors in the middle, one of which was open. A tractor was parked out in front, and through the door they could see a hay baler and other farm machinery.

They passed a large stable that stood at a distance in the field on their right. A row of small windows ran along the side of the building, one window for each stall. Each window was shuttered to keep the winter air from blowing in on the horses. Off in the distance, about a dozen cattle were clustered around a large hay bale.

When they reached the house and climbed out of their truck, Sylvia appeared on the front porch and waved. They braced themselves for the confrontation that would erupt if she wanted to open the boxes and inspect the load.

Their reputations and paychecks hung in the balance. The moment of truth having arrived, they put their game faces on and stepped forward to meet her.

Sylvia extended her hand to Scotty, so it fell to him to speak first. Relieved that Scotty would be handling the introductions, Miguel held his breath and waited. Forcing a thin smile, Scotty shook her hand. "Scotty Warfield, ma'am. It's a beautiful ranch you've got here, Ms. Finley."

Sylvia looked puzzled and hesitated. "Nice to meet you. I'm Susan Finley's friend, Sylvia Ricketts."

"Oh, I'm sorry. I thought she'd be meeting us here. Is she around?"

"I've been expecting her to call, but I'm not sure where she is. Let me show you where to unload her things, and I'll write you a check when you're finished."

Smiling broadly, Miguel reached out to shake her hand, bubbling over with artificial enthusiasm. "I'm Miguel Buello. We work in lots of places, but it's a real treat to see a farm like this." He cast his gaze across the nearest field to emphasize the point. "I'm sorry we won't get to meet Ms. Finley. She sounded real nice on the phone. She called us about a week ago and gave us directions. We figured she'd be here."

"I did, too. Something must have come up." Sylvia paused for a moment, trying to suppress her fear that Susan was in trouble. The men glanced at a dog pen and then studied the gravel at their feet as they waited for her to continue. Regaining her composure, she invited them to follow as she walked to the fence near the guest cottage. Resting one arm over the top board, she pointed to the stable in the field, several hundred yards away. "I'm afraid there's not a lot of space, but I'm hoping everything will fit in a few stalls in that barn. Do you need me to go with you out there?"

"No thanks," Miguel answered quickly. "I think we're all set. We'll give a yell if we have any trouble."

They walked back to the truck, and Sylvia told them to let her know when they finished. They agreed and guided the truck back down the driveway, confident that Sylvia's check would clear long before anyone discovered that some of Susan's books and other items were missing. Scotty drove across the field at a moderate pace, just fast enough to avoid getting stuck in the mud and slush. Small piles of dung were scattered across the pasture like visible land mines, but the men were eager to finish the job and get away, so they didn't try to avoid them. They would flip a coin to see who had to wash the truck.

Inside the stable, several fluorescent lights ran along the ceiling over a central aisle that extended from one end to the other, separating two rows of stalls. The lighting was uneven, and the first stall was darker than the others. Its rear wall was barely visible in the shadows, and they put the first boxes in the darkest corner. They couldn't be sure what items had been stolen, but it was clear that these boxes, packed near the back of the truck, had been opened. They carried most of the furniture into a large double stall in the middle of the barn and covered it with tarps that Sylvia had left in a stack nearby.

They carted most of the boxes from the middle of the load into the second and third stalls, and then filled the rest of the first stall with the boxes that were at the front of the truck. They packed the dark stall as tightly as possible, putting some of the heaviest boxes near the entrance so it would be harder to reach the ones on the bottom in the far corner. The sun was low on the horizon when they shoved the last box into place.

Back at the house, Sylvia offered them something to drink, but they politely declined and made small talk while she wrote out a check. She thanked them, and they got in the truck and headed up the driveway. There was just enough time to cash Sylvia's check in Aberdeen before the banks closed.

CHAPTER 15

Susan awoke early. Several days of rest in the hospital had helped to heal the worst of her physical pain, and had tempered the raw emotions that gripped her when she fled from Virginia. She felt rested and was eager to join her friend in South Dakota. Annie was still asleep across the room. As quietly as she could, Susan lowered her bed rail and sat up, slowly adjusting to a new position after lying down for several days.

There was little activity in the hallway outside her room, as the staff for the morning shift had not yet arrived. Only a dim glow of daylight crept through the window shades, as the sun was still below the horizon. She took advantage of the relative quiet to gather her thoughts. From what Dr. Nokes told her, she knew that her money had been in her coat pocket when she was pulled from her car, but she still had little memory of the accident or her rescue.

In planning her escape several weeks earlier, she initially considered carrying all the money she would withdraw from the bank in the form of cash. Then it occurred to her that transporting $45,000 in cash would require her to carry a huge stack of $100 bills. It would be almost impossible to hide that much money in her pockets, and risky as well. She had a vague recollection that banks kept records of large cash transfers, so she had done some research online and found that certain transactions of $3,000 or more were reported to the authorities.

It didn't matter if the $45,000 withdrawal was reported because Channing would find out about that anyway. She had withdrawn the money and then visited fourteen other banks, buying a cashier's check at each bank in the amount of $2,900. She kept the rest of the money in cash, stuffing a wad of $100 bills into a Ziploc bag and filling her wallet with the checks and the rest of the cash.

She had assumed that $45,000 would be enough money to tide her over until she could begin divorce proceedings and force Channing to start paying her an allowance or alimony, if he hadn't blown the rest of his money by then. She hadn't planned on losing her car and paying a hospital bill, but she would have to make do with the money she had.

She slowly eased off the bed, cautiously lowering her feet to the floor. She clutched the bed rail and gradually put more weight on her legs, making sure she was strong enough to stand upright. She was light-headed for a short while, but soon felt comfortable on her feet and guessed that she would feel better after eating breakfast. Taking short, deliberate steps, she crossed the room to reach the locker. Her clothes had been washed, but faint mud stains were still visible. She slipped into the bathroom and took a long, hot shower before returning to the locker. She fretted that she would be leaving the hospital with lifeless hair and no makeup on, but it felt good to get out of her hospital gown and into real clothes. She decided to check out and then return to her room to see if Annie was awake, so she could say goodbye. If not, she would leave a short note beside her bed.

She ambled out of the room and down the hallway to an elevator. She studied a floor directory, then entered and pushed the button for the third floor. A short, chubby woman in the bursar's office clipped the patient ID bracelet from her wrist, reading some numbers on the plastic band as she typed them into her computer. She disappeared briefly into an adjoining room before returning with Susan's wallet and the bag stuffed with cash. She set it on the counter and smiled. "I guess you don't travel light. Do you want to count it?"

Knowing that she couldn't prove how much cash had been in the bag, Susan replied diplomatically. "No, thanks. I trust you."

The woman chuckled. "Maybe you should see the bill before you say that." She paused for an instant and then returned to her computer and resumed typing. "Just kidding. We'll take care of filing the paperwork for you. We copied the health insurance card from your wallet. Is it still current?"

Susan hated to part with her cash, but she couldn't afford to leave a paper trail for Channing to follow. "Actually, I'd like to pay now and not bill it to my insurance. I'm kind of sensitive about keeping my medical records private."

Amazed, the woman stopped typing and looked Susan in the eye. "You're kidding, right? Nobody pays out of pocket. It's unheard of."

"I'm serious. How much is the total?"

"Hold on a minute, honey." She typed again on her keyboard, then studied the computer screen while Susan waited nervously, fumbling with the plastic bag in her pocket. "Let's see. It looks like we already sent some initial information to your insurance company to get authorization for treatment. Normally we would have contacted your next of kin, too, but we've been shorthanded because of the snowstorm. We're several days behind on our paperwork. You can pay now, but I can't cancel the initial claim information because it's already gone to the insurance company. If you pay today, your insurance company might close their claim file and not send you a statement. I'm not really sure. I've been here five years and I've never had a case like this. My supervisor's not here today."

"I see. Well, how much is the bill?"

"One second." She hit a button, and a printer behind her began spitting out pages of itemized charges. The woman picked up the pile, stapled the pages together and turned to the last one. "Twelve thousand, three hundred seventy eight dollars and ninety-six cents. She watched Susan's face as she spoke, unsure whether her expression was one of shock or indifference. Susan said nothing until the lady spoke again. "Did you want to put that on a credit card?"

Susan knew that was not an option, as it would create an electronic record that could be tracked. She also knew that she had less than $5,000 in cash with her. Somewhat awkwardly, she responded. "Possibly. Let me give it some thought. Is there a bank nearby?"

"Well, there's an ATM on the ground floor, but you can't get twelve grand there. The closest bank is about two blocks east of here."

"Okay. I'll be back soon."

"I trust you. I'll be here. But if you change your mind, I can submit it to your insurance company."

"Thanks." Susan turned and made her way out of the hospital. *I think I'll need that pain medication*, she thought. She walked carefully up the sidewalk, taking small steps and avoiding any slick spots. She had little stamina and was starting to feel hungry, having forgotten to eat breakfast before checking out. She felt self-conscious about the bare patch in her scalp, and ran her fingers through her hair in an attempt to cover it. She stepped into the first clothing store she saw and bought a warm fleece hat.

At the bank, she presented one of the cashier's checks and waited patiently while the teller studied her driver's license and made a phone call to get authorization to cash it. The teller counted out twenty-nine $100 bills in several neat stacks on the counter then pushed them toward Susan before making a sales pitch.

"With a deposit of just $100 more you'll qualify for our high-interest money market checking account." Sliding a slick pamphlet across the counter, she continued. "This brochure also explains some of our other financial opportunities. Would you like to speak with our investment counselor?"

"No, thanks, but I appreciate the offer. What I really need is something to carry this cash in. Do you have anything I could use?"

The teller handed her an oversized plastic pouch with the bank's logo on it, and Susan stuffed the cash inside. Glancing around to be sure no one had been watching the transaction, she exited the bank and paused to get her bearings. She visited three other banks and repeated the process, hoping that she had successfully evaded all of the cash transaction reporting rules.

About a block up the street from the last bank she spotted a phone store. Her cell phone was missing, and she assumed it was still in her car, probably smashed to bits. Sylvia would be frantic by now, and she had to call her with news of the accident. Susan went inside and chose a base model phone with a simple calling plan, waiting while the clerk struggled to program it with a South Dakota area code. She paid in cash and returned to the hospital to settle her bill.

Arriving back at the checkout counter, she was greeted with a look of surprise. "To be honest, I didn't think you'd come back," the woman said. "I have never seen anyone pay in cash."

"It's a new experience for me, too," Susan replied. She pulled out a huge wad of $100 bills and peeled them off one by one, as if she were dealing cards from a deck. She took some smaller bills from her wallet and added another $80 in a separate pile. "Keep the change," she said with a hint of sarcasm and a look that was either a tight smile or a smirk.

"Sorry, sweetie, I have to give you your change," the lady answered, sliding a dollar and four pennies across the counter. "It's regulations." She printed a receipt and handed it to Susan. "I think I can feel your pain now. Good luck out there."

"Thanks. I'll need it." Susan pulled her coat tightly around her and exited the hospital without a specific destination in mind. She thought about renting a car but decided to talk to Sylvia first. She passed several shops and bought a newspaper before stopping at the entrance to a diner. Stepping inside, she chose a booth in a quiet corner, away from the cashier and kitchen.

Moments later a perky waitress appeared from a back room and set a laminated menu on the table. "Hi, sweetie, my name's Marie Aston, and I'll be your server today. Our special's sold out, but everything else is real tasty."

Susan returned her smile, ordered an omelet and toast, and read the paper as she waited for breakfast to be served. She scanned each page quickly, searching for any story about a local car wreck. There were articles about several recent accidents caused by slippery roads, but none of them mentioned her car. When the waitress returned with a breakfast platter, Susan asked if she had heard anything about a car running through the guardrails on the Interstate a few days earlier. "There were a lot of fender benders all around here, but I haven't heard of anything like that," the waitress replied.

Susan savored her food, a welcome change from hospital meals. After a few minutes she slipped the phone from her pocket and tried to remember Sylvia's home phone number, which was unlisted. She had memorized it shortly before leaving home, but now it escaped her. All she could recall was the area code, but that was enough for her to get Sylvia's office number from information. She dialed the number for The Pet Vet and was surprised when Sylvia herself answered the call.

"Sylvia, it's me," she whispered, hoping no one else in the restaurant would overhear her conversation.

"Susan! Thank God it's you! What happened? I've been worried sick about you. I was afraid to call you at home. You said you weren't going to tell your parents where you were going, so I didn't call them."

"It's so good to hear your voice, Sylvia. It's a long story, but the bottom line is I'm okay."

"Where are you?"

"I'm in Charleston, West Virginia. I had an accident and was in the hospital for several days. I didn't want to call you until I could think straight and figure out what to do. I'm sorry for the delay."

"Oh, no! That's terrible! I'm so sorry. I was afraid something awful had happened. I'm so relieved to hear from you. How are you doing? Are you able to travel? Do you want me to come get you?"

"Thanks, but I'll be all right. I was thinking of renting a car and getting on the road today. What do you think?"

"Susan, take my advice and fly. You shouldn't be driving right now. There's an airport in Aberdeen. Sit tight and I'll book a flight for you and call you back. How soon can you get to the Charleston Airport?"

"I don't know where it is, but I'm downtown and taxis are running again. We've had a ton of snow here. I should be able to catch any flights that leave this afternoon. Let's say anything after two. The sooner the better after that."

"Stay put and I'll get right back to you."

Susan set the phone on the table and took another bite of her omelet. She returned to the newspaper and leisurely perused it as she continued to eat. After a while the waitress finished a second cigarette and came over to check on her. Susan ordered more toast and coffee and waited for Sylvia to call back. Eventually the phone vibrated on the table, and Susan put it up to her ear.

Sylvia sounded apologetic at first. "The good news is that you'll be in Aberdeen tonight. But it's going to be late, and it won't be fun getting here. You'll have to switch flights in Pittsburgh and Minneapolis. I'm sorry, but it's the best I could do. Aberdeen's not exactly the hub of the Midwest."

"Well, it beats driving all night, I guess. I don't have any luggage, so that should help with the transfers."

"Really? What happened to your stuff? You know, the movers brought all your boxes here a couple of days ago."

"Everything was in the car. A deer ran in front of me on I-64, and I must have run off the road. I'm lucky to be alive. I guess the car is buried under snow because I don't think anybody has found it. Someone took me to the hospital before the cops got there, so I don't think there's even a police report. And I'd like to get out of here before anybody finds the car. Channing might be looking for it."

"I'm so sorry. Are you sure you're okay?"

"I'm a little sore and kind of weak. I had a concussion and got a few stitches on my head. I'm doing pretty well, though, considering."

"I'm really sorry. Just take it easy and I'll be waiting at the airport tonight. It's small, so you can't miss me there. Do you have a pen?"

Susan signaled the waitress, who brought a pen over, along with the check. She had written "Thanks!" in large letters and signed her name above a hand-drawn smiley face. Susan wrote on a napkin as Sylvia gave her the flight information and reservation numbers. She paid the check and stepped outside, walking up the street until a taxi approached and picked her up.

At the airport she bought a toothbrush and other essential items before settling into a chair with a magazine. It was hard to concentrate, so she skimmed the pages casually, without absorbing much content. She had planned to take every conceivable precaution when she left Channing. She hired a moving company from another city, giving them a drop point far from South Dakota so they wouldn't know her ultimate destination. The second mover would not know that her property had come from Charlottesville. She had purchased a new cell phone back home and avoided using her credit cards, planning to replace them when she got to Sylvia's farm. Now that phone and her car were gone and might be discovered after the snow melted. Her supply of cash was diminished, and there was a paper trail at the hospital if Channing could find it.

She boarded the plane as soon as her flight number was called and found her seat. Deciding not to wait for the light dinner that would be served later, she reached into her pocket for a sandwich and cookie, touching the money pouch at the same time to make sure it was still secure. The plane taxied down the runway and began to lift through the crisp afternoon air. She wrapped a blanket around herself, pushed back her seat, and fell asleep.

CHAPTER 16

Billy shivered as he walked among rows of trucks that were parked behind the sales office at the Midway Moving Company on the edge of town. This was the fourth lot he had investigated, and the results so far were ridiculously unproductive. He slipped a photo from his shirt pocket and studied it as he moved along, glancing frequently at the tires on each truck that he passed. The picture showed the tire treads that were pressed into the ground in front of Channing's house, where the moving van had parked before it hauled Susan's furniture away. There was no distinct tread pattern in the picture, and it seemed to match practically every tire he had seen.

Channing's description of what he was looking for was pathetically incomplete. He said a neighbor thought the truck was large and perhaps brown in color. "Sorry, I know it's not much to go on," Channing had told him, shrugging his shoulders. Some of the vans he had checked were coated with fresh yellow or blue paint, while most others were a dull gray or white or some other color that defied description. None of them could fairly be called brown. In Billy's mind, the hunt for a large brown moving van was a colossal waste of time and a wild goose chase at best. Nevertheless, if Channing wanted to pay him to look for it, then he was glad to oblige.

Near the end of the last row of trucks, a scrawny cat appeared from behind a bush. Seeing Billy nearby, it hissed and darted under one of the vans before disappearing through a hole in a privacy fence. Shoving the photo back into his pocket, Billy turned and walked toward the small, windowless structure that served as the company's office.

He tapped twice on the door, then opened it and stepped inside to escape the cold air that had settled over the area. The cramped office had all the charm of an abandoned garage. The walls were dingy and bare, with paint peeling in several spots. A noisy upright furnace blasted hot air into the room.

Billy stepped up to the counter, warming his hands as he peeled off his gloves.

A thin, middle-aged man was sorting through a stack of papers behind the counter. He looked up, pushed the papers aside and greeted his visitor. "Can I help ya with somethin'?"

Billy had struggled to invent a credible reason for his inquiry but had failed to come up with anything impressive. Nevertheless, most of the other movers in town had answered his questions without seeming to be suspicious. Surprisingly, none of them had asked to see any identification. "Yeah, thanks. My wife messed up and threw away her paperwork from a move about two weeks ago. She forgot which company it was, so I'm not sure I'm in the right place. I need to get a copy of the invoice so we can write it off on our taxes. Her name's Susan Booker, but she might have put it under the name Susan Finley."

"The names don't ring a bell, but I'm only here three days a week. She might have talked with the manager."

"Sorry to bother you with this. I should've handled it myself, but I didn't think she'd screw it up. Do you have a log book or something you could check?"

"Yeah, let me think where to look. What day was the move?"

"Saturday the eighth."

"Okay, hold on a second." The man rummaged through several piles of paper on the counter, and then hunted through a drawer. "I don't see anything under Booker or Finley. You sure we did the job?"

"Not really. I'll double-check with her, but she probably gave me the wrong mover. Sorry to bother you." Billy paused before turning to go. "She said she thinks the truck was brown. Do you have any like that?"

"Not that I know of. There's a few out on the road today, but mostly all we've got is what's on the lot here. Take a look if you want to."

"Okay, thanks." Billy slipped his gloves on and stepped out into the bleak afternoon air. Glancing at his watch, he decided there was enough time for a trip to the Division of Motor Vehicles. Channing had told him to check the DMV records to see if Susan had sold her car or changed her address. They both knew it was a long shot, but few leads were available, so it had to be checked out.

As always, the DMV office was jammed with customers. Billy chewed through a pack of gum before it was his turn to be served. A heavyset clerk wearing large round glasses finally called his number and invited him to step forward. "Next," she announced in a tired voice.

Billy spit his gum into a foil wrapper and leaned his elbows on the counter. "Hi. How's it going?"

The clerk nodded slightly and replied automatically, "Can I help you?"

"Yeah, thanks. I need a copy of the registration on my wife's car."

The clerk reached down and produced a sheet of paper, placing it on the counter and pointing to several blanks on the page. "Just write in the make, model and year of the vehicle, and then have your wife sign at the bottom."

"Well, she's not with me today. How about if I sign for her?"

"I'm sorry, sir. Only the owner of record can request a copy of the registration. You said it's your wife's car, right?"

Billy thought for a moment before speaking. "Okay. Actually, I think we titled it in both of our names. Can you check and see, because I don't remember for sure."

"All right. What names would it be under?"

"Booker. Channing and Susan Booker."

The clerk typed on her keyboard and checked the computer screen. "I have a vehicle that's titled in both names. I need you to confirm the make and model, please."

Billy pulled a slip of paper from his pocket and read Channing's notes. "It's a Volkswagen Passat."

"Yes, that's it. You can use the same form and sign it yourself. I'll just need to see some identification, and the fee is $8.00, or $12.00 if you want a certified copy."

"Unfortunately, I don't have my ID with me today. I didn't think I would need it."

"Any photo ID is fine. Your driver's license will do."

"Oh, sure. Well, except I don't have it on me. Are you sure you need it? I'm not changing the registration. I just want a copy of it."

"I'm sure, sir. I've been working here for six years. That's the rule we have to follow. It's for privacy protection."

Billy could see there was no point in trying to negotiate the point. Channing would be furious at having to come down to the DMV with proper identification, but there was nothing Billy could do. He hoped there would be a different clerk on duty when Channing arrived, or that this one had a short memory for faces. Sliding into his car in the parking lot, Billy sat behind the wheel and called Channing with an update. "Channing, the car's still titled in both names, but I can't find out if she changed the address. You'll have to request a copy of the title in person."

"Oh, all right. I'll take care of it," Channing said in a grumpy voice. "What have you found out so far?"

"Not a damn thing of any use," he replied. "Nobody in town has any brown moving vans that I could find. Most of the guys were willing to talk to me and check their records. Nothing turned up. I'm sorry, man. Have you come up with anything?"

Channing was silent for a few seconds before responding. "Well, I checked our phone records online. She hasn't used her cell phone since the day she moved out. I didn't see any unusual calls before that, and there aren't any long distance calls on our land line that look suspicious. She knew how to cover her tracks, but she's bound to slip up sooner or later. I want you to stay on this until we catch a break. Go ahead and check some moving companies in Orange and Waynesboro. If she hired somebody from out of town, she probably went there."

"You sure you want me to do that? It seems like a long shot."

"Yeah, I'm sure. I really need to get hold of her. And remember, if you find her, let me know and don't move in. I want to handle this myself."

"Okay, my man. It's your money. But if we keep this up, it's all gonna be mine before long."

"We'll see." Channing ended the call and opened a desk drawer. He dug down below a wad of papers and felt a small plastic sandwich bag. Slipping it out, he set it down in front of him on the desk. Without opening the bag, he looked through the clear plastic and reread Susan's note inside.

He got angry every time he looked at Susan's note. If she had waited just a couple of days before leaving, he would have had time to hide the lottery ticket in a safe deposit box. She would never have found it there. Now she had stolen the ticket and taken a camera that held the only evidence that proved the ticket was his. He could have signed his name on the back of the ticket to keep her from stealing it, but he had planned to let Sully sign it and claim the jackpot. As things stood now, Susan could claim the unsigned ticket if she found it. Or anyone else, for that matter.

Channing doubted that Susan would open the Dickens book anytime soon. She hardly ever opened the rare books because they were old, and she wanted to preserve them. But there was no guarantee, and, since Billy seemed to be getting nowhere with his investigation, Channing decided to seek assistance from the police.

He had hoped to avoid that step because he didn't want any publicity in the matter. If the police got involved, they might ask uncomfortable questions. If Billy had to take any drastic action in his search for clues, and he got caught, the cops might discover a link between the two of them. Billy knew an awful lot of unsavory information about Channing. Who knows what he might reveal in order to save himself?

With the plastic bag in his shirt pocket, he put on a coat and left his office. On the way to the downtown police station, he pulled into a parking lot beside a Taco Bell restaurant. Glancing around his car to make sure no one was nearby, he took a $5 bill from his wallet and placed it on the passenger seat beside him. Next, he carefully slid Susan's note out of the plastic bag. He folded it twice and held it between his thumb and forefinger, close to one edge of the paper, and picked up the $5 bill with his other hand. He slipped the bill between his thumb and the note and put his hand in his coat pocket before exiting the car.

Inside the restaurant, he approached the counter and spoke to the cashier—a young, heavyset woman who took his order for a large coffee. He held out the $5 bill, concealing the folded note underneath it as he placed it in the cashier's hand. Without seeing the note, she took the bill and began to move her hand toward the cash register before Channing stopped her. "I'm sorry, I think I gave you a note that I had stashed in my wallet. It must have gotten stuck to the money."

The cashier turned the bill over and smiled before handing the note back. "No problem. Here it is." Channing accepted it with his thumb and forefinger, holding it near one edge before slipping it into his pocket. He got his change, and the coffee arrived a few seconds later. He carried it to the nearest trashcan, dropped the cup in, and left the restaurant. In his car, he placed the note back into the sandwich bag and put it in his shirt pocket. Reaching into the glove compartment, he extracted another plastic bag and shoved it in his coat pocket. Then he headed downtown.

Emerging from a parking deck, Channing walked a short distance to the city's main police station and stepped inside. He approached a counter and spoke to a receptionist who sat behind a large window of bulletproof glass. There was no need to introduce himself, as he was well known to most of the employees at the station. This was not an advantage. Many of the officers on the force, and a substantial portion of the clerical staff, detested him. Over the years he had thwarted their efforts to put a number of criminals behind bars, either through sharp practices in the courtroom or by less visible means. At various times witnesses had changed their stories unexpectedly, and on a few occasions they had disappeared altogether. Neither the police nor the prosecutors at the Commonwealth Attorney's office had ever been able to prove that Channing obstructed justice, but a cloud of suspicion hung over him as the receptionist unlocked a door and allowed him inside.

Officer Tolbert was sifting through a stack of arrest warrants when Channing stepped into his office. Tolbert's first instinct was to throw him out and slam the door, but he knew better than to give in to his initial impulse. There was no doubt that Channing would retaliate with some kind of civil rights lawsuit at the drop of a hat.

"Hello," he said dryly, remaining seated without extending his hand.

He motioned to a chair in front of the desk. Channing knew that if he found his lottery ticket, he would no longer have to deal with the police or prosecutors or, for that matter, the kind of low-life clients he often represented.

Seeing no advantage in antagonizing Tolbert, Channing decided to forgo his usual confrontational approach.

"Thank you, sir. I appreciate your taking time to meet with me this afternoon," Channing offered, knowing that Tolbert had little choice in the matter. He couldn't refuse to talk to someone who wanted to report a possible crime.

Somewhat taken aback by this unexpected courtesy, Tolbert was curious about Channing's intentions. Pointing to the papers on his desk, he replied with a trace of sarcasm in his voice. "Well, I don't see any new warrants on you, so I guess you're not here to turn yourself in."

Channing forced himself to laugh, feigning affability. "There's no one else I'd rather surrender to than you, but I guess we'll drive off that bridge when we get to it."

"I suppose so," Tolbert answered, longing for the day when he could arrest Channing for something. "So what brings you in today?"

Channing pulled the plastic bags from his pockets and emptied their contents on the desk. "These are clues to a possible burglary and kidnapping. I think my wife may have been abducted, but I'm not sure."

"Abducted? When did this happen?"

"About two weeks ago."

"You're joking, right? You waited that long to report a kidnapping?"

Channing squirmed in his chair but stuck to his story. "Well, as I say, I'm not sure. I wanted to do some investigating on my own before I came in. I didn't want to file a false report."

"I see," Tolbert replied skeptically. "Well, what has your investigation turned up?"

"I came home one night and my house was half empty. My wife was gone and a lot of furniture was missing. I found this note," he said, pushing it forward with the tip of his fingers.

Tolbert reached in a drawer and brought out a pair of tongs. He squeezed them around a corner of the note, placed it in front of him and read it. "Is that her handwriting?" he asked.

"It looks like hers. But she could have been under duress when she wrote it."

"Anything's possible, but it's not unheard of for a wife or a teenager to run away, particularly when there's domestic trouble or other problems at home. Have you and your wife—this says Susan, right?"

"Yes. Her maiden name's Finley."

Tolbert jotted it down on a note pad. "Has there been any conflict in your marriage?"

"Well, I guess you could say there's been some friction at times." Not a surprise, Tolbert thought to himself.

"And you don't think she just decided to move out?" Tolbert asked, believing that would be the most logical course for any woman who found herself married to Channing.

"It's a possibility, but I haven't heard anything from her, and the neighbors said she didn't tell them anything about leaving."

"Has anyone contacted you? Has there been any ransom demand?"

"Well, no. Not so far."

"I see." Tolbert scribbled some more notes on his pad. "Any signs of forcible entry at the home?"

"No. I don't think so. A neighbor said she saw a moving van in the front yard."

"Any signs of a struggle?"

"No."

"I see. Now, you said there was furniture missing?"

"Yes. All of the pieces she had when we got married. All of her clothes, her books. All of her things, basically."

"Mmm. Did she take anything of yours?"

Channing frowned. "You're assuming she took the stuff herself. It could have been a burglar."

"All right, I'll rephrase the question. Is any of your property missing?"

"My camera is gone. I think that's all."

Tolbert put down his pen and looked up at the ceiling, wishing someone else had been on duty when Channing walked in. Returning his gaze to Channing, he wondered what he could say that would make him go away without filing a complaint. "Mr. Booker—may I call you Channing?"

"Sure."

"Well, Channing, we don't have much here to suggest a burglary or kidnapping. Normally a kidnapper demands money within hours of seizing his victim. There's no indication of violence—no physical evidence that you mentioned, or statements from the neighbors that they saw anything unusual. I've never heard of a kidnapper taking the time to bring in a moving van. Obviously it's not typical for a burglar to take only property that belongs to one occupant in a house. We could check the pawn shops for your camera if there's any way to identify it as yours."

"That's okay. I already did that."

"Well, what did you have in mind for us to do?"

"I'd like you to search for my wife and her car. I'm worried about her."

Tolbert thought for a moment before responding. "I could put out an alert for her car. If it's pulled over, we would be notified. It would also show up as a stolen car if someone tries to get new plates for it or transfer the title. I'm afraid that's all we can do based on the evidence that you've presented."

Channing leaned forward and pointed to the bottle of mouthwash that he had placed on the desk. "The alert would be fine, but I also want you to check the note for fingerprints. Susan left this bottle in the bathroom. It's the one she always used, so her prints would be on it. If the note has other fingerprints on it, that would indicate foul play."

Tolbert decided not to argue the point. It would be easy enough to check for prints, and maybe Channing would let the matter drop if no foreign prints showed up on the note. He slipped the note and bottle into evidence bags and took Channing's fingerprints to compare with any that might appear on the two items. He assured Channing that he would keep in touch, then ushered him out of his office before getting back to more pressing business.

CHAPTER 17

Winston sat at his desk, watching the clock on the wall ahead of him. His office was roughly the size of a typical jail cell. The desk and chair, which were the only pieces of furniture in it, were squeezed against one wall. There was enough room for one client chair, but the partners never trusted rookie associates to meet with clients, so one of them borrowed the chair several years earlier and never returned it. The walls were bare except for Winston's law school diploma and state bar certificate. They were uninspiring from the standpoint of office décor, but they did serve a limited purpose at times. Winston glanced at them whenever he needed a reminder that even the lowliest associate had more status than the firm's secretaries.

At one time there had been a small window in the office, but several years ago one of the partners hired a carpenter to cover it over with a set of tall bookshelves. He told a junior associate who was in the office at the time that it would make the place more functional. "No use wasting billable hours by looking outside all the time," he explained.

Winston watched apprehensively as the clock's minute hand crept toward the top of the hour. He dreaded meeting with Channing again to discuss the mystery client's lottery case. His research had uncovered nothing particularly useful, and certainly no cases that allowed a spouse to hide assets during a divorce proceeding. Although there was apparently no case that directly discussed the propriety of lending a lottery ticket to a third party until a divorce became official, and then taking the jackpot proceeds back as a gift, the idea clearly would not pass the smell test. As the clock ticked down to the hour, Winston headed for Channing's office.

"Well, what have you got?" Channing demanded.

Winston slumped down in a chair and reviewed some notes before responding. "Well, sir, as you recall, the question was whether your client could give his lottery ticket to a friend until his divorce becomes final, and then take back the funds after the friend cashes in the ticket."

"Yes, I do recall the question. So what's the answer?"

"Well, it's somewhat complicated. Evidently there's no prior case just like this."

Channing sat up straighter, a look of anticipation in his face. "So there's no case that says he can't do it, right?"

"Uh, well, I'm not sure it's that simple. When I say there's no case like this, I mean no case with identical facts. I found lots of cases that say all assets must be disclosed during a divorce. I think a gift like this would be viewed as a fraudulent conveyance, or at least a fraud on the court. Assuming all the income and gift taxes were paid by the third party, I don't know that it would be a criminal matter, although there might be some kind of conspiracy charge. If the client's wife found out about it, she could probably get the divorce decree modified and claim her share of the jackpot. Just on principle, the judge might give her most of the money to punish the husband."

Channing frowned and leaned back in his chair as Winston cowered in front of the desk. "Okay, let's back up a minute. How do we know the wife has any claim to a share of the money in the first place? If the husband bought the ticket with his own money, why doesn't the whole jackpot belong to him anyway?"

Having researched the matter ad nauseum, Winston was prepared to answer. "It depends on the facts. If he bought the ticket with truly separate funds, then he might have a decent argument for keeping it all. But he would have to buy the ticket with funds that were completely separate property, such as money he inherited or held before he was married. If he paid for the ticket out of his salary from work, that would not count as separate property. You can't buy lottery tickets with a check or a credit card, so as a practical matter it would be extremely hard to establish a paper trail to trace the money anyway."

Channing looked away and stared through a window at a bare tree across the street. He began to absorb the full measure of his difficulty. Every time he talked with Winston the picture got more complicated. His original plan was gradually being picked apart, and so far he had not devised another scheme that might work. He was willing to take certain risks, but the problem was not his own appetite for risk. The problem was that Sully might be unwilling to take the same chances that Channing would. The risk would be about the same for Sully, but the potential reward would be much smaller—a mere percentage of the jackpot. He could not gauge Sully's reaction without disclosing the plan, and if Sully balked, then the element of secrecy would be lost.

As Channing pondered the situation, Winston watched intently, nervously awaiting his response. Finally Channing turned his head back toward Winston, who took that as his cue to speak again. "So the question is: was the ticket purchased with separate funds?"

Channing responded without thinking carefully. "No, I didn't." Seeing the look of confusion on Winston's face, he realized his mistake and quickly corrected it. "I mean I didn't know—I don't know. I'll have to check with the client." He decided to change the subject and then send Winston on his way.

Knowing that Billy had difficulty getting information from the DMV, and expecting similar problems as their investigation continued, Channing assumed it would be easier to have a power of attorney from Susan. This would authorize him to act on her behalf and allow others to disclose information about her to Channing.

Of course, Susan would not be around to sign it, but he or Billy could probably forge a convincing signature. Channing would notarize the document himself.

He brought the meeting to a close with a request for Winston. "All right. I'll update the client and see what he thinks. I'd like you to prepare a power of attorney for his wife to sign. She's going to be traveling abroad for a few weeks and he needs to handle some transactions while she's away. That's all for now."

"Yes, sir." Winston hesitated, waiting for more information.

Channing tapped his fingers on his desk, expecting Winston to scurry off to his office. A few seconds passed before he realized that Winston wasn't ready to leave. "Well, is there something else?"

"Uhm…well, I was just wondering if you wanted the husband and wife's names on the document."

"Actually, that's confidential. Just draft a basic form that covers everything and leave the names blank."

"Covers everything?"

"Yeah, every transaction under the sun, plus the kitchen sink. I'll fill in the names. But don't email it to me. Put it on a flash drive and give it to me. I'll take it from there. Oh, I almost forgot. Put something in there that says a copy is as effective as the original. His wife doesn't want to hassle with signing a bunch of originals."

Winston nodded and departed quickly. It appeared that Channing's client was up to no good, and probably Channing, too.

Nevertheless, it seemed that his involvement with the case was almost over, at least temporarily. Rather than trying to sort it all out, he could just draft a power of attorney and leave it on Channing's desk when he was out of his office.

Channing watched Winston leave and then stared at the door after it closed behind him. The investigation was going nowhere and he was running out of ideas. Unless they were completely incompetent, the police would discover a stranger's fingerprints on Susan's note.

Assuming that the unidentified prints couldn't be traced to the Taco Bell clerk who had served him coffee, Channing hoped the police might suspect foul play. Unexplained fingerprints could convince them to make an effort to find Susan, although Channing doubted that Tolbert would do much to help him.

He took out his smartphone and called a number. "Hey Billy, it's me. Has anything turned up?"

"Not really. I'm checking movers in Waynesboro, but it looks like it's a waste of time. Nobody's heard of your wife so far. I think there's a couple more places I can try, but this seems like a long shot. She could have hired a mover from just about anywhere within 100 miles of Charlottesville."

"Yeah, you're probably right. Go ahead and finish up in Waynesboro, then I want you to stake out her parents' house for a few days. Don't break in—just watch the place and see if she shows up there. Keep in touch. Call me at this number if you need to talk. Don't use the office phone unless you have to. You still have the address I gave you, right?"

"You bet. I'll let you know when I get there."

CHAPTER 18

Susan opened her eyes and saw the faint light of dawn as it began to illuminate her bedroom. She pulled the sheets and a thick quilt up around her neck and curled her body into a ball under the covers. The house had cooled overnight as a frigid wind howled outside, sweeping across the flat, snowy plains around Aberdeen. It was Saturday morning and the wind had moved on toward the eastern part of the state, leaving behind wide snowdrifts that rippled across nearby fields.

The house was quiet. She lay in bed for half an hour, listening to the occasional barking of a dog outside, somewhere off in the distance. Several weeks had passed since Sylvia met her at the airport and drove her to the farm. Only in the past week had Susan begun to relax completely and unwind from her ordeal. Her mind and body were healing slowly, and she could feel her condition improving. Hair was starting to grow into the patch on her skull that had been shaved and stitched at the hospital. Her right hand was now free of its bandage, and the dark skin had faded into a light pink color. The stiffness and aching in her muscles had gone away.

Susan had tried to put Channing out of her mind after she arrived in Aberdeen, preferring to wait until her head cleared before attempting to sort out her future plans. In the weeks before leaving Charlottesville, she had hired an attorney to handle her divorce, but no timetable had been set for filing the papers to get the suit underway. She realized there was probably no longer any urgency in the matter, as Channing might have few remaining assets to fritter away at this point. Assuming that he didn't destroy his health with drinking and cocaine, he would continue to earn a good salary at his law firm, which would provide a steady source of alimony payments.

Knowing that the divorce would be an emotionally wrenching experience, and would bring her back into contact with Channing, she wasn't ready to begin the process. Sylvia hadn't pressed her to talk about Channing, allowing her to recover fully from the accident before addressing the next phase of her life. The invitation to stay at the farm was open-ended.

As the light in her room gradually brightened, Susan heard sounds of stirring downstairs. Sylvia opened her animal clinic at noon on Saturdays, and usually slept late in the morning before driving into town. Pushing aside the covers, Susan crawled out of bed and walked across the cold hardwood floor to the closet. She put on a heavy housecoat and slippers and went downstairs. A pleasant aroma was in the air as she made her way to the other end of the house.

Sylvia was in the kitchen with a pot of fresh coffee and a pan of sausages frying on the stove top. "Well, good morning, kiddo. I thought you might stay in bed all day. I'm glad you're able to sleep so well now."

Susan yawned and then smiled before replying. "Thanks. It's great to be coming alive again. Can I help with breakfast?"

"No, thanks. It's just about ready. If you'll get some orange juice out, we'll be all set."

They sat down and began to eat. Between sips of coffee and juice, Sylvia explained her plans for the day. "I'll be at the clinic until three, and then I have to check on a horse just north of town. She's due to have a foal any day now, so I need to keep an eye on her. If you'd like to go along, I could swing by here before I head out there."

Susan was eager to get out of the house and see the countryside. "That sounds great. I was thinking of going into town after lunch to pick up some groceries. I might drive around a bit before I get to the store, but I'll make sure I'm back by around three."

Sylvia put down her coffee cup and frowned. "I can pick up some things at the store. I've already got a list. I told you I've got everything covered until the dust settles and you get back on your feet. It's no problem at all. I want you to save your money for your lawyer. If he's going up against Channing and his firm, it'll cost you big time. If he's good, he won't be cheap."

"You're an angel, Sylvia. I can't believe how good you've been to me. But I've been thinking about this, and I want to help out with expenses. I've got a bunch of furniture and other stuff in your barn that I really don't need right now. I doubt that I'll be moving into a house as big as the one in Charlottesville for a long time, especially while I'm single." Sylvia cut a piece of sausage and remained silent, letting Susan continue. "I saw a consignment shop in Aberdeen a few days ago. I was thinking of taking a few things there to see how that works out. If they sell at decent prices, I'll keep going back there with other items."

Sylvia looked out the window and thought for a moment as she watched several small birds clustering around a feeder, pecking at sunflower seeds. Then she looked back at Susan. "I don't know about being an angel, but I'm so happy I can be here to help you through this mess. You know I went through a lot of grief when Kevin left me two years ago. I remember how much you did for me back then. We must have talked 100 times on the phone, and when you came to visit that first week—I can't tell you how much that meant to me." Sylvia stopped and looked down at the table as her eyes moistened.

Susan reached out and touched her arm as Sylvia rubbed her eyes with a napkin. "It's okay, it's okay," she whispered.

Collecting herself after a long pause, Sylvia raised her eyes again. "I'm sorry. It's still difficult for me." She drank some orange juice and then continued. "Anyway, I was going to suggest another option, at least for some of your smaller items. I have a friend in town who runs a small business out of her home. Her name's Lilian Leslie. It's a part-time thing, but she's been successful at it."

"What does she do?"

"She's got several things going. She makes some craft items and sells them, and does some knitting, too. But she also buys and sells a lot of items online. She watches eBay auctions over time to see what certain products are worth, and then buys them when she sees a good deal. She can usually resell them later at a profit. She also sells items for other people and charges a small commission."

"Sounds interesting. That might be something to try."

"Well, just think about it. You could take a few things over to her place and see how it goes. If it doesn't work out, you could try something else."

Susan swallowed the last drops of her coffee. Seeing that Sylvia was finished with breakfast, she gathered their plates and began fitting them into the dishwasher. "You know, I think I'll do it. It's worth a try at least. I could go through some of the boxes in the barn this weekend. I'll pick out a few loose things and take them over to your friend. We'll see what happens."

"Sure, why not? If you'd like, we can go over there together whenever you're ready. Take your time. Just let me know when, and I'll introduce you to her." Sylvia handed her cup to Susan and wiped the table with a sponge before turning to go. "Well, I'd better head on to work. I'll see you when I get back this afternoon."

After she left, Susan showered and dressed and then walked down the driveway to retrieve the morning newspaper. The paper box was at the entrance to the highway, beside the mailbox. The sun was bright, but not warm enough to melt the coating of white powder that had blown onto the evergreen trees along the driveway. The January air was bitterly cold. Sylvia had warned her that the winter weather in South Dakota would last weeks longer than in Virginia. Normally the idea of an extended winter would have been depressing, but Susan didn't care now. She was happy just to be free and far away from Channing. The past few weeks had been little more than a blur. Although she was feeling better after arriving at the farm, she had not mustered enough energy to celebrate the arrival of another year. Sylvia turned down a party invitation to stay at home with her on New Year's Eve. They spent the evening watching old movies in the den, and Susan fell asleep on the couch well before midnight.

As she walked back to the house with the newspaper, Susan wondered where she would be next Christmas, and what kind of life she would be living. One possibility would be to move to Northern Virginia to be near her parents, perhaps looking for a job in Washington. She assumed that her parents would enjoy having her close by, but had not discussed it with them. If she had brought up the subject, it would have signaled that she was planning to leave Channing. She kept her plans to herself, protecting her parents from being pressured by Channing to reveal her location. On the day she left Charlottesville, Susan mailed them a letter to say she was moving away and would contact them later. She explained that her marriage had become unbearable, but left out the gory details of Channing's abusive and erratic behavior. She told them not to worry, assured them that she was going to a safe place, and said it would be better if they didn't know her location until she could gauge Channing's reaction.

As she reached the parking lot at the end of the driveway,

Sylvia's dog appeared from behind the guest cottage and bounded over to greet her. He jumped up in front of her, waving his paws across the paper and tearing off the corner of the front page. "Easy there, Trotter," Susan said sternly, pushing him aside before reaching down to rub the back of his neck. He followed closely behind her as she stepped up onto the porch, and then curled up to lie on the doormat after she went inside.

Susan retreated to the kitchen and poured a cup of coffee before reading the day's news. The newspaper was thin, consisting mostly of advertisements, and in a short time she was fully informed of current events in Aberdeen and the surrounding counties. Fortified by the fresh blend of hot coffee, she was ready to begin sorting through her possessions in Sylvia's barn. Wrapping herself again in a heavy coat, she left the house and met Trotter on the front porch. As she turned away from the driveway and passed through a gate into the field, her boots sank into the snow that covered the frozen ground. Trotter moved ahead of her toward the barn, lunging through the snow with short hops, occasionally stopping to rest and shake the powder off his back and face.

Once inside the barn, she sat down on a straw bale and rested while her eyes grew accustomed to the dim light. Trotter explored several open stalls, sniffing about in an effort to catch the scent of a raccoon or squirrel. Gradually Susan's energy returned, and she found a light switch and began to explore the barn. At the far end of the central passageway, two stalls were occupied by horses. She reached through the bars and stroked their noses, then walked to the large central stall, where most of her furniture was stored.

Some of the dressers were still stuffed with clothes, as there had not been enough time for the movers to remove and pack them in boxes. She made a mental note to retrieve some pants and blouses when she had more time. She opened several drawers to look inside, and then closed them tightly to prevent mice or birds from crawling in to make a nest. Sliding out the drawer of a small table, she peeked inside and noticed a camera and a wad of paper slips. She picked up several slips and examined them closely. Realizing what they were, she threw them on the floor in disgust. All of the worthless lottery tickets that Channing had bought over the years would probably fill up this whole barn, she thought. She dropped the camera into her coat pocket, closed the drawer and pulled a tarp back over the table, smoothing out a few wrinkles with her hand.

She continued down the corridor, stepping into a stall that was filled with cardboard boxes. She was too tired to sort through them all, but she opened a few of them with a utility knife from Sylvia's kitchen. One box contained China dishes, which would be too heavy and unwieldy to carry back to the house. Another one was full of towels and wash clothes, items that probably would not bring a good price on an eBay auction. The next box was full of electronic devices, which seemed more promising. Rummaging through it, she found a brand new miniature TV, still in its original packaging. She set it down in the corridor and continued her search.

After spending about two hours in the barn, she had filled a box with items to sell. She called out to Trotter, waking him from a nap inside one of the vacant stalls. "Come on old buddy, it's time to head back."

She walked slowly to the house, following the tracks she had left earlier. She stopped several times to catch her breath and shifted the box from one hand to the other. Her arms began to ache, but she resisted the urge to set the box down, not wanting to get it dirty or wet in the snow. Eventually she reached the porch, where Trotter was waiting patiently by the front door, licking traces of mud off his paws. Nearly exhausted, Susan climbed the steps, set the box on a bench and sat down beside it. She leaned her head back against the wall and closed her eyes, waiting several minutes until her heavy breathing subsided. As her strength gradually returned, she opened her eyes and gazed at the snowy landscape in front of the house. She watched water dripping from a row of icicles along the edge of the porch.

After a few minutes she felt refreshed. She scooped up the box and went inside, pressing the door shut with her foot after Trotter slipped in behind her. Fetching a glass of orange juice from the kitchen, she took the box into Sylvia's study and placed it on the desk. Removing the TV, she inspected it closely and jotted some notes on a sheet of scrap paper. Using Sylvia's computer, she explored eBay's website, attempting to master its rules and selling procedures.

She searched for portable TVs to get an idea of their value, and with some effort succeeded in setting up an account. To maintain her anonymity, she chose "Trotter" as her trading name, and listed her location as "Midwest, USA."

By the time Sylvia returned in the afternoon, Susan felt confident enough to list her TV for sale. Sylvia complimented her for mastering the process, and seemed relieved that Susan had found something to occupy her time.

"Not bad for a beginner," she commented as Susan gave her a demonstration, scrolling through several sale items that she had put on her watch list. "So you decided to do it yourself, I see."

"Yeah, it's really not that hard to figure out. It seemed intimidating at first, but I think I've got it now," Susan said with a smile. "All I need to do is take pictures of the items I want to sell and then upload them to eBay. I found my camera in the barn, so I'm all set."

"Why not sell your camera? I've got one that I never use. It's the last gift Kevin gave me before he left, and it makes me sick when I think of using it." Sylvia slipped out of the room and returned a moment later with a slim black camera. "It's all yours. You can save your pictures on my computer and upload them to eBay."

"Thanks. I'll probably get started in a day or two. I think I'll sell the TV first and see how that goes. Right now I'm ready to take it easy. It's Saturday night, you know."

CHAPTER 19

Channing struggled to align the margins of Winston's power of attorney. He had copied the document from a flash drive that appeared on his desk while he was out at lunch, but now that it was on his computer screen he had made a mess of it. His typing skills were minimal, and when he tried to fill in the blanks with Susan's name he mangled the document. The formatting was now a wreck, and several paragraphs had disappeared. Ordinarily he would have yelled for a secretary and told her to fix it, but he couldn't risk getting anyone else involved in his plans. His temper nearly reached the boiling point as he fumbled with the keyboard, but eventually he cleaned up the document, printed out eight originals on cotton bond paper and placed them on his desk.

Next to them was a copy of a check that Susan had signed several years before. Her signature had an elegant style, with graceful strokes and flourishes. It would have been much easier to forge a name that was scrawled in everyday handwriting. Channing knew there was some way to scan the check and electronically insert an exact replica of her signature into a power of attorney, but the technology was beyond him.

Sliding the check closer to the desk lamp, he studied Susan's signature. On a yellow legal pad he practiced signing her name. For several minutes he struggled to replicate the flowing lines of her handwriting, with gradual improvement. Eventually he was ready to test his skill on a power of attorney. After six attempts he was satisfied with the result, and he pressed his notary public stamp on the document to make it official. He admired his handiwork for a moment, then balled up the other papers and dropped them into his trashcan.

He walked quickly down the hall to run some copies, then folded one and put it in his pocket.

Opening a phone book, he flipped to the yellow pages. He found the listings for banks and was surprised at how many there were. With the book in hand, he grabbed his overcoat and gloves, left the building and headed to the first bank on the list.

After a short drive through moderate traffic, he parked in front of Albemarle Savings & Loan. He watched an elderly couple enter the building while he collected his thoughts. Susan had been gone for several weeks, and so far his investigation into her whereabouts had been long on expense but short on results.

He had considered hiring a professional investigator but was not yet ready to take that step. It was better to keep as few people as possible involved in the search, at least for now. The lottery ticket would not expire until late spring. It was too early to panic or take desperate measures to find Susan. There would be time enough for that later if it became necessary. For the moment, he would rely primarily on Billy and himself, and hope the police might turn up a lead. He thought there was a chance that Susan might have opened a new account to hold the funds she had withdrawn from their joint accounts. It was a long shot, but if there was a money trail, it might provide some clues. Ideally he could discover her current address.

Turning off the ignition, he exited the car and entered the bank. Only one teller was on duty, and several customers were ahead of him in line. He waited impatiently, glancing at his watch and wondering how many banks he could cover in one afternoon.

"Good afternoon. How may I help you today," the teller chirped as Channing reached the front of the line.

"I'd like to close my wife's account," he replied.

"Well, we'd hate to lose her business if we could avoid it. If there's a problem with the account, I'd be glad to try to straighten it out."

"No, thanks. There's no problem. We just want to simplify our finances."

"Certainly, sir. Is it a joint account?"

"Actually, it's only in her name. Unfortunately I don't have the account number with me."

"I can look it up, but if she's the only person on the account I'm afraid she'll have to come in and close it herself. I'm sorry for any inconvenience, but it's a bank regulation."

"Okay, I understand. That's no problem. To be honest, I may have made a mistake. She has several accounts in town, and I'm not sure I've got the right bank. Her name is Susan Booker. Or she may have put it under her maiden name—Susan Finley." Channing pulled a slip of paper from his shirt pocket and placed it on the counter. "Here's her Social Security number." Unfolding another paper, he laid it beside the first one. "I have her power of attorney here. She's on crutches for a few weeks and doesn't get around much right now. If you could just check to see if she has an account here, then I can close it out as her agent."

The teller picked up the two papers, glanced over them, and typed some information into her computer. She handed the papers back to Channing. "I'm sorry. There's no account under this number. You must have the wrong bank."

He repeated the same process nearly twenty times over the next few days, with the same result, until he checked off the last bank in the phone book. As he left Virginia Trust Bank in frustration, he muttered a string of obscenities and threw the book into a trashcan.

His next stop was the police station. He had called Lieutenant Tolbert off and on for two weeks without getting through, and his voice mail messages had been ignored. Now it was time to be more persistent. He was a good liar, and he easily tricked the desk clerk into believing he had an appointment. He knocked on the door and stepped inside as soon as he heard a reply, sitting down before Tolbert had a chance to object.

"Hi, Channing. Thanks for your calls. I've been meaning to get back to you, but it's been pretty hectic around here."

Channing thought about launching into a tirade about the urgency of his wife's disappearance, and how unprofessional Tolbert's response had been, but concluded that it would probably do no good at the moment. "Right," Channing replied in a matter-of-fact tone. "I just need an update on my wife's case. What's the status of the investigation?"

"Yes, of course. Let's see..." Tolbert leaned to one side and searched through a cabinet beside his desk. He pulled out a thin file and opened it to review the contents before looking up. "Well, I'm afraid there's not much here," he said. "We found some prints on the note. Most of them matched you and Susan. There were two others that we can't identify. We ran them through the FBI database, but there was no match."

"So that's proof she was kidnapped!" Channing exclaimed, leaning forward in his chair.

"Well, not exactly," Tolbert answered. He held up a plastic baggie with Susan's note inside. "Your wife wrote the note on a piece of thick brown paper that was torn from a bigger piece. It's the same type of paper that's used to make shopping or grocery bags. Most likely that's where it came from because it's much thicker than ordinary stationery or note paper. These prints could be from a bagger or stock handler or cashier in any of dozens of stores. They don't all use plastic, you know."

Channing frowned as he continued to lean forward. "Well, it certainly suggests a possibility of foul play," he asserted. "I think this justifies a thorough investigation. My wife could be in real danger out there. You have no idea how worried I've been. I've just got to find her!"

"I understand your concern. We take every case seriously. But we have to be realistic. There's been no contact from anyone demanding a ransom. No sign of forced entry or a struggle." Tolbert looked at another sheet in the file. "My notes say there was some friction in your marriage?"

"Well, some, I suppose. But lots of couples have marital problems."

"That's true. But it's far more common for a woman to move out than to be kidnapped. You know, we've had only one confirmed kidnapping in Charlottesville in the last six years."

"I see," Channing said with an air of resignation. "Well, have you got anything else in the file?"

"Nothing of substance. We put out a bulletin on her car, but it hasn't been spotted." Tolbert paused, waiting for Channing to leave. Instead, Channing sat quietly, so Tolbert continued. "Well then, we also made a few calls to your neighbors to see if they noticed anything unusual." He glanced at some notes in the file. "Nobody told us anything useful," he reported. Tolbert paused again. "So there you have it," he said, closing the file.

Channing continued to stare at him until Tolbert spoke again. "If you know where your wife usually shops, I suppose we might be able to confirm the source of the paper on her note. To be honest, that probably wouldn't get us anywhere, though. The store could have dozens of employees, and even if one of them was involved in your wife's disappearance, he probably wouldn't tell us anything.

It's easy for people to say they can't remember what they were doing several weeks ago."

Channing had no earthly idea where Susan usually shopped, or whether she preferred paper or plastic bags. He was blissfully unaware of all the routine tasks she had performed to keep the household running. He had already searched through credit card records and their checking account statements, without finding any leads. He could look through them again and figure out where she had shopped, but it was clear that Tolbert would not be impressed with that information. Channing was convinced that there must be something further the police could do to search for Susan, but he could think of nothing specific to demand. He would have to give it more thought. With as much bluster as he could summon, he gave Tolbert a parting shot. "All right. I'll check back soon. This is an important case. I really need to find my wife before anything happens to her. I've been worried sick about this."

"I'll let you know if anything turns up," Tolbert replied, remaining in his seat. Neither man offered a handshake, and Channing left. He exited the building, got in his car and pulled out his smartphone.

Billy answered on the second ring. "Yeah. What's up, Channing?"

"You tell me. What have you found out?"

"Nothing at all. I've been watching the parents' house, but there's no action there. It's damn cold and I'm freezing my ass off."

"You haven't seen anything?"

"Her parents have been out a few times. The mail and paper get delivered, but that's it. There's no sign of Susan. I'm watching the place about fifteen hours a day, at different times. I've looked inside the garage when they open the doors to drive out, and there's no Volkswagen Passat in there or out on the street. I've poked around outside the house a few times and looked in the windows. When the parents are out there's no sign of anything going on inside. There's no way she's here. I couldn't have missed her."

Channing tipped his head back and rubbed his eyes. After a long pause he spoke to Billy again. "Okay. I'm out of ideas. Come on back to Charlottesville."

"Okay. Sorry, man."

Channing was starting to shiver. He turned on the motor and let the car idle until the heater began to warm up. The sun was low on the horizon and would soon dip below the Blue Ridge Mountains in the distance. Susan's trail was completely cold. She had vanished without a trace.

CHAPTER 20

Lee opened his eyes, and the bedroom gradually came into focus. It was almost noon, and brilliant sunlight flooded the room. Birds chirped in the trees outside his window as a wasp buzzed against the glass. He had fallen asleep while reading, and a paperback book and an empty pretzel bag lay on the bed beside him. Through a window he marveled at the beautiful day outside. Flowers were blooming in the yard, and a squirrel bounced across the grass before disappearing under a shrub.

He shuffled down the hall and gradually descended a staircase, pausing several times to catch his breath. On his way to the kitchen he stepped out to the front porch, picked up the morning paper and retrieved several items from a mailbox on the wall by the door. As he waited for two slices of bread to toast, he sorted through the mail on the kitchen table. He tore the brown wrapping from a small box and opened it.

Removing the bubble wrap that secured its contents, Lee found the camera he had ordered on eBay. It had arrived just in time for his departure to Charlottesville that afternoon. The camera had been used, and it came without an instruction book, but he had gotten it at a bargain price. Between bites of food he scanned the newspaper and studied the buttons and symbols on the camera.

After a cool shower he hunted through the house in search of an empty travel bag. With no wife in the house to maintain order, Lee had fallen into a habit of tossing travel bags on the floor and leaving them there after returning from trips to Virginia. Occasionally he would go on a cleaning binge and gather them up, emptying out the junk he found inside.

He switched on his computer and pulled up his eBay account.

Auctions for several items on his watch list would end while he was out of town, and he scrolled down the list before deciding not to increase any of his bids.

The flight to Charlottesville took less than three hours, with a short layover in North Carolina. The weather in Charlottesville was cooler than in Charleston, and the trees had not yet started to bloom. He washed up in his hotel room and then went down to the bar. He chose a small table near a window, ordered a whiskey sour and lit a cigar. He spread out a *Daily Progress* newspaper and immersed himself in the sports pages. Occasionally he looked up and surveyed the room, hoping an unattached female might show up.

For a long time after Andrea's murder he had not even thought about the possibility of romantic involvement. As time began to heal his physical and emotional wounds, his thoughts had gradually turned to the possibility of sharing his life with someone else. He remained in the bar for the next hour but saw no women who were likely prospects for his attention. At one point an attractive brunette ventured in and glanced around the room, but she quickly left in search of a bar with a more suitable clientele. Eventually Lee accepted the fact that this was not his evening to meet a lady, and he ambled back through the lobby and up to his room. He ordered a thick sandwich from room service and settled into bed to watch an old black and white Western movie on TV, falling asleep before it ended.

The weather the next day was perfect. At the baseball game he brought out his camera and took several test shots of players warming up on the field, and then settled into a spot along the third-base line. During the game, he snapped pictures as players ran from second base and slid into third, or rounded third on their way to home plate.

Arriving back home late on Sunday night, he crawled into bed without unpacking. The next morning, he fished through his travel bag until he found the camera, and popped it open to extract its memory card. He slipped the card into a slot on the computer and transferred the images, eager to see how the baseball players would look on a larger screen.

He was surprised when he opened the first image file. Instead of the baseball field, he saw a close-up view of a bookshelf with a slip of paper propped against the spines of several books. The paper was partially washed out in bright light, indicating that a flash had been used at close range. The books were bunched tightly together on the shelf and were all of the same height. Each one had leather binding in the same dark brown color. The spines were somewhat faded and appeared to be old. Because of their uniform height and binding, Lee guessed that the books were part of a set. Four titles were legible just above the slip of paper: *The Chimes, The Cricket on the Hearth, The Battle of Life,* and *The Haunted Man and the Ghost's Bargain.* The book spines did not show an author's name, but Lee logged onto the Internet and quickly discovered that all four books were written by Charles Dickens in the 1840s.

The slip of paper had the words Mega Millions at the top and was obviously a lottery ticket. Five rows of numbers were visible, as well as some fine print. At first he saw no pattern, but in a moment he noticed that three numbers in the third row matched his birth date. Nine, seventeen and fifty-five could be read as September 17, 1955. On the screen, he enlarged the picture and scrolled down to the bottom of the ticket. He could read its date as December seventh. With a few key strokes, he printed a copy of the photo and slipped it into a pocket.

Lee could think of no particular reason why he should spend any time investigating the source of the photo, but his curiosity began to get the better of him. Memories of another trip to Charlottesville began to surface, and he recalled reading an article about an unclaimed winning lottery ticket. Something about the numbers matching his birth date seemed familiar.

He thought about searching for the lottery article on the newspaper's website, but decided to start with a more traditional approach. There was a good chance that the paper might still be stuffed inside a travel bag or stacked in one of several piles of old newspapers and magazines that lay around the house. He could look for it and clean up some of the mess at the same time.

By late afternoon he had filled several recycling bins and garbage cans with a variety of papers and assorted junk. As he turned a large duffel bag upside down and shook it, an old issue of *The Daily Progress* tumbled out. He flipped through its pages until he spotted the article that he remembered reading weeks before. The details seemed familiar as he scanned the text. *Single lucky ticket...Mega Millions...Wally's Quick Mart in Charlottesville...$241 million...lump sum value of $124.6 million...cash option...winning numbers were 2, 6, 9, 17, 55 and 12...*

Lee compared the numbers from the mystery photo with those in the newspaper article. He couldn't believe his eyes at first. The numbers matched exactly.

CHAPTER 21

Channing tossed the stack of daily mail on the kitchen table and set his briefcase down. The house was cold, and through the windows he could see darkness approaching. The days were gradually getting longer, but it was early March, and in Charlottesville the sun disappeared not long after the office closed.

In happier times, he had eagerly awaited the arrival of spring every year, looking forward to long drives in the country and time spent outdoors on the downtown mall. He had often prowled the bars until he could find a woman who wanted to join him for dinner at one of the tables in front of the restaurants that lined the brick mall, which covered the surface of what had once been Main Street.

Everything was different now. As each day went by without any progress in his search for Susan, the winning lottery ticket was one day closer to becoming worthless. In less than three months the deadline for presenting it at the lottery office would pass. At that point the jackpot would be forfeited, and the ticket would become a worthless piece of paper—nothing more than a cruel symbol of what might have been. His frustration grew as each day passed.

He had called the police a few times, but they had no new information to report. Billy had burned through thousands of dollars as he investigated moving companies in a hopeless, if not lucrative, search for information about the van that Susan had hired. Billy had bugged the telephone and several rooms at Susan's parents' home, and periodically watched the place from a safe distance, but it was apparent that they had no idea where she was. In fact, Billy learned that they had hired their own investigator to look for her. He intercepted several phone calls from their investigator, who told them he was coming up empty.

Channing searched through the refrigerator but found nothing that was particularly appetizing. He settled for a few slices of pre-cut ham and some macaroni. He poured a large glass of scotch and began nibbling the food, pausing now and then to wash it down with a swig from the glass. He glanced through *The Daily Progress* as he ate, but there was little news that interested him. Every few weeks the paper ran a short update that the lottery ticket was still outstanding, that it was sold in Charlottesville, and that it would expire in early June.

He finished dinner and began sorting through the mail. There were the usual bills and advertisements, but nothing of note until he was nearly at the bottom of the pile. An official-looking brown envelope was addressed to "Booker, F. Channing & Susan F." It was from the Municipal Court, Traffic Division, in Charleston, West Virginia. The mere sight of Susan's name was enough to pique his interest, and he tore off the perforated edges to open it. Inside was a legal document that referenced a court date in February, with some small print that explained the option to waive an appeal and mail in a $150 fine, which included court costs. The document listed the offense as parking in a loading zone, followed by a reference to a city ordinance. The next line identified the date and time of offense as December ninth, five-oh-five p.m. He read the vehicle description and license number. They matched Susan's car.

He leapt from his chair and grabbed the phone, selecting a name on his contact list. After a long pause a voice came on the line, sounding irritated at first.

"Yeah?"

"Billy, it's me," Channing replied breathlessly.

"Yeah, I know. I wouldn't have answered for anybody else."

"I'm honored," Channing said, with a hint of sarcasm.

"So, you watching the Knicks game, or what? It's getting real tight. I don't think—"

Channing interrupted and got straight to the point. "Yeah, I know. Listen, what are you doing right now? You busy?"

"Well, I was kind of watching the Knicks game, you know?"

"Right. Yeah, of course. Look, we need to talk, but I don't want to use the phone."

"Chan, what the hell are you worried about? It's not like you're a suspect or anything. From what I can tell the cops don't give a damn about your wife disappearing. What's so top secret?"

"Billy, I told you before, I want to keep this quiet. I have my reasons. Are you at the store?"

Billy sighed. "Yeah. You want to come over?"

Channing thought for a moment. Billy would probably be happy to drive over to the house so he could watch the rest of the game on a decent TV. Often the ones at the pawn shop were small or had a distorted picture. Channing wasn't eager to leave the house on a cold night, but he didn't want to run the risk of having the neighbors see Billy. It would be better to keep him at a distance, just in case Billy's work got dirtier. There was a chance that he might have to rough somebody up to squeeze out information. "No, that's okay. I'll come on over in a few minutes. Keep an eye on the door or leave it unlocked. I'll get there soon."

"You don't want to wait till the game's over?"

"No, it's fine. I didn't get around to picking this one. I'm on my way." Throwing on a wool coat, he grabbed his keys and slipped out into the darkness. The streets were fairly quiet, but he had to drive at a moderate pace to avoid skidding on patches of ice that were scattered throughout the city.

He arrived at the pawn shop and pulled up close to the front entrance, flicking his headlights on and off to divert Billy's attention from the game, which he was watching on a small TV near the back of the store. Channing left his coat on as the two men walked behind the counter and stood near the TV.

Billy spoke first. "I'm surprised you didn't wait until the game was over. It looks like it might go into overtime."

"Yeah, I had it on the radio just now. I didn't think it would be this close."

"You should've put something on it. Even just a few bucks. It's no fun to watch it if you don't bet."

"Yeah, you're right." Channing glanced around the shop to make sure they were alone. He reached into his pocket and pulled out the traffic document, then placed it on the counter.

Billy took his eyes off the game for a moment and glanced at it before looking back at the TV. "So what's that?"

"This could be the break we've been hoping for," Channing replied.

"For real?"

"I don't know, but at least it's a clue. Something to go on."

Billy glanced back at the document. "Well, we're due for a break.

It's been a wild goose chase so far." He read over it quickly, listening to the game announcer at the same time. He slapped his hand on the counter as a desperate three-point shot bounced off the rim and time expired. "That's fifty bucks for me," he said with a smile.

Channing was not in the mood to celebrate Billy's win, and he motioned toward the TV. "How about cutting that off?"

"Yeah, sure. So what's the deal? Did you get a parking ticket?"

"Not me, Billy. Susan got one. Looks like she was in Charleston, West Virginia, the day after she disappeared."

"No kidding? You think she's still there?"

"I don't know, but I need you to find out. Can you head out tomorrow?"

Billy scratched his chin and thought for a moment before nodding. "Yeah, I think my brother can cover the shop for a few days. So how did you get this ticket?"

"It came in the mail today. I've been getting some mail for Susan, but nothing interesting until now. Mostly just catalogs and junk. Susan didn't give the Post Office a forwarding address, for obvious reasons. I've been hoping something might come in that would help me find her. At least we know which direction she went."

"Well, I could go to the courthouse and see if she shows up," Billy offered.

"No. She already missed the court date. This says she was found guilty in her absence. It's called a default judgment. Maybe she thought they mailed a summons to the house, and she was afraid I'd be there if she showed up in court." Channing paused for a minute while he thought about that. "Wait a second. Why didn't she just pay the fine right away? She could have just paid it and avoided a court hearing."

"Maybe she figured you would pay it, Channing."

"Maybe, but she went to great lengths to hide from me. I don't see why she would risk leaving a paper trail. If she had paid the fine right away, that would've been the end of it. It doesn't make much sense."

"Well, to be honest, I don't think any of this makes much sense. Why bother trying to find her? I'd just let the bitch go. You've got plenty of other girls to take her place, right?"

"Billy, I told you before. I've got my reasons. It's personal. I don't want to go into it. Maybe after we find her I'll tell you more, but for now just take my word for it. I need to find her, and soon."

"Okay, man, it's your money. Speaking of which, I'll need an advance to cover my expenses in West Virginia."

Channing found his wallet and pulled out a handful of $100 bills, which Billy shoved into his pocket. "Okay, Chan, I'll head out tomorrow. But this isn't much to go on. It's one lousy parking ticket from last December. What am I supposed to do in Charleston?"

"I don't really know, but this is better than nothing. It's the first trace of her that we've had. We know she went straight to West Virginia after she left here. Maybe that's where she's hiding. Who knows? Maybe she's got a place near where the ticket was issued. Go to the clerk's office in traffic court and see if they have a copy of the ticket, or anything else in their file." Channing pulled an envelope from his pocket and set it on the counter in front of Billy. "These are powers of attorney for me and Susan, if you need them. I don't know if the cops or the clerk will help you without these. The car's registered in both our names, so they should talk to you as my agent. If somebody won't cooperate, give me a call."

"Okay. I'll check it out."

"Good deal." Channing watched as Billy pulled a handful of potato chips from a large bag on the counter. Billy caught his glance and tilted the bag toward him. As Channing ate some chips, Billy turned the TV back on and found another basketball game in progress. Channing motioned toward the plastic cup that Billy had sipped from as they talked. "What are you drinking tonight?"

"Bourbon and Coke. I've got half a bottle left."

"I'll help you finish it off."

Billy mixed another drink and handed it over. "I've got some other coke in the back, if you know what I mean," he offered.

Channing smiled. "I can help with that, too."

൞൞൞

Lee rolled over in bed and rubbed his eyes, straining to read the illuminated face of his clock radio. It was the middle of the night and the house was still. He couldn't remember what time he had dropped off to sleep, but a call of nature had awakened him. After a visit to the bathroom he crawled back under the sheets, but was still awake twenty minutes later. His thoughts turned to food, and a short time later he settled into an armchair in the den, with a plate of cookies and a soda nearby. For several weeks he had been mulling over an idea but had dismissed it as being a waste of time. Curiosity had finally overcome inertia. Switching on his laptop, he browsed some sports sites for the latest scores and then signed into his eBay account. Scrolling down a list of recent purchases, he found the digital camera that had arrived with the unusual photo on its memory card.

The seller's eBay identification was "Trotter," and the item location was listed as Midwest, USA. Checking a record of other transactions by the same seller, he saw several sales by "Trotter" within the past month. The list included several antique bowls, a small TV, a handcrafted picture frame and other items that were of no particular interest. Some earlier sales were on the list, but detailed item descriptions were unavailable for older items. There were no recent transactions involving books.

Lee had paid for the camera using an online payment service. He logged into his PayPal account and searched until he found the transaction. In less than a minute he determined that "Trotter" was one Susan Finley of Aberdeen, South Dakota. With a few keystrokes he ran a Google search for her address and located a website for a vet in Aberdeen. The web page listed the owner as Sylvia Ricketts.

He opened the picture file he had saved from the camera and enlarged it on his laptop screen. As he had done weeks before, he studied the image of a lottery ticket and the books on a shelf behind it. Turning back to his eBay account, Lee typed in a book search for each of the four titles he saw in the photo: *The Chimes*, *The Cricket on the Hearth*, *The Battle of Life*, and *The Haunted Man and the Ghost's Bargain*. A few of these titles were currently offered for sale, but none by "Trotter." Lee saved each search, requesting automatic notification if any of the four books was listed for sale in the future.

He signed off eBay and logged onto the Virginia Lottery's website. After several attempts he was able to locate a list of unclaimed prizes, including a jackpot of $241 million from last December. For reasons that Lee could not imagine, whoever took the photo had not yet presented the ticket to claim the money. South Dakota was a long way from Charlottesville, Virginia, where the winning ticket was sold. Lee pulled up a map of the United States and found South Dakota. It appeared that Aberdeen was a long way from just about everywhere.

He set the laptop aside, leaned his head back against the chair and closed his eyes. Although he was beginning to feel drowsy again, he was afraid of forgetting his train of thought. Before nodding off, he forced himself to get out of the chair. He searched for the camera and found it on a shelf near the fireplace. Returning to the kitchen, he tore a paper towel off a roll and located a Ziploc bag, and then retraced his steps to the camera. With the paper towel covering his fingers, he carefully picked up the camera and slipped it into the plastic bag before putting it back on the shelf. Popping another cookie in his mouth, he returned to bed and went back to sleep.

CHAPTER 22

Boz settled into his chair and sipped his morning coffee, savoring its robust flavor. Ordinarily a newspaper would be spread out on his desk to occupy him for the first hour or two at the office. With no one caring to monitor his activity, or more typically his inactivity, he was free to while away the hours as he pleased. On any given day he might devote two or three hours to what could loosely be called work, in the sense that the time was devoted to reviewing documents that had some relationship to the firm. Whatever else he did each day was a mystery to his colleagues and subordinates at the offices of Dunlap & Cranston, but it made no difference to them as long as he kept out of their way.

He would have abandoned all work entirely some years ago, but he had convinced himself that his paper shuffling actually served some purpose. The fact that neither he nor his partners could identify it was beside the point. He generated meticulous charts and reports on each associate's billable hours, client contacts, travel expenses, research efficiency and numerous other attributes. He presented them each month at partnership meetings, where they were received and then discarded at the earliest opportunity.

Although Boz was utterly bereft of most rudimentary legal skills, he did have one attribute that was shared by many of his colleagues. He had a high tolerance for boredom. It was the one quality that sustained him through years of monotonous recordkeeping and pointless tasks. On most days at the office his mind was on auto-pilot as he crunched numbers and flipped through associates' research files.

Today was different. His interest was piqued, and he sensed that he was on the verge of a major discovery. He had logged many hours in front of his secret recording device, listening to conversations captured by the bugs he placed in two offices. He had pored over every research trail that Winston generated on Westlaw since he first became suspicious of the young associate. He had waited long enough to see that Winston was not going to bill any client for time spent on his unusual research.

For weeks he had studied Winston's and Channing's movements and activities. He had even slipped into their offices periodically, searching for physical clues. As best he could tell, nobody was aware of his investigation. At last the picture was becoming clear. He was definitely onto something.

Sliding his chair over to a credenza, he opened a compartment and lifted an index sheet from a stack of audio CDs. He ran his finger down the list until he came to the one that seemed to be the most explosive. Noting the number, he found the corresponding disc and popped it into a player. He kept the volume low to make sure that no one in the adjoining offices could overhear the recording. The voices of Winston and Channing were somewhat faint, but still audible.

Winston: "Yes, sir. As you recall, the question was whether your client could give his lottery ticket to a friend until his divorce becomes final, and then take back the funds after the friend cashes in the ticket."

Channing: "Yes, I do recall the question. So what's the answer?"

Winston: "Well, it's somewhat complicated. Evidently there's no prior case just like this."

Boz pressed the forward button to skip ahead.

Winston: "I think a gift like this would be viewed as a fraudulent conveyance, or at least a fraud on the court. Assuming all the income and gift taxes were paid by the third party, I don't know that it would be a criminal matter, although there might be some kind of conspiracy charge. Perhaps something like criminal fraud. If the client's wife found out about it, she could probably get the divorce decree modified and claim her share of the jackpot."

Boz advanced the recording again.

Channing: "All right. I'll update the client and see what he thinks. I'd like you to prepare a power of attorney for his wife to sign. She's going to be traveling abroad for a few weeks and he needs to handle some transactions while she's away. That's all for now."

Boz paused the recording and returned to the credenza, where he rummaged through several large envelopes before selecting the one with the proper label. He removed a yellow piece of paper and several sheets of wrinkled cotton bond paper and set them on his desk, pressing a heavy dictionary on top of the stack to flatten the documents further. He had fished the papers out of Channing's trashcan one night when the building was empty.

On the yellow sheet the name Susan Finley Booker was signed multiple times. The other papers were powers of attorney in the same name. Two of them were blank and five were signed. Some of the signatures were erratic, as if scribbled while in a state of intoxication. Checking his notes, Boz confirmed that these documents had been retrieved from the trashcan a few days after Channing and Winston had discussed a "client" who wanted to give away some lottery winnings and who needed a power of attorney for a wife who was apparently about to divorce him after returning from overseas.

Boz pulled another item from his credenza, a draft of a tax article that Winston had left on his desk some time ago. There was nothing in it about lottery tickets, divorce law, or powers of attorney. It was a short discussion of the tax treatment of like-kind property exchanges. It was not only dry and boring, it was poorly written and well below the quality of Winston's typical work product. Boz was not surprised that no law journal had agreed to publish it. In fact, he suspected that Winston had not even submitted it for publication. Apparently Winston's story about collaborating with Channing on a tax article was a complete fabrication, but it was not so clear that Boz could prove it.

Moreover, there was now a bigger fish to fry than Winston. Channing was conspiring with Winston and was obviously involved in some unsavory scheme. Boz gathered up all of the evidence he had collected and packed it neatly back in the credenza. Leaning back in his chair, he began to consider his next move.

He could call a meeting of the partners and confront Channing. He could picture Channing melting in his chair, squirming under the weight of damning evidence. Ideally, the partners would recognize Boz's dedication and devotion to the firm and reward him in some way. They might even force Channing to withdraw from the partnership. The two of them had never gotten along, and Channing's departure would be a blessing as long as he didn't take many clients with him.

On the other hand, it was not clear that Channing had actually done anything illegal or detrimental to the firm. As an experienced litigator, Channing was well versed in shading and recasting the truth. He might invent a plausible explanation for whatever he had done. Boz would have to reveal the source of his information, and the partners would be aghast to learn that he had bugged offices and sifted through trashcans without their knowledge. There was a considerable risk that Boz himself would end up in the hot seat.

He considered a more lucrative possibility. Channing apparently had some connection to a winning lottery ticket. If he was engaged in an illegal conspiracy, or a scheme that could damage the firm's reputation, perhaps Boz could turn the situation to his advantage. If he could catch Channing red-handed, he might be able to collect some hush money. Blackmail might be a profitable option.

It was clear to Boz that he would have to give more thought to the matter before deciding what to do with the information at hand. There was no pressing need to confront Channing right away. He could continue his investigation and wait until he had a better grasp of Channing's activities.

There was also something fishy about Winston. Normally Boz would pounce on an associate at the first sign of trouble. The slightest breach of protocol or company policy was enough to get his adrenalin flowing. In fact, the only part of his job that Boz enjoyed was making his subordinates miserable. It annoyed him to think that he would have to postpone Winston's day of reckoning, but if he confronted him now, he might never find out what he and Channing were up to. Satisfied that he had accomplished enough for one day, he decided to go out for an early lunch and take the afternoon off.

CHAPTER 23

Channing glanced up at the sky as he squeezed the pump handle and squirted just enough gas to top off his tank. The sun was high overhead, and it was an unusually mild April afternoon in Charlottesville. In happier times, Channing would have been tempted to enjoy the weather and delay returning to the office. On days like this in the past, his lunch break had sometimes extended into the afternoon to allow for a trip along the country roads of Albemarle County, or a stroll on the downtown mall.

But these were not happy times. As each day passed without any information about Susan, Channing's situation was becoming more desperate. He had until June fifth to find the ticket and turn it in at the Virginia Lottery's headquarters in Richmond. The deadline was absolute. If he failed to produce the ticket on time, his fortune would simply evaporate.

Billy had returned from West Virginia several weeks earlier with nothing to show for his trip. The fine for Susan's parking ticket remained unpaid, and the clerk's office in Charleston had no information other than what was written on the ticket. The clerk and the judge refused to bestir themselves to track down a scofflaw who had failed to pay a $150 fine. The effort would simply not be cost-effective, and Billy couldn't give them a convincing reason why it was so important to find Susan. Billy himself didn't know why Channing wanted to find her. He managed to locate and interview the officer who issued Susan's parking ticket, but the cop had written dozens of other tickets that same day and had no recollection of her car.

As he walked toward the entrance to Wally's, Channing contemplated the hopelessness of his position. When Susan disappeared, his first thought was to delay any divorce proceedings until he could find the ticket. He had expected to find her, steal the ticket, and make arrangements with Sully before getting divorced. But Susan's plan of escape had been executed flawlessly. As time passed and Channing's efforts to find her led nowhere, he began to hope that she or her lawyer would contact him to discuss a divorce. Susan's note had said she would be in touch, and her silence after four months was puzzling. At this point he was willing to try almost anything to initiate contact with her.

He said a quick hello to Wally and then headed toward downtown Charlottesville. Along the streets, dogwood trees were budding, and tulips sprouted in front of several shops. A group of construction workers in T-shirts and overalls were taking a lunch break on a grassy hill in front of the main library, while several teenagers were sprawled nearby under a large oak tree. Across the street in a park, two elderly men were hunched over a chess board, while several dogs cavorted in a boxwood garden. A young couple strolled hand in hand on the sidewalk.

Channing observed the scene with disgust. Everyone but himself was enjoying the April afternoon. Women who had thrown themselves at Channing in the past now kept their distance, their affections waning as his income declined. He should be lounging on a beach in St. Croix with a blonde at his side, not running around aimlessly in a futile search for a stolen lottery ticket. He didn't belong in the same neighborhood with these ordinary chumps and losers. The whole situation was grossly unfair.

The injustice of his predicament weighed on his mind as he turned onto a side street and parked in front of an old brick structure. It was separated from the sidewalk by a small yard that was shaded by magnolia trees. A bed of pink azaleas ran along a decorative iron fence encircling the lawn. The building had been converted to a law office years before, but on the outside it still resembled a typical family residence.

Beside the front entrance, a handsome gold plaque identified the building as The Law Offices of J. Sullivan Pendleton, III. Channing paused and took a deep breath before knocking on the door. He was not sure how much he should tell his friend. The original plan to have Sully cash in the lottery ticket and quietly transfer the proceeds to Channing was still on hold. He had continued to see Sully socially, but had not said a word about the lottery win.

He knocked on the door and stepped inside. The front hall opened into a reception area, which had once served as the home's elegant dining room. A large fireplace was still present but had been sealed with plaster and was no longer in use. The hearth was now occupied by a bookshelf, and modern furniture had replaced the Victorian-era antiques that once graced the room.

The receptionist was an attractive woman in her late thirties, but Channing refrained from flirting, knowing that her relationship with Sully was not strictly professional.

"Good afternoon, Mr. Booker," she said cheerfully. "Is Mr. Pendleton expecting you today?"

"Not today, Karen, but I'm sure he'll have time to see me."

She invited him to wait while she called Sully's extension on her phone. "He has a client with him at the moment but will be free shortly. Would you like some coffee or tea while you wait?"

"I'll take a Coke." As he waited for the drink, Channing settled into a chair and chose a magazine at random from the coffee table in front of him. He went through the motions of flipping through its pages to keep his hands occupied. He debated with himself whether to tell Sully everything, before deciding that there was no particular advantage in mentioning the ticket until he could find it. Apparently no one knew about the ticket except himself, and he would keep it that way for now.

In a few minutes Karen motioned for Channing to see Sully. His office was at the far end of a hallway, past several rooms where Sully's paralegals toiled. Sully greeted him with a smile and a firm handshake. "Hey, buddy, come on in. How've you been?" Noticing the soda can in Channing's hand, Sully motioned toward a small table in a corner of the room. "Can I get you the usual today?"

"Sure thing, thanks." Channing waited while Sully poured bourbon into a glass, and then added some Coke and waited while the fizz evaporated. Before taking a sip, Channing tapped a finger against the label on the bourbon bottle. "You must be doing well, Sully. You always serve the best."

"It's pretty good, isn't it?" Sully agreed, sipping from his own glass as they sat down on a couch. They enjoyed their drinks and swapped sports stories before Channing turned the conversation to business. "I've been thinking of doing something to clean up this mess about Susan. I thought she would have filed for divorce by now, but nothing has happened. I'm thinking it may be time to go ahead and get things rolling. I think it would be better to use someone on the outside. We've got enough gossip at the office already."

Sully nodded in agreement. "Yeah, these things can get ugly. I know from personal experience."

"I remember. Sorry you had to go through all that yourself."

"Well, it's water under the bridge now. You live and learn. It was an expensive lesson, though," Sully added with a smile. "So, how long has it been since she left?"

"About four months. I don't know why she hasn't filed anything yet."

"Maybe she's decided not to make a big fight out of it. She might be waiting a year so she can get a no-fault divorce."

Channing took another sip of bourbon. "I really can't figure it out. She planned everything out so perfectly, so I thought she'd have some pleadings already drafted and ready to file. It's a mystery to me."

"Hmmm. Well, we could wait a while, you know. If you wait eight more months, we could file for a no-fault divorce. The only requirement is that you live apart for twelve months. There wouldn't be any negative publicity."

Channing frowned. "I can't do that, Sully. I want to get this resolved sooner than that."

"I see. Well, since you don't have any kids, another possible option would be to negotiate a separation agreement and file the case after you've lived apart for six months. Who knows? Maybe she'll be reasonable and we can work out a simple settlement. We could file the pleadings as early as sometime in June."

Channing frowned again. "But I can't negotiate a separation agreement until I find her. There's got to be some way to speed up the process."

Sully drank the last drop from his glass and set it down. "Well, we can speed it up in the beginning, but it would probably take longer to litigate it. And it would get messy to say the least. You'd have to accuse her of fault."

Channing's face brightened and he leaned closer to Sully. "Now you're talking. If anyone's at fault, it's her. She was a real pain in the ass to live with."

"Well, unfortunately the statute doesn't list bitchiness as a ground for divorce. Hang on a second." Sully stood up and walked to his desk. He typed on his keyboard and waited for the statute to appear on the computer screen. "Okay, here it is. Let's see…grounds for divorce…adultery, sodomy or buggery committed outside the marriage—"

Channing laughed. "I don't think we can get a witness to prove buggery!"

Sully rolled his eyes and continued reading. "Conviction of a felony with imprisonment for a year…cruelty…apprehension of bodily hurt…willful desertion or abandonment."

"Go on."

"That's it. That's the whole list."

Channing took another sip and thought for a moment. "Apprehension of bodily hurt. Well, she did throw a candlestick at me once when I came home late from a bar. But that was a long time ago. She got used to it after a while and quit hassling me as much."

"Yeah, I remember you mentioned that when we were out drinking one night. But look, that's not enough to work with."

"Right, I know. But what about desertion? She moved out! She deserted me. There's no two ways about it. That's as clear as it gets."

Sully marveled at the look of satisfaction on Channing's face, understanding that Channing had no experience handling divorce cases. He weighed his words carefully before responding. "Look, Channing, we're good friends. We've had a lot of great times together and met a lot of fine women. But right now I have to level with you and speak as your lawyer, not just your friend."

Channing's smile evaporated. "Well, that's unfortunate, but go ahead."

Sully exhaled slowly. "Okay. The thing is, there's no doubt that Susan left you. But she can claim that she was justified in leaving because of your…well, you know."

"Yeah."

"And your case would be handled here locally. The judges know you. Now sometimes that's an advantage, but sometimes it's not. I can't predict what a local judge might do in this case. You do hold the record for contempt citations in this district. You've kept me pretty busy defending you over the years. Maybe I could get the local judges to recuse themselves and bring in somebody from out of town, but there's no guarantee. There's just a lot of risk and uncertainty here. You know I'll do the best I can, but—"

Channing held up his hand to cut him off. He appreciated Sully's loyalty and was prepared to rely on it even more if he could find the lottery ticket in time. At that point there would be plenty of time to talk about cashing it in. For the moment, though, there was no need to reveal everything to Sully. All he needed to do now was find Susan. "Sully, I know you'll do a great job. There's nobody else I'd rather have handling my case. Let's just file the thing and take it from there."

"Okay, it's your call to make. Of course, we'll have to get an order of publication and put a notice in the newspaper because Susan's disappeared. We don't know where she is so we can't serve the papers on her. Well, theoretically I suppose we could have the papers served at your residence, but if we say she deserted you, the judge will know we're not really trying to bring her into court. I don't think that would pass the smell test. Maybe we'll get lucky and she won't read the newspaper notice. It'll be much easier to get a divorce on favorable terms if she doesn't file a response."

Channing had to feign enthusiasm for the prospect of Susan's default. "Yeah, that would be great. How often does that happen?"

Sully thought for a moment before responding. "Good question. I haven't really kept track of that in my practice. If I had to guess, I'd say about a third of the time the spouse shows up in court. We'll just have to see if Susan or her friends read the legal notices in the classified ads."

Channing drained his glass of bourbon, wiped his lips with the back of his hand, and stood up. He shook Sully's hand and thanked him. "All right, you go ahead and draft something up and let's get it filed right away. I want to get this started as soon as possible."

"I'll get right on it. I can email a draft to you sometime tomorrow. You can fill in a few blanks with full names and dates and send it back, and I'll file it."

"Good. I'll watch for the legal notice in the paper. See you later. Keep me posted."

Channing started down the hall on his way out of the building, satisfied that he had done all he could to find Susan. His satisfaction lasted until he reached the front door. Realizing that he had overlooked a possible lead, he stepped back to the reception area and borrowed a phone book from Karen. He jotted down some numbers and slipped out to the front porch to make a few phone calls to the subscription offices of the local newspapers and weekly magazines. He explained that his wife may have accidentally opened duplicate subscriptions, using their vacation address by mistake. It took only minutes to confirm that he had reached another dead end. Susan had not ordered any subscriptions with a new address. If she was monitoring local news, she was doing it online or buying papers individually. Channing trudged back to his car. The only option now was to wait.

ᏋᎧᏋᎧ

Lee returned to his hotel room and looked in the mirror. The face that stared back at him was red and covered with sweat. He had neglected to wear his trademark Virginia Cavaliers baseball cap to the game that afternoon, believing that the April sun was not intense enough to cause a sunburn. Vowing not to repeat his mistake at tomorrow's lacrosse game, he stepped into the shower to cool off. At first the blast of water was painful on his sensitive cheeks and forehead, but gradually he felt better and dabbed at his face with a soft, soapy washrag.

He was in no hurry to head out for dinner, having eaten several snacks at the baseball game. Lying back on the bed and closing his eyes, he offered no resistance to the fatigue that crept through his body. When he awoke from a nap an hour later, his body was cool and partially dry under a thick towel. His hair was still slightly damp and lifeless, flattened against his head by a pillow. He slowly gathered his strength and sat up on the bed, then leaned across it to pull his laptop case off the floor.

He switched the computer on and typed some notes into a diary that tracked the baseball team's progress through the season. In the past he had sometimes written sports articles for a local newspaper in South Carolina, and had developed a habit of documenting some of the key plays in games that he attended. As he finished typing, Lee decided to check his eBay account before going out to dinner. He ran a search for vintage novels by Charles Dickens, which yielded a few sale offers. None of the sellers was located in South Dakota, so he searched for items listed by the seller whose trading name was Trotter. Two items appeared on the screen: an antique Christmas tree ornament and an old edition of the Sixth McGuffey Reader.

He read the item description for the reader. It was the first edition of a book that was originally published in 1885. The seller noted that the book included several selections from the Bible, as well as quotations from numerous acclaimed authors such as Shakespeare, Longfellow and Dickens. No one had placed a bid so far. The auction was set to end in three days.

Lee's interest was piqued, but before bidding he opened another web page and confirmed that the jackpot from last December's Mega Millions drawing was still unclaimed. It was a shot in the dark, but there was at least a slim possibility that the winning ticket was somehow associated with this eBay seller, and perhaps there was some connection to an old book. Maybe it was crazy to think that someone had hidden the ticket inside a vintage book, but it had to be somewhere unless it had been destroyed by accident. The only clue that potentially linked the ticket with a book was the photo he had found in his camera.

Lee had no interest in reading an old school textbook, but the thought of discovering a missing jackpot ticket was truly enticing. He knew that the odds of winning a Mega Millions jackpot were astronomical. Conceivably the odds of finding the winning ticket in this *McGuffey Reader* were lower than that. He had certainly frittered away good money in the past on eBay purchases of less practical value, so he had no great aversion to acquiring another collectable. He placed a bid on the book and then got dressed for a night on the town.

CHAPTER 24

Susan pushed a rocking chair across the wooden planks on the front porch until it rested a few feet in front of the railing, and then settled into it. Trotter was sprawled out along the top of the staircase, with most of his body exposed to the afternoon sun. He wagged his tail and lifted his head as he watched Susan's movement, but relaxed when he saw that she was not leaving the porch. Susan stretched her legs out and placed them atop the porch railing, gently flexing them to rock the chair back and forth.

She looked out at the green fields that extended all the way to the horizon. Hay was beginning to grow, fed by recent rainstorms that had rolled across the prairie. In some places it was about a foot high, tall enough to bend back and forth in waves whenever the wind blew. Several horses crowded under the shade of a tree near the barn where she stored her furniture, and cattle grazed in the distance. Two butterflies flitted about the front yard before landing on yellow daffodils.

The emotional scars from her abusive relationship with Channing had faded, along with the physical signs of her car accident. There were no lasting marks on her hands or face, and the scar from the stitches in her scalp had disappeared as her hair grew back. Her face had a fresh, vibrant appearance, and her eyes often sparkled when she smiled.

She was finally at peace. Almost five months had passed since she fled from Charlottesville. She no longer had nightmares about Channing coming to find her.

The window behind her was open, allowing spring air to circulate through the house. She closed her eyes and let her arms rest loosely on the sides of her chair. The sun warmed her face as she breathed deeply, enjoying the scent of freshly cut grass. An occasional breeze teased her hair as her body relaxed and her mind wandered. Soon she and Trotter were both asleep.

She was happily dreaming when the sound of Sylvia's phone echoed inside the house and through the window, jarring her awake. She considered ignoring it, but guessed that Sylvia could be calling from the office.

Rubbing her eyes, she slipped inside to answer the call. At first she didn't recognize the deep male voice on the line. For a brief instant she mistook the caller for Channing, and her pulse quickened as she listened silently to avoid revealing her identity. A moment later she recognized the voice and responded with a hello.

The caller was on a speakerphone from his law office in Culpeper, Virginia. Susan had met him there a month before leaving Channing. Her attorney was an earnest man in his late forties. On days when he had no hearings in court he wore a rumpled shirt with its sleeves rolled up, and a tie that hung loosely around his collar. His office was functional but not physically impressive. The room appeared to be smaller than it was because it was crammed with bookshelves and filing cabinets, and the floor was littered with numerous legal files. Some of them were stacked in thick piles that bulged with reams of paper and exhibits. Two windows of modest proportions overlooked an alley that ran perpendicular to Main Street. A diploma and some ink drawings hung on the walls, which were painted in a nondescript color. A faded wooden desk stood at an angle near one corner of the office, almost invisible under layers of paperwork. There was nothing remarkable about the place other than its cluttered appearance.

"Ah, yes, good afternoon. This is Lucas Morton. Is that you, Mrs. Booker?"

"Yes, sir. You're welcome to call me Susan."

"I'll make a deal with you. I'll call you Susan if you don't call me 'sir.' Please call me Lucas or you'll make me feel older than I am."

"Of course. Sorry for the formality. I was just surprised to hear from you. Is everything all right?"

"Well, probably so, but I needed to call you because there's been a development here."

Susan held her breath in anticipation, unsure what he meant. "I see. Has Channing done something?"

"Yes. He's gone ahead and filed suit. As you know, my staff has been monitoring the legal notices in the paper. This is not really a surprise under the circumstances. You might recall that I predicted this when you came to see me last fall. November, I believe it was."

"That's right. I know you advised me to file the papers first, but I appreciate your understanding about that. I just wasn't up to it for a long time. I needed to clear my head and let things settle down before dealing with all of the legal business. I'm not even sure I'm ready for it now."

"Susan, I understand completely. How are you doing now?"

"Not bad at all. Thanks for asking. I can't say I'm eager to jump into this, but I'm doing well and I think I'll be able to handle it."

"That's great. I'm so glad to hear it. Divorce is always a difficult process, but since no children are involved this case may be more straightforward than some are."

"I hope so."

"Now, at the same time, I have to warn you that it won't be a pleasant experience. My paralegal saw the notice in today's paper and has just sent me a copy of the pleadings from the clerk's office in Charlottesville." Lucas leafed through the complaint as he paced back and forth, carefully weaving his way around loose files to avoid tripping over them. "Channing has alleged that you deserted him, which we had expected. Of course, that's a complete load of crap. I'm sure we can prove you were justified in leaving home. You may recall that we discussed this when we met last year. A wife is not guilty of desertion if her husband creates intolerable conditions or she reasonably believes her health is endangered by remaining in the marital home."

"Yes, I remember you gave me advice about that when I was planning my escape. I discovered a gun in his closet one day, and he hit me several times. I was afraid he was going to kill me if I stayed there. To be honest, I'm still afraid of him."

"Well, you did the right thing in leaving. We'll be very careful to keep your location a secret to the best of our ability."

"Thanks, Lucas. When you say 'the best of your ability,' what does that mean? Can Channing force me to say where I've been staying?"

"Unfortunately that's not clear. The circumstances of your departure are important facts in the case. Channing may argue that evidence of your location is relevant. He might try to prove that he made a big effort to find you to seek a reconciliation. Maybe he'll pretend he was worried about you and you made it impossible to find you. Who knows? We both know he's a slick lawyer. If he persists, I'll file a motion to try to keep your location a secret. There's no guarantee what the judge will do, but I think I can persuade him that Channing's a threat to your safety and we need to keep you hidden."

"Thanks. I know you'll do your best."

"I sure will. I'll file our response with the court just before the deadline and keep you posted."

Susan thanked him, and their conversation ended. She paced back and forth several times before going back out onto the front porch. She sat in the rocking chair and tried unsuccessfully to relax. To keep herself occupied and her mind off Channing, she retrieved a radio from the house and set it on the porch railing, pointing the speaker out into the yard. She checked several stations before settling on one that was playing soft rock, and then gathered flowers in the yard. She retreated to the kitchen to arrange them in a vase before returning to pick up small sticks that cluttered the lawn. She made several trips to the fence at the edge of the yard to throw them into a field. After a while she began to calm down, and before long she heard Sylvia's van rumbling down the gravel driveway.

She helped her carry several grocery bags into the house. As they passed through the hallway on the way to the kitchen, Sylvia admired the vase of fresh flowers. Susan didn't mention the phone call from her lawyer at first, but after a few minutes of small talk her friend detected a tone of concern in her voice.

"Susan, is everything okay? You seem a little bit on edge."

Susan leaned against a counter and took a deep breath. "I guess I am a little nervous," she acknowledged. "I wasn't sure when to mention it, but my lawyer called from Virginia. Channing filed divorce papers."

Sylvia stopped unpacking the grocery bags and moved closer, gently placing her hand on Susan's arm. "I'm sorry. I thought there might be more time before you had to deal with all that." Sylvia pulled a bottle of red wine from one of the bags and held it up. "How about some wine and cheese on the front porch? We can talk about it out there. Things always seem a little better when you're sitting on the porch with a glass of Merlot."

They settled into chairs and looked out over the green pastures. The sun was slipping lower in the sky, casting shadows across the lawn.

Sylvia sipped her wine and waited for Susan to start the conversation.

"Lucas Morton's my lawyer. He called this afternoon while you were out. Channing claims that I deserted him."

"Yeah, right. What a crock! He's got a lot of nerve."

"You got that right. Anyway, Lucas says he'll try to keep Channing from finding me, but there's a chance he'll have to reveal my location." Sylvia frowned as she spread some cheese on a cracker, and then nibbled it as Susan continued. "I'll feel a lot safer if he doesn't know where I am."

Sylvia tried to sound reassuring as she replied. "We're a long way from Charlottesville. A lot of time has gone by. I'm sure Channing's cooled off by now. He's probably as anxious as you are to get this over with and move on."

"Maybe you're right. I hope so, anyway."

"And your lawyer's pretty good, right? So he can probably keep your location a secret."

Susan drained her wine glass and set it on the floor beside her chair. "He said he can't be sure what the judge may do, but he'll try to keep Channing from finding out where I am. Lucas is a good lawyer, and I know he'll work hard on my case because he has a grudge against Channing. That's one of the main reasons why I chose him to represent me. I wanted to get someone from out of town so there would be less chance that a secretary or paralegal in the office would know Channing. I don't want anybody blabbing around Charlottesville about my case, or giving Channing my address. But mainly I knew Lucas despises Channing and would do whatever it takes to beat him."

Sylvia leaned forward, anticipating some good gossip. "So give me the details. Sounds like there's a history between Lucas and Channing. What's the story?"

Susan reached for the plate and grabbed a handful of crackers. It was late in the afternoon, and clearing sticks from the yard had increased her appetite. She spoke between bites as Sylvia listened. "Lucas used to be a Commonwealth's Attorney in Charlottesville, when Channing was just starting to practice law."

"What's a Commonwealth's Attorney?"

"Sorry, I forgot that Virginia has some unusual quirks in its legal system. In most states he'd be called a prosecutor or District Attorney. You know, a DA."

Sylvia smiled and replied, "I get it. I thought maybe you were trying to show off with some fancy legal talk."

"No way! Channing did that all the time and it was really obnoxious."

"Yeah. A lot of lawyers think it makes them sound smart to use all that legal mumbo jumbo, but it just annoys me."

"Exactly. Anyway, Channing had a client who was charged with raping a thirteen-year-old girl, and Lucas was the prosecutor. The client was a real scumbag. He had several prior convictions for assault and drug possession. He drove around in fancy cars and lived like a king. Everybody knew he was a big dope dealer, but the cops could never get enough evidence to put him away. But he slipped up when he went after the girl. He grabbed her in a parking lot at a mall and shoved her into his car. He drove out into the county and took her to an abandoned warehouse, where he raped her and left her tied up. After he drove away, she managed to get free and walk six miles before someone found her. The girl said he blindfolded her as soon as he shoved her in his car, and she couldn't identify him. He wore gloves and used a rubber, and no DNA evidence was recovered. But there was a witness at the shopping mall. A young boy was asleep in a car, lying down in the back seat. The rapist must not have seen him because he wasn't sitting up at first. The girl screamed when she was grabbed, and the boy woke up in time to see the attack. He noticed an odd tattoo on the man's leg and saw the license plate on his car. It was a vanity plate with two short words that the kid could remember. 'Big Dog' or 'Hot Dog' or something like that."

Sylvia shook her head and looked disgusted as Susan continued her story. "The judge was going to keep the jury sequestered in a hotel during the trial, but Channing hired a private detective and found out that the victim attended the same school as the judge's daughter and had been to a birthday party at the judge's house about a year before the crime occurred. Channing was able to get the judge disqualified or recused, or whatever the word for it is, and he convinced the new judge to let the jury go home each night. Everyone in the jury wanted to convict the defendant, except for one man. He held out until there was a mistrial, and he moved out of town soon after the trial was over. Some reporter tracked him down later and found him living in a fancy house with a new car and a boat and stuff, but nobody could prove that he had been bribed to vote not guilty. Lucas was prepared to have a second trial, but the kid who had witnessed the crime disappeared and was never found. Lucas had to drop the case for lack of evidence."

"That's awful. Do you think Channing had anything to do with all that?"

Susan shrugged her shoulders. "I honestly don't know. He never said much to me about the case. He acted pretty cocky after the trial ended, and collected a big fee for handling the case. Most of what I know about the case came from the radio and newspapers. I'm sure somebody bribed that juror, and it wouldn't surprise me if Channing knew about it. And I hate to think what may have happened to that little boy. It's very suspicious." Susan slouched back in her chair and watched a crow fly past the porch and land on the fence at the edge of the yard. Sylvia waited to see if she wanted to say anything else about Channing's possible involvement in bribing a juror or getting rid of a young witness. Susan decided to steer the conversation back to her own case. "Anyway, I knew Lucas would never trust Channing again and would keep my plan to leave him a secret. He can't stand Channing, and he'll do everything he can to help me."

"That makes two of us."

CHAPTER 25

Channing rested his hands against the window sill, glaring out at the neighborhood. The weather was ideal, with a perfect temperature in the high seventies. Feeling caged in his office, he had opened the window, and a soft breeze wafted in, gently rippling the curtains. In the distance, dozens of townspeople meandered in the park across from the library. Some were tossing Frisbees, while others chatted with friends or leaned back on large wooden benches, relaxing under the shade of tall mulberry trees. A man in a dirty T-shirt, with a dense beard and a dark suntan, dozed on the ground, resting his head against a canvas knapsack.

The tranquil scene had no calming effect on Channing as he nervously tapped his fingers on the wooden sill. His anxiety and anger were increasing as each day passed, along with a sense of gloom and helplessness. Assuming that his desk calendar was accurate, today was May fifteenth. In three weeks his lottery ticket would become worthless. Its location would become completely irrelevant at five p.m. on June fifth. At that point the slip of paper would be nothing more than a collector's item, a map for a treasure that would never be found.

He fumed and cursed his bad luck. For a moment he was tempted to jump out of the window and put an end to his misery, but the thought scared him and he slammed the window shut. He turned away and retreated to his chair, where he slumped into a disheveled heap. His mind raced as he cast his eyes about the room, desperately sorting through all the steps he had taken to search for Susan, wondering if he had missed something. For several minutes he hunted through the papers on his desk before remembering that his scheduling calendar was stuffed in his back pocket. He searched its pages until he found the publication date of his divorce notice, and counted forward. If Susan had somehow seen the notice, she would have to file a response by the following week.

He called the clerk's office and asked if any pleadings had arrived in the case. He could hear the frustration in the voice at the other end of the line. "Mr. Booker, the situation is the same as yesterday. There's still nothing in the file." The clerk hung up before Channing muttered a perfunctory thank you. Disgusted, he hurled the calendar across the room. It struck a leg of the display case, bounced to the floor, and slid underneath. He waited a few minutes to let his anger subside, and then pulled a bottle of bourbon from his desk to pour a drink. His hand shook with tension as he lifted the glass to his lips, as if his fingers were about to crush the glass into pieces.

He took a quick gulp and then rose to retrieve the calendar, which had come to rest several feet under the case. He extended his leg toward it, trying to nudge it out with the sole of his shoe, but it was out of reach. Setting his glass on top of the case, he lowered himself to the floor and prepared to crawl underneath the case, grumbling to himself. Turning onto his side, he extended his arm as far as possible. As he groped for the calendar, he noticed something out of the corner of his eye. At first it looked like a strand of bubble gum, stuck to the underside of the case, perhaps left by some uncouth staff member. On closer inspection it appeared to be an air freshener, but he detected no odor. He scooped up the pocket calendar and turned his attention to the mysterious item. He touched it gently and then peeled it away from the furniture.

Crawling out from under the display case, he examined the item and manipulated it with his fingers until its outer skin folded back to reveal a thin electronic device. He was fairly certain it was a microphone. Shocked at the thought that his office had been bugged, he locked his door and spent the next hour methodically searching the entire room to look for other devices. Finding none, he sat down at his desk to consider the magnitude of what he had discovered. There was no way to know how long the bug had been in place, and he nervously recalled various meetings that had taken place in the office. What incriminating conversations had transpired in recent weeks, and who may have heard them? Was he under police surveillance? Were his partners spying on him? Various conspiracy theories swirled around in his head.

He made a mental list of clients whom he had met recently, but could not recall dealing with any unusually sensitive cases in the past few months. He could think of no obvious reason why one of his clients might be trying to set him up. Could Susan have paid someone to bug his office and get damaging evidence to use against him in the divorce case? Anything was possible, but that seemed highly unlikely, and he dismissed the thought.

He recalled that Winston seemed particularly ill at ease when the two of them discussed the lottery. The young associate had squirmed in his chair while they talked and had generally avoided him whenever possible. Maybe Winston realized that the story about an anonymous lottery winner was simply a ruse, and that Channing was trying to locate the ticket so he could steal it. Or maybe Winston believed his bogus tale and was trying to identify the mystery client for the same purpose. The idea seemed preposterous at first, but a $241 million jackpot was a tempting target for even the most honest person.

The situation was delicate to say the least. If he confronted Winston directly and he was not the culprit, Channing's scheme might be exposed. Winston would surely squeal to the other partners if he falsely accused him. At the very least, Winston would think he was a raving, paranoid lunatic. Channing would have to handle the matter with a light touch. He gathered his thoughts and headed down the hall to Winston's office.

He knocked on the door and went inside, where he found Winston leaning over his computer keyboard, typing at a furious pace. He stepped forward and stared at Winston without saying anything, closely observing the associate's demeanor and searching for any sign of duplicity. Winston looked up and said nothing at first, waiting for Channing to explain his presence. After an uncomfortable silence, Winston decided to speak. "Hello, Mr. Booker. Could I help you with something?"

Channing paused before responding. Winston's puzzled expression seemed genuine, and there was nothing obvious about his body language to indicate that he knew why Channing was there. He finally spoke. "Winston, someone is bugging me."

Winston waited for him to continue, but Channing simply looked at the associate in silence. The two men faced each other like gunfighters in a street, waiting to draw, until Winston finally spoke. "I'm sorry, I may have misunderstood. Did you say someone is bugging you?"

"That's right," Channing said firmly. He continued to stare at Winston. "Do you know who it is?"

Winston shrugged. "I'm sorry, I don't understand. I'm not sure I'm following you, Mr. Booker."

Channing maintained his icy stare, watching Winston's reaction carefully before speaking again. Sensing that Winston's confusion was real, Channing decided to back off. "Well, I'm sorry to disturb you. It's no big deal. I kept hearing an odd noise in my office and thought it might be coming from this end of the building. It was an annoying buzzing sound, and it bugged me. It must be outside. Maybe a car alarm went off or something. I don't hear it at this end of the hall now. Well, I'll let you get back to work. I hope I didn't interrupt anything important."

"Okay, no problem. If I hear any buzzing, I'll check it out."

"Thanks. I'll see you later." Channing offered a weak smile and quickly returned to his office. He called Billy on his cell phone and reached him at the pawn shop. "Billy, I need to talk with you right away. I'll be there in ten minutes."

こうこう

Lee removed his cap, leaned back in his stadium seat, and let the afternoon sun warm his face. The place was virtually deserted. A few fans were still strolling across the parking lot at a leisurely pace, and a dog was sniffing along the fence at the far end of the playing field. Except for several workers who were picking up trash, everyone had left to celebrate Virginia's lacrosse victory, or to drive home to North Carolina in the wake of a lopsided defeat.

Lee savored the moment. Football season was months away, and it was possible that he would not return to Charlottesville over the summer. He hoped that the thrill of a successful lacrosse season would stay with him, as happy memories might relieve the boredom of a summer without college games to attend. Virginia's baseball team had also enjoyed a successful run in recent months. Lee had enjoyed this year's athletic campaign more than most.

He had even had some success in his quest for female companionship during his visits to town. One of the waitresses at a downtown restaurant had gotten to know him and had accompanied him to several games earlier in the year, but their brief relationship had cooled after she moved away from the area to accept a better job. Still, she had given Lee some hope that he might find someone to fill the void in his life after Andrea's untimely death. He slowly folded his portable stadium seat and descended from the bleachers. A lone usher remained at the gate as he left and headed to the parking lot. His car had been exposed to the sun for several hours, and a wave of hot air escaped when he opened the door. He started the engine and ran the air conditioner at full blast as he waited for the car to cool off.

He sat there for several minutes, wondering if it was worth his time to run the errand he had tentatively planned. For several months he had been monitoring "Trotter's" sales on eBay, hoping to see listings for Dickens novels. He also routinely checked the Virginia Lottery's website. "Trotter" had been selling a variety of items on a regular basis, and had recently listed a few books, but no Dickens volumes so far. The $241 million jackpot was still unclaimed, and the winning ticket would expire in less than three weeks. As each day passed, it seemed more likely to Lee that the ticket had been lost or misplaced. He could think of no reason why someone would intentionally wait so long to cash it in. He was convinced there was some connection between "Trotter" and the ticket, but there was little time left to prove it or benefit from it.

He had to make a choice. He could get serious about searching for the ticket, or he could go home for the summer and wait to see if anyone claimed the money by June fifth. His flight back to Charleston would leave tomorrow afternoon, and there was nothing that he had to do before then.

He could go get a beer and forget all about the ticket. It was a simple and tempting option. The other alternative was probably a fool's errand. He could spend a lot of time and money and end up with nothing to show for it. He would probably have to bend some rules and break others, and there could be significant risks ahead. The odds of finding the ticket seemed ridiculously low. Still, $241 million was an awful lot of money.

The trip across town to an office supply store took about ten minutes. He had stopped briefly at Wally's on Friday and knew what he needed. Wally still had his DVD of surveillance photos on the counter, and Lee had memorized the color of the plastic case, the brand of DVD and the writing on the disc. Arriving at a strip mall, he entered the store and hunted for the items he needed. He left with a small bag and emptied its contents onto the front seat of his car.

With gloves on, he opened a package of clear green plastic jewel cases and pulled one out. He scribbled a notation on one of the DVDs, inserted it into the case, and tucked it inside his shirt.

He lowered the windows and headed to Wally's, enjoying the rush of spring air that swirled through the car. Trees along his route were thick with fresh green leaves. In a short while he spotted the sign in front of Wally's and pulled into the parking lot. Wally had taken the day off, and a young sales clerk was behind the cash register, watching a tiny TV set. He glanced up and nodded his head as Lee came inside, then returned his gaze to the screen. Seeing no other customers, Lee pretended to examine some merchandise as he waited to make his move. He knew that the surveillance cameras would record what he was about to do, but nobody would ever see their photos unless a robbery occurred in the next few days. If nothing unusual happened in the store, presumably the recording disc would be overwritten as soon as it was full. He decided to proceed in full view of the cameras. He waited until another customer approached the clerk to check out, and then quickly switched the discs. Apparently oblivious to what had occurred, the clerk never turned his head in Lee's direction.

During his flight home, Lee copied the disc onto his laptop's hard drive. Without more information, there was little to be gained from reviewing the disc's contents, but he couldn't resist taking a look. The first photos were taken five days before the winning ticket had been drawn, and the last one was dated the day after the drawing. There were hundreds of photos of customers standing in front of the checkout counter, each with a time and date stamp in the lower right corner. Apparently the surveillance cameras were activated by a motion detector and snapped photos only when someone was in the front area of the store. He spent a half hour reviewing the pictures before concluding that they were useless until he had some other clues to help him narrow his search.

CHAPTER 26

Channing unlocked the back door at Dunlap & Cranston and peered into the darkness as Billy slipped inside the building. Nothing out of the ordinary was apparent outside, and Channing had confirmed that all of the offices were unoccupied. He had hoped to address the matter sooner, but Billy wanted time to examine the bug and research its capabilities, and to round up the equipment he needed. It was Sunday night, and there was little chance that any of the firm's attorneys would show up at this hour. They were free to proceed.

Channing had taken the bug to the pawn shop as soon as he discovered it. Billy had carefully pulled it apart, photographed its internal components, and reassembled it. He advised Channing to put it back in his office, thinking that if it stopped transmitting for an extended period, whoever planted it there might realize it had been detected.

The two men went directly to Channing's office. Once inside, they said nothing as Billy peeled the bug from the display case and expertly pried it open. He removed the tiny battery and snapped in a replacement whose power was exhausted. He pressed the bug back into place. From a toolbox, he removed a device with a circular antenna and a control panel with dials, switches and an illuminated screen. He attached an earpiece and then carried the device silently around the office, pointing it in different directions and passing it over every piece of furniture. He watched an electronic green line on the screen as he moved about, but it barely moved. When he was satisfied that he had taken enough readings, he switched the machine off. "The room's clean," he announced.

"Okay, good. What kind of range did that thing have?"

"Probably several hundred yards with a fresh battery. The receiver could be in a building down the street, or as close as the next office. It's not as powerful as the ones I put in your wife's parents' house, but it's not a cheap model, either."

"And you never heard anything at the house, right?"

"No, man. Well, I mean, I heard some kinky stuff every now and then in their bedroom, but Susan never called or visited them. I couldn't hack into their Wi-Fi. The encryption's too good. I don't know, maybe they call her when they're away from the house, or maybe they've been in touch by email."

"Well, it's probably a dead end, but go ahead and watch their house for the next few days." Channing sat down behind his desk and looked over at the display case. "Man, I hate to think what I might have said in here while that bug was working."

"Yeah, I know what you mean. I can't tell how long it's been there. A new battery can last three or four months—sometimes even longer—and whoever bugged your office could have come back and changed the original battery. The one I put in there is out of juice, so whoever planted the bug should come back soon to replace it."

"Well, I hope the bastard does come back. Let's set up the cameras."

Billy lifted three tiny surveillance cameras from the toolbox and set them on Channing's desk. As Channing watched, he inserted a battery into the first camera and switched it on. "Okay, you see how to put the battery in, right? You'll have to replace it every two weeks. These things eat up power like crazy."

"Got it. I hope I won't need it that long, anyway."

"We'll see. Now, we could plug them into the wall outlet instead of using batteries, but someone might see the cords. They'll be harder to see if we use batteries." Billy pulled out another box and removed an instrument that was slightly larger than an iPod. It had a small touch screen on the front and a few jacks and switches on one side.

Billy inserted a battery and connected the device to the camera with a short cable. He showed Channing how to download video images and play them on the small screen. "You can download everything onto your computer, or you can play it back right out of the machine here. Each camera can store up to fifty hours of video. Switch them on whenever you're out of the office. They automatically shoot in infrared at night."

Billy loaded batteries into the other cameras, tested them, and then looked around the room. Channing followed him as he moved around the office to place the cameras in strategic, hidden locations. Channing placed the video monitor in his pocket, and the two left through the back door, disappearing into the night.

Channing arrived at the office the next morning around nine-thirty and poured a cup of coffee before settling in. He glanced over at the display case and reminded himself to be careful with his words. Someone could be listening to every conversation. There was a stack of files on his desk and a pile of mail that had come in over the weekend, but he had little appetite for digging through it all. He opened the middle drawer of the desk and found his calendar. It was May twenty-third, and a little over two weeks remained before all would be lost. If he didn't catch a break soon, it wouldn't really matter who had bugged his office.

Recalling Billy's instructions, he walked over to the bookshelf and plugged his video monitor into the surveillance camera. The small screen flashed the message "no images recorded," so he disconnected the cable and switched off the camera. It was aimed at the office door and was set to record images at a wide angle, so Channing knew the other cameras had not detected any activity after he and Billy departed the night before.

He reached for a stack of mail and flipped through it until an envelope caught his eye. The return address indicated that it was from the Law Offices of Lucas Morton, PC. Channing instantly recognized the firm name, recalling past legal skirmishes with one of his fiercest adversaries.

His curiosity was piqued because he had no open cases against Lucas. He removed a document from the envelope and unfolded it. As he read the first page his pulse quickened. *In the Circuit Court of the City of Charlottesville...Fordham Channing Booker vs. Susan Finley Booker...*

He skimmed through the following pages, but the contents meant very little to him. The important thing was that he had a trail that might lead him to Susan's hideout.

He reached for his desk phone and dialed a number. A pleasant female voice answered. "Law Offices of Lucas Morton. How may I help you?"

"Hi, this is Channing Booker. I'd like to speak to Mr. Morton."

There was a brief pause. Channing's reputation had preceded him at the law office in Culpeper. "Is he expecting your call, sir?"

"That's hard to know, but I need to speak with him right away. It's urgent."

"I see. Hold please."

Channing read through Susan's allegations as he waited for Lucas to come on the line. Soon he heard a voice, with a tone of ice-cold formality.

"Hello, Channing. I was expecting your call."

"I'm sure you were," Channing replied.

The situation was unfamiliar to him, and he was unsure how to make a pitch to his old nemesis. Lucas was under no obligation to cooperate in speeding up the divorce process, and it was unlikely that Channing could convince a judge to expedite the proceedings. At the same time, it was against his nature to be conciliatory, and if he told Lucas outright that he wanted to settle the case quickly, Lucas might see no point in allowing him to take Susan's deposition. Susan would probably object to giving Channing her prized Dickens novels in a property settlement, and she might inspect them closely if he overtly fought to get them. The situation was delicate to say the least. "Lucas, I'll be honest with you," Channing began.

"I'm sure. As always," Lucas replied tartly.

"Well, I know we've had some differences in the past," Channing acknowledged, stating the obvious. "But I'm prepared to handle this matter professionally. Of course, I want to protect my interests, but I'm ready to put aside any personal feelings and see if we can resolve this case fairly. It may be hard to believe, but I have some fond memories of my time with Susan. I know this has been difficult for her. Just between the two of us, I can understand how she might feel that this was in some way my fault. Of course, that's off the record, and I'm not conceding that our breakup was my fault, but I can understand her view of things."

Lucas rolled his eyes, having witnessed the effect of Channing's silver tongue on juries over the years. Nevertheless, he had no interest in prolonging Susan's pain. If there was a way to get a favorable property settlement for her without a lot of wear and tear, he could suppress his revulsion and endure Channing's insincerity, at least for the moment. "I appreciate your candor. I'm listening."

"Yes. Well, obviously with no children, we only have to work out the property situation."

"Very true. Channing, let me break in here for a second. As you know, technically I'm not supposed to talk with you directly since you're represented by an attorney. I assume you're waiving the right to have your attorney speak for you?"

"Yeah, no problem there. As the pleading indicates, Sully Pendleton is acting as my counsel, but I think you and I may be able to work out some details without involving him at this point. I know it would be difficult for Susan to have to testify in court. And I realize that if we take this to a judge, there would be a lot of unfortunate publicity. That's why I'd like to explore the possibility of a quick settlement. I have to consider the reputation of myself and my partners in this town."

Lucas could barely contain himself, but he replied without laughing. "I'm sure Susan has no interest in damaging your reputation, such as it is."

Channing continued without acknowledging Lucas's sarcasm. "I think we can probably work things out quickly. I'd like to put this behind me, and I'm sure Susan feels the same way. I'm even inclined to make some concessions in order to move it along. I think if Susan and I could meet in person to discuss this we could work out a solution that she'll like. I'm willing to meet at her place any time. And, of course, you would be there to mediate the discussion. If you'll give me her address, I could meet the two of you there in the next few days."

"Channing, I don't think that would work, but we might be able to meet at my office soon. I'll have to get back with you after I talk to Susan."

"I just thought she might be more at ease if we meet on her turf. Are you sure that won't work? I can adjust my schedule to meet at her convenience."

"Well, Channing, I'll be honest with you, too. This whole thing has been extremely hard for Susan. She actually told me she was afraid of you. I won't go into that right now, but if we went to trial, there would be some evidence in that regard."

Channing realized he wasn't going to get Susan's address out of Lucas, so he tried another approach. "Well, I'm sorry she feels that way. Really, I just want to get this over with, and I feel sure we can work out the property distribution if both of us are open-minded about it. I assure you that I'm prepared to meet her more than halfway, but only if we can get this done quickly. If she insists on dragging this out, I'll have no choice but to take a hard position and make this a dogfight."

"I see. Channing, I think you know me well enough that I don't need to tell you I can go to the mat any time, any place, if it comes to that. But if you're serious about resolving this quickly, we may be able to work something out. What are you proposing?"

"I'd like to get a list of all property she removed from our home and its present location."

"I think that will depend on what you mean by 'location.' I don't believe we're obligated to tell you its precise location at the moment. Susan told me she didn't take anything that she didn't own before you were married. As you know, those items aren't marital property. They're not subject to equitable distribution by the court."

Channing had no idea if Lucas was correct about the definition of marital property, but his voice sounded confident and convincing. Channing would have to tread lightly. He hoped that Susan hadn't already sold her books, but if she still had them, she would probably hold onto them if she thought the divorce could be settled soon. "Okay, Lucas, here's what I'm proposing. Let's take her deposition within the next week and we can get everything on the record. You can take my deposition at the same time. I'll voluntarily produce my tax returns from the past five years. We filed jointly, so Susan won't have to bring any tax records. Each side will bring a sworn affidavit of all our assets, and I'll send you a proposed settlement agreement within three days after the depositions. Or you can draft one yourself and I'll review it and get back to you quickly. I really think we can work this out. I don't know what Susan has told you, but I'm prepared to be reasonable if she cooperates to get this resolved soon. To show my good faith, I'll even waive any claim to the money she took out of our bank accounts when she moved out."

"Will you put that in writing?"

"I'll get a letter to you this afternoon."

"Okay. And, Channing, not to cast any aspersions on you, but your property affidavit had better be complete. You're certainly aware of the consequences if you don't disclose all of your assets."

Channing was also aware of what would happen if he *did* disclose the lottery ticket. Lucas would fight to the death to get at least half of the jackpot for Susan. "Absolutely. I assure you everything will be out in the open and above board."

"Okay. At this point, I think Susan will agree to your proposal, but I'll have to check with her and see what she wants to do. It's her call to make, as you know."

"I understand. I'll get that letter to you this afternoon. Be sure to mention it to her. And tell her I'm sorry things didn't work out better for us. I truly hope she'll be happy in the future, once we get this over with."

"I'll let you know, Channing."

As soon as the call ended, Lucas telephoned his client with an update. "Susan, we know Channing's a skunk, and he may have some ulterior motive, but he's certainly acting in a gracious and conciliatory manner."

"Wow, I didn't expect that," she replied.

"Frankly, I didn't either. Maybe he wants to remarry, and he needs to get the divorce out of the way. Maybe his partners have told him to take care of this quietly to avoid negative publicity for their law firm. It's hard to know what Channing is up to, but if he's ready to negotiate a fair settlement, there's no reason to put you through the ordeal of a trial."

"Well, I guess we should go ahead and schedule the deposition, then. I'll make a list of the property items and see you soon."

♥∂♥∂

At one-fifteen on Monday afternoon Lee settled into a booth at Rollo's Steakhouse and waited for Alex Charleton and Anna Cortez to arrive. He sipped iced tea and scanned the sports section of the morning paper while he waited. They arrived a short time later and spotted him from across the room. Alex was tall and athletic, with a hint of a suntan. He had been promoted from patrolman to detective several years ago, but he still maintained his hair in the short, closely cropped style that he had worn on the streets. He was dressed in a plain business suit with a blue shirt and conservative tie. Anna wore a brown pantsuit with a tasteful blouse. Her blazer sported a gold pin in the shape of a racehorse. Her dark hair was parted in the middle and hung down past her collar. She was quite a bit shorter than Alex but carried herself with authority. They greeted Lee warmly and slid into the booth, across the table from him.

Lee set his paper aside and smiled broadly. "Thanks for seeing me on short notice."

"Are you kidding? We're always happy to see you," Alex replied.

"We've been meaning to check in with you. It's been too long since we've seen you, Lee," Anna added. "How are you doing?"

"Not bad at all," Lee answered. "I'm walking better and getting my stamina back. It's gonna take more time, but I can feel the improvement."

"Well, you look great," Alex said. "We've missed you at headquarters. The place isn't the same without you."

"Thanks. I'll try to stop by sometime."

A waiter approached and distributed menus to Lee's guests, and then recited a list of daily specials before disappearing to get their drinks. The three chatted constantly, reliving war stories from their time together as detectives on the Charleston police force. Midway through the meal, Lee finally broached the subject that had prompted him to call them. "Listen, I'd like to ask you guys a favor. I've got a camera that may have some fingerprints on it. I was wondering if you'd mind dusting it to see if you can identify anything on it."

Alex and Anna stopped eating, and a look of concern crept over their faces. Anna spoke next. "Does this have anything to do with Andrea's case?"

Lee smiled reassuringly. "Oh, no. It's not a big deal—not a crime at all. I'm trying to locate someone without going to a lot of trouble. It's not urgent or anything, but if you can help me out, I'd really appreciate it."

Alex and Anna exchanged glances with each other, and then both nodded at the same time. "That shouldn't be a problem if you can wait a few days. Do you have any information that might help us narrow the search?" Alex asked.

Lee pulled a Ziploc bag from his pocket and placed it on the table. "Not really. I just want to know whose prints are on this camera."

Anna took the bag and slipped it into her purse. "We'll see what we can find out and give you a call."

CHAPTER 27

Boz opened his office door just far enough to peek out into the hallway. It was six-thirty in the evening, and there was no sign of activity nearby. He held a manila folder in his hands as he stepped out and headed toward Channing's office. The folder was stuffed with blank sheets of paper but gave the appearance of being a collection of important documents. If anyone surprised him, he would point to the folder and explain that he was working late. Boz had perfected the technique of projecting a businesslike air, unaware that most of his colleagues knew he performed no real function at the firm. He could alter his facial expression in an instant to portray a man carrying the weight of the world on his shoulders.

Fortunately, the building was empty, and he quickly arrived at Channing's door. Slipping inside the office, he set the folder down on the display case and went to work. He peeled the microphone from its hiding place and pressed a new battery inside before sticking the device back underneath the case. He paused to listen for any sound of activity, and then sifted through the contents of Channing's trashcan. Finding nothing incriminating, he looked through papers on top of the desk, being careful to leave them in their proper place. He searched the desk drawers, but found little of interest. Although there was nothing new, he already had enough evidence to expose Channing's misdeeds. Satisfied that he was ready to present his case to the partners, and blow the lid off Channing's scheme, he was on his way home by six-forty-five.

⁊ɔɛɔ

Susan awoke to the sound of Trotter scratching at the screen door.

The dog had made his early rounds, exploring the yard and several barns before returning to the front porch. Sylvia opened the door, and he followed her back to the kitchen to find his breakfast in a large plastic bowl. Susan lay in bed for a few minutes but got up as the smell of fried bacon grew stronger. She put on a bathrobe and joined Sylvia at the kitchen table.

"Well, I guess you and Trotter think alike. He begged some bacon from me, but I saved some for you, too," Sylvia said with a smile.

"Thanks. It really smells good. I need some energy today. I have to make a list of all my assets for the divorce case."

Sylvia rolled her eyes. "That sounds like a fun day. I guess I'd rather be going to work. I don't remember if we did that when Kevin and I got divorced."

"My lawyer says it's not unusual, but I'm kind of surprised because all I took was stuff that was mine before we got married. Channing can just look around the house and see what's missing to figure out what I've got." Susan laughed and then continued. "Well, except for a bunch of cash I took out of the bank. But I only took half of it."

"So you'll be spending the day out in the barn, I guess?"

"I'm afraid so, unless you have a better idea."

"Well, if the stuff is yours, I guess you could sell some more of it before the divorce is final."

"I don't know. My lawyer told me to be honest and list everything. He says Channing's hinting that he'd like to settle this thing without a big fight. That's really surprising if it's true. I still don't trust Channing. I don't know what he might be up to."

"Well, your deposition is next week, right? And that's when you have to turn in the asset list?"

"Yeah. I was planning to carry it with me or email it to Lucas before I leave for Charlottesville."

Sylvia thought for a moment as she crunched a piece of bacon and washed it down with coffee. "You're going to need some money to pay your lawyer. You could sell some more things before you leave next week. Then you could pay the proceeds to Lucas and not have to include the money on your list."

Susan liked the idea. "That'll make it easier to prepare the list, too. I won't have to itemize every last thing that I've stored in your barn."

"And it'll free up some stalls for the horses."

They finished breakfast, and Susan volunteered to clean up the kitchen. She watched Sylvia drive off to work and then put on some old clothes. She filled a jug with ice and lemonade and found a pad of paper before heading to the barn. The midmorning sun was oppressive as she and Trotter waded through tall grass in the field that separated the barn from the yard. Panting rapidly, Trotter lagged behind Susan instead of running ahead, which he often did when he had more energy.

It was cooler inside the barn, and Susan waited for her eyes to adjust to the darkness before making her way down the aisle to the last stall. She set the jug and paper down and walked back to retrieve a small stool. She shoved several boxes aside to make a narrow pathway to the back of the stall. The movers had been in a hurry when they packed her belongings in December, so some of the boxes were not labeled. With a pocket knife, she sliced open several boxes before finding one that contained books. She struggled to slide it to the front of the stall, closer to the overhead light in the aisle that ran between the rows of stalls. She placed the stool next to the box and sat down to begin work, as Trotter curled up next to a bale of straw to watch.

She noticed that the box was not full, and the books inside were loosely packed, as if the box had been jostled or tipped over in transit from Charlottesville. She lifted the books out and wrote the titles on her note pad. There were about a dozen volumes by Chaucer, Voltaire, and Dickens, in addition to some more recent art history books. Reviewing the list, she was shocked to find that several of her Dickens and Chaucer books were missing. Hoping that they had been packed in another box, she continued her inventory for several hours until every box had been checked. Her list of assets filled three pages, but the missing books were nowhere to be found. It had taken her years to collect antique copies of the complete works of Charles Dickens, and she couldn't believe her bad luck. She assumed that the movers had lost some of the books or she had forgotten to pack them when she left home.

She set her list down and poured a cup of lemonade. Trotter followed her to a bench just outside the barn's main entrance, flopping down on the grass at her feet. She sipped the cool liquid and looked out across the fields as she thought about her possessions. She had not read any of her rare books in years. They had generally rested untouched on the shelves at home in Charlottesville, and she never thought about them after moving to Aberdeen. The books had some sentimental value, but she could no longer feel the satisfaction of owning a complete collection of either author's works. Channing had probably frittered away most of the couple's remaining funds, and she would need money to pay Lucas and to tide her over until she got a job. The books would command an impressive price on the market, and she could no longer afford the luxury of keeping them.

She finished her lemonade and went back inside the barn. A large open area was occupied by farm machinery. She rolled a compact utility vehicle into the central passageway and started its engine. Slowly she guided it to the other end of the barn, parking next to one of the stalls. She loaded its bed with several boxes of items to sell, then drove back to the main exit and started toward the house. Trotter followed along behind her, pausing occasionally to sniff the ground.

෬൚൚

Channing brushed by the receptionist without saying hello and headed to his office. The hearing in court that morning had been a routine matter. He had filed several evidentiary motions in a burglary case, hoping to prevent the jury from hearing of his client's prior felony convictions when the case came to trial in two weeks. The judge had agreed to suppress the evidence as long as his client wouldn't testify that he had a clean record or a good reputation in the community. His client congratulated him and invited him to lunch as they left the courtroom, but Channing declined.

His mind was on other matters. In less than two weeks the lottery ticket would expire, but he would have at least one good chance to find it. In three days Susan would be at her lawyer's office in Culpeper for depositions. Channing had arranged to have Billy wait outside the law office, watching for Susan to leave the building when the business was concluded. Billy would follow her wherever she went. Channing had not told Billy about the books, fearing that he might inspect them and find the ticket. If he did, he would surely steal it.

He instructed Billy to call him as soon as he knew where Susan had been staying. Channing would take it from there. If the books were not at Susan's hideout, he would have to resort to more dangerous tactics. He or Billy would threaten her, and use whatever force was necessary to make her talk.

Stepping inside his office, he set his briefcase on the floor beside his desk. Remembering the surveillance cameras, he closed the door and downloaded the contents of their hard drives. Immediately he could tell they had recorded some activity since he last checked them. He played the first recording on the small monitor Billy had given him. The electronic date stamp showed that the video was shot yesterday, beginning at six-thirty-three p.m.

He watched his office door open slowly, almost imperceptibly at first. A figure entered the room, clutching a folder in one hand. He put on a pair of gloves before switching batteries in the bug and then hunted through Channing's trashcan and desk. The recording lasted just over ten minutes, and Channing watched it twice. The intruder's identity was unmistakable. The man in the video was clearly Boz Dunlap.

Channing spoke before remembering that the bug was still transmitting. "I've got you now, you sorry little weasel!" He placed the video monitor in a pocket and returned to his desk, wondering what he should do next. Suddenly Winston burst into the room without knocking. The young associate's face was flushed and sweaty. His shirt was damp under the armpits, and his tie was loose. He had a grim look and was breathing rapidly. Panic showed in his eyes. Before Channing could say a word, Winston blurted out the reason for his visit.

"Mr. Booker, we're in a real mess. I just came from Mr. Dunlap's office and—"

As soon as he heard Dunlap's name, Channing held up his right hand and put his forefinger over his lips. He silently mouthed the word "quiet," and Winston stopped in his tracks, standing with his mouth open.

"Don't say anything else," Channing commanded. He stood up and approached Winston, placed an arm around his shoulders, guiding him out of the room. When they were out in the hall, Channing motioned ahead. "We'll talk in the conference room." Arriving there, Channing closed the door and pointed to a cluster of chairs in one corner. They sat down, and Channing spoke first.

"Now, what's the problem, son?"

Winston wiped his forehead and spoke quickly, in a hushed voice. "I just got out of Mr. Dunlap's office. He said I've violated all kinds of firm policies. He's been tracking everything I've done for several months. He said I lied about my reason for writing that tax article and that I've been doing work without billing it to a client. He accused me of being in some kind of lottery and tax evasion conspiracy with you. He forced me to tell him everything I knew about the work I did for you." Winston stopped for a moment to catch his breath. "Basically, he scared the crap out of me. I don't know what's next, but he said he's meeting with the partners tomorrow morning. He said he's going to 'blow the lid off this conspiracy.'"

Channing sat impassively as Winston continued, waiting until he had gotten everything off his chest. "I asked if I could talk to you, but you were out of the office. I think Mr. Dunlap planned it that way, but that's just a guess. He wouldn't let me leave his office until I told him everything I knew. He threatened to fire me. I didn't know what to do. He made me write out a statement and sign it."

Channing finally interrupted. "Do you have a copy of the statement?"

"No, sir. He wouldn't let me keep a copy. He said he would put it in a big dossier that he's prepared. He plans to show everything to the partners tomorrow. What should I do?"

Channing tapped his fingers on the arm of his chair as he thought. Deciding on a plan of action, he replied. "All right, here's what you do. First, don't worry about this. I'll handle Dunlap. He talks a good game, but I know how to shut him up. Second, I need you to do some quick research for me. And I mean quick." Channing looked at his watch. "It's about two-fifteen now. I need your response by four today. Assume that somebody puts a bug in a lawyer's office and records conversations without telling the lawyer. Also, assume the same person sneaks into the lawyer's office at night and searches through his trashcan and desk. Now, get me a list of all federal and state statutes and regulations that would be violated under these facts."

Winston's eyes widened and he gasped. "You mean Mr. Dunlap did all that."

"I didn't say that. Just consider it a hypothetical situation. I need that list right away."

"Yes, sir. By four. Got it."

"And don't tell anybody about this conversation. I'll be in my office until you report back to me."

"Okay, I understand." Winston stood up, but thought of one question before leaving. "In this hypothetical research, did Mr.

Dunlap—er—I mean, did the person remove anything from the lawyer's office?"

"Assume that he did."

"Yes, sir. I'll get right on it."

"Good. And don't worry about all this. I know how to make it go away."

Winston managed a weak smile. "I hope you're right. I'll try to make the list as thorough as possible."

"That'll help."

✐✑✐

Boz guided his car into the usual parking space behind the firm's building. Uncharacteristically, he had arrived early at the office, eager to sort through his dossier and make copies to hand out at the partners' meeting. Channing's secretary had confirmed that her boss would attend the meeting, which as far as she knew would be the routine weekly gathering to discuss the firm's business. Boz had ordered Winston not to tell anyone about yesterday's confrontation. He knew Winston had visited Channing soon afterward, but the hidden microphone had not captured their conversation. Winston may have warned Channing, but it didn't matter. Boz had all the evidence he needed to bury both of them. There was no doubt that the partners would admire his detective work and reward his initiative. He would remember the morning of May twenty-seventh for a long time.

He turned off the engine and slipped the car keys into his pocket without noticing the man who was approaching from behind his vehicle. The passenger door opened without warning, and Channing was sitting beside him in an instant. Boz recoiled in horror, pressing his body against the door to his left. There was no time to gather his thoughts before Channing spoke. "Well, what a coincidence. We both got here early today."

Boz found the door handle with his left hand and gripped it tightly as Channing shut the passenger door and leaned toward him. Shock turned to fear as Boz felt the intensity of Channing's glare. His mouth began to quiver, but he managed to reply. "Uh, yeah, I gotta get ready for the meeting. I really should be going—" Boz began to open his door, but froze when Channing grabbed his arm.

"Not so fast. We need to talk about your little visit with Winston yesterday."

As the shock of seeing Channing began to wear off, Boz tried to assert himself. "Well, let's discuss that at the meeting. I have some papers to show you then."

"Maybe you do and maybe you don't. I stopped by your office last night after you left. Winston told me you had a special file. It was an interesting read, especially the documents that were stolen from my office. Did you happen to make any copies?"

Boz's jaw dropped and he gasped. Realizing that Channing had stolen his secret dossier, he was unable to control his anger. Boz had the emotional range of an atom bomb. His body shook with rage as he shouted, "You son of a bitch! You think you're so smart, don't you? Well, I'm taking you down, tough guy. For your information, I made a copy of the whole file and put it in a safe deposit box. What do you think of that?" Boz watched Channing's face but was surprised when his expression didn't change.

"What do I think? I think if anybody's going down, it's you." Channing reached into his pants pocket and pulled out his video monitor. He switched it on, turned the screen toward Boz and began to play it. As Boz watched himself sneaking into Channing's office, he struggled to catch his breath and then waved his hand at the screen and screamed at Channing. "That doesn't prove anything! I can say I was just trying to protect the firm. I needed to get evidence to prove your conspiracy. You and Winston are up to no good. You've got some kind of tax evasion scheme going on, or you're trying to steal a lottery ticket. That's what I'll tell the partners."

"You think they'll believe that crap? Winston does some research and uses the wrong billing code, and you start bugging offices and stealing documents? Sounds like you're the one who's trying to steal a lottery ticket."

"Well, you can't prove that. The partners won't believe it. In case you haven't noticed, they're a stupid bunch of incompetent fools! I'm the only guy with a brain in this firm! There's no way they'll believe you."

Channing smiled and paused for effect and then pulled a small recorder from his shirt pocket. "I think they'll believe this. I just recorded our whole conversation." He slipped the device back into his pocket, pulled out a sheet of paper, and handed it to Boz. "Here's a list of laws and regulations you broke during your so-called investigation. I didn't have much time to compile this list, so there's probably a few others I could add. But believe me, the list is long enough. I'm sure the Commonwealth's Attorney would be interested in seeing it."

Boz slumped in his seat, knowing he was trapped. "Look, maybe I went a little overboard, but you're not clean either. I've got proof that you forged your wife's signature on a power of attorney, and you made Winston violate the firm's billing policies. What's it going to take for you to forget about all this?"

"You got nothing on me, sucker. You're lucky you even have a job here. You're also lucky that I don't have time to screw around with you right now. I've got business to take care of." Channing leaned forward and pointed a finger in Boz's face. "Here's the deal. You go to your office and keep doing whatever the hell it is you do around here, and keep your mouth shut. If you ever bother me or Winston again, I'll turn all this stuff over to the partners and the Commonwealth's Attorney, and that'll be the end of you. You got that?"

Boz frowned and nodded his head, knowing there was nothing to negotiate. Channing got out of the car, slammed the door shut, and hustled away.

"I swear I'll get that bastard," Boz muttered to himself.

CHAPTER 28

Lee was dozing on his front porch when the phone rang. He reached for it with his right hand, nearly knocking it off the table, but managed to catch it before the voice mail kicked in. He mumbled a groggy "Hello."

"Lee, it's Anna. Sounds like I woke you up."

"Yeah, I came out on the porch at halftime and must have fallen asleep. What time is it?"

"Doesn't matter now, Lee. The game's over."

"Don't tell me who won. I'll replay it. The Lakers were up by six at the half."

"I missed it, but I heard it was a good game. There was a murder last night, so I had to come in to work. So much for my Memorial Day weekend."

"Sorry, Anna. How's the investigation going?"

"There were some prints at the scene and two witnesses, so we've got some leads. Anyway, since we were running prints I included your camera in the batch. I've been waiting for a chance to check all the databases without doing a special request."

"Thanks. I was going to call you soon to check on it. It wasn't a rush, but I need to know pretty soon, or it'll be too late."

"Okay. Well, I have good news and bad news. The bad news is we couldn't get any clear prints on the camera. The only ones we could identify are yours."

"Too bad. I was afraid of that. I used the camera several times, so I must have wiped out any others."

"That's the way it looks. There are some partial prints that don't look like yours, but not enough to trace."

"All right. You said there's some good news?"

"Well, it depends on what you need. We checked the memory card inside. There was a good print there. We got a hit on a database in Virginia, but I don't know if you're interested in prints that aren't on the outside of the camera."

"I'll take whatever you can give me."

"Okay. The print belongs to Fordham Channing Booker. It looks like he got into the system when he visited someone in a Virginia prison. They often take prints and run a background check on visitors, like we do in South Carolina. I don't have any other information on this guy. He doesn't have any criminal convictions on record."

Lee grabbed a pen and jotted the name down. "That's okay, Anna. No problem at all. It's a good lead. I didn't have much to go on before. Thanks a lot."

"Sure. Listen, I don't want to pry into your business. I know you said you'd like to keep this confidential, but if it's something criminal we could help you investigate it further."

"Thanks. I really appreciate it, but for now that's all I need. I owe you one."

"No problem. I'm glad to help. I hope you'll stop in at the station and see us. We miss you down here."

"Great. Thanks again. Say hi to Alex for me."

"I sure will. He should be back in on Tuesday. Take it easy, Lee."

Lee said goodbye and leaned back in his chair. He was still a little sleepy and decided to enjoy the warm afternoon air before gearing up his investigation. The traffic on the street in front of his yard was light on a Sunday afternoon. He wanted to thank Alex and Anna, but that might have to wait. The lottery ticket was set to expire in ten days. After the dust settled he would take them out to a nice dinner and get the camera back. He went inside and settled into his favorite reclining chair.

Switching on his laptop computer, he logged onto the Internet and checked alerts for new eBay listings from "Trotter." This time the seller had listed two books by Chaucer, and Lee quickly placed bids that were generous and well over market value. As he watched the replay of the basketball game, he conducted multiple searches to find any available information about Fordham Channing Booker. He pursued every lead to its end, getting distracted only a few times when his searches veered off course into sports topics and a few titillating websites.

By the time he finished he had collected various details about his target. According to the website for the law firm of Dunlap & Cranston, F. Channing Booker was a partner at the firm, specializing in criminal law. He was a graduate of Temple University Beasley School of Law and practiced primarily in Central Virginia. The firm's website showed a picture of Channing and his partners, all with broad smiles on their faces, sitting at a large round conference table with rows of law books on shelves in the background. Channing's home address was listed in the Charlottesville telephone directory. He had married Susan Marie Finley in Virginia almost eight years ago and had honeymooned in Europe. A wedding announcement in a newspaper's online archives added some biographical information and showed a picture of the happy couple. It listed their parents' names as well. There were dozens of newspaper articles reporting on cases that Channing had litigated over the years, most of which involved serious criminal charges.

Lee logged onto the camera manufacturer's website and searched for product registration information, but was unable to access records for his camera without knowing the date of purchase. There was a customer service number, though. He located the file he had created before giving the camera to Alex and Anna and opened it on his computer screen. Reaching for his phone, he called the number. A voice with a foreign accent answered and asked how he might be of service today.

"Hello. I bought one of your cameras a while ago but lost my paperwork. I'm trying to find out if it's still under warranty. Can you look that up for me if I give you the serial number?"

"I'm very sorry you're having a problem with the camera, sir. I can transfer you to our repair technicians and they can help you troubleshoot the issue, or they can tell you where to get warranty service in your area."

"No, thanks. All I really need is to see if it's still under warranty." Lee identified the camera model and read the serial number and then was put on hold. Gentle music played on the line while he waited. Finally the voice returned.

"I believe I can help you with this request. Please tell me your name and the place and date of purchase."

"My name is Channing Booker, but it's possible that I registered the camera under my wife's name. Her name is Susan Booker. She gave it to me as a birthday present, and I don't know where she bought it, but it was probably in Virginia or Pennsylvania."

"I see. And the date of purchase, please?"

"Yes. Well, you see, that's why I called you today. I can't remember how long ago we got the camera, so I can't tell if it's still under warranty. If you could just look it up and tell me, that's what I need."

"I see, sir. Yes, I believe I can assist you with that request. Please hold."

In a few minutes he came back on the line. "Mr. Booker, I must inform you that the warranty has expired for this camera. It was a one-year, parts-and-labor warranty. However, if you pay today for an extended warranty, we can waive fifty percent of the cost of repair, or we can—"

Running out of patience, Lee stopped him in mid-sentence. "Look, I'm sorry to interrupt, but I just wanted to confirm the warranty information. So you have it listed under my name, is that correct?"

"No, sir. The original purchaser registered it under the name Susan Booker."

"Great. Thanks a lot."

Lee was now convinced that Channing or Susan Booker had taken the photo of the winning lottery ticket. He copied Channing's picture from the law firm's website and printed it out. He began a slide show on his computer, playing the surveillance photos he had copied off the DVD from Wally's gas station. He hoped he could identify Susan or Channing buying a lottery ticket at the counter. After more than an hour he decided it was probably not worth the effort. Most of the photos were out of focus, and the camera angle was off to one side. Many of the customers approaching the counter were not looking directly at the lens. Some wore caps that partially obscured their faces. There were hundreds of photos taken over a period of several days. He could try looking at them later if he got desperate, but for now his time would be better spent investigating in the field.

∽∾∽

Billy sat inside his car and watched pedestrians strolling along the sidewalk near the Law Offices of Lucas Morton. He had managed to find a parking space with an unobstructed view of the office entrance, and earlier in the day a tree had provided shade from the intense heat. As the sun moved westward the shade had shifted away from his car, and his shirt was moist with perspiration. Occasionally he rolled the windows up and ran the air conditioner, but decided that he might attract too much attention if he kept the engine running all day.

He had picked out his spot early in the morning, well before most of the shops opened. Channing was not sure when Susan would arrive, and had told Billy to be on the street in time to identify her vehicle when it approached. Apparently she had parked several streets away and walked to the office. By the time he spotted her she was already near the building. The photo that Channing supplied did not match her appearance. She wore sunglasses and was either wearing a wig or had dyed her hair blonde. She carried a large tote bag in one hand.

Channing and Sully had arrived at nine-thirty. As soon as they went inside, Billy pressed an earphone into place and switched on the receiver at his side. Channing had hoped to meet Lucas in his office before the depositions began, and was carrying two transmitters in case he had an opportunity to plant one of them there. Channing suggested they meet in his office to discuss the case, but Lucas insisted that they wait in the lobby until it was time to go to the conference room. Given his past experience with Channing, Lucas was taking no chances.

Billy began receiving the audio signal shortly after the receptionist ushered Sully and Channing into the conference room to begin the depositions. Susan testified first. Sully asked the questions while Channing sat quietly at his side. Billy was surprised at how gently Sully treated Susan. He had expected that Channing would turn the divorce proceedings into a dogfight, but that was simply an assumption because Channing had said little about the case. He thought Channing's lawyer would pry embarrassing information from Susan, ammunition to be used against her at trial.

Sully began with some basic questions about the marriage and Susan's employment history. It soon became apparent that Susan was not going to volunteer any information. She answered each question briefly, without offering to elaborate. Apparently Sully was fishing for a clue as to where she had been living, but she gave no hint. Finally, Sully asked her directly, but Lucas objected. Evidently there was nothing that Sully could do during the deposition to overcome the objection, but he did state for the record that he would be filing a motion to compel an answer to the question.

Sully moved on to some other routine questions and then raised the issue of Susan's assets. He reviewed the items on the list that she provided, asking innocuous questions about the value of various items. He asked about the history of certain pieces of furniture, and Susan dutifully explained which ones were gifts, which ones she had purchased, and when she had acquired them. Billy was puzzled by Sully's line of questions, but his job was not to analyze Susan's testimony.

During the lengthy discussion of Susan's assets, Sully asked about her books. He asked about specific titles that she owned and whether she had complete collections of the works of several authors. He asked if any of the books had particular sentimental value.

She seemed willing to answer, but Lucas objected and instructed her not to respond. He advised Sully that only the books' market value was relevant, and Sully moved on to other questions. At one point, he asked about the condition of the books and their whereabouts. Lucas objected as to the books' location, but allowed Susan to testify about their condition. She gave a general answer but could not recall details about specific titles. Sully moved on to ask about other items of property, giving no overt indication that all he really cared about was the books. The whole process mystified Billy, but if Channing wanted to pay him to sit in his car and eavesdrop all day long, that was fine with him.

There was a short break after Susan's deposition ended, and Channing and Sully excused themselves to go use the restroom. As soon as they left, Susan began asking Lucas questions, but he told her to wait until they got back to his office. They chatted for a few minutes about the weather and the drapes in the conference room, and then Susan left the room before Channing and Sully returned.

Lucas questioned Channing for about two hours, asking him to disclose information about his drug use, gambling habits, income, and assets. He probed relentlessly for intimate details about Channing's affairs with other women during his marriage. The difference in tone between the two depositions was striking. Surprisingly, Sully objected only a few times, and Channing seemed to handle the brutal questions with a modicum of dignity. Billy had expected Channing to explode with anger, but he kept his cool.

When the deposition ended, Sully suggested that the parties retire to Lucas's office to discuss the possibility of settlement. Lucas dismissed the idea but promised to get in touch soon.

Having failed in his effort to bug Lucas's own office, Channing stuffed his notes and documents into his briefcase, and he and Sully exited the building. A few minutes later a paralegal came outside and glanced up and down the street to confirm that the two had disappeared. The bug that Channing had placed in the conference room continued to transmit, but all Billy could hear was the sound of a door closing as Lucas and Susan left. As Channing had instructed, Billy waited in the car and kept a close eye on the front entrance, while Channing was watching the door at the rear of the building.

About a half hour later, two blonde women wearing sunglasses emerged from the front entrance and began walking down the street. One of them followed the other at a short distance while speaking on a cell phone. The woman in front was dressed in the outfit Susan had worn when Billy saw her earlier in the day, and she carried the same large bag. Billy waited until they were about a block away and then started his engine. The women headed to a parking lot next to a department store. They spoke briefly, and then the first one got into a car while the second one went into the building.

Billy reached for his phone and called Channing, who was still watching the back entrance at the law firm. "Channing, two women came out front, and one just got into a car. The other one went inside a store. I think your wife's the one in the car, but I'm not sure."

"Follow the car and don't lose it. Give me the store name and I'll get there as soon as I can."

"Okay, I can't see the name from here, but it's a furniture store about four blocks up from the office. There's a green sofa in the window. You can't miss it. She went in the side door. I have to go. Susan's leaving."

"Stay with her, whatever you do. Let me know where she goes. I'm on my way to the store."

Billy followed the car at a distance. It circled around the block and turned back onto Main Street, passing a movie theater and a row of shops before leaving town. The car maintained a moderate speed as it headed west. About five miles beyond the edge of town, it turned in at an apartment complex and parked near a stairwell. Billy drove past the car and backed into a space at the far end of the lot. The woman exited her vehicle and climbed up the stairs to the third floor. Billy got out of the car and walked in her direction, keeping her in sight as she pulled keys from the tote bag and went inside. He memorized the apartment number and walked back to his car to phone Channing, who was breathing rapidly when he answered the call.

"What've you got, Billy?"

"She's in number three-fifteen at the Blue Ridge Apartments. It's a few minutes west of town. I'm in the parking lot with her door in sight. What do you want me to do?"

"Stay there for now," Channing answered. He paused to catch his breath before continuing. "I've been running all around this store and can't find the woman you were following. A sales clerk said a blonde woman came in through the side door and went straight to the front door and left. She said the lady was in a hurry. I think they pulled a switch on us. That was probably Susan. Are you sure they didn't talk about Susan's books or where she lives when we left the conference room?"

"Yeah, I'm sure. You can listen to the recording if you want to, but they didn't talk about that stuff. So what are you going to do now?"

"I'm desperate, so I'm going to the Charlottesville Airport. I'm guessing she's not living in the area, since she got a parking ticket in West Virginia after she left me. It's a long shot, but maybe I can find her at the airport and see where she's going. Watch the apartment until the woman leaves, then stick with her. Give me the license number on her car, and I'll have an investigator run it down to see who owns it. I've got to get going. I'll check with you later. Let me know if anything happens there."

Channing ran as fast as he could back to the parking lot behind Lucas's law office. A short time later he was traveling south on Route 29 toward Charlottesville. He drove only ten miles over the speed limit, hoping to avoid being pulled over. He considered driving faster, but Susan could not have more than a fifteen-minute head start, and if she was going to the airport, she would probably have to wait for a flight. He arrived at the airport in forty minutes, driving quickly through the main parking lot as he searched unsuccessfully for Susan's Volkswagen Passat.

He parked in a spot that allowed him to watch most of the terminal's entrances. There was moderate traffic circulating outside, as travelers were dropped off and picked up near the large glass doors that faced the parking area. Channing waited in the car for about an hour, occasionally glancing away from the terminal to watch activity in the parking lot. He was unable to monitor the movements of every vehicle and pedestrian and was unaware when Susan drove a rental car through the parking lot and down to the far end of the terminal.

She guided the car around to the back of the small rental office building and went through the rear entrance to return the car. A few minutes later she exited the office with a small suitcase in tow, no longer wearing her blond wig. She had changed out of the dress she wore at the deposition and was now wearing an old pair of blue jeans. She had a baseball cap pulled low over her forehead and kept her sunglasses on as she walked along the front of the terminal to reach the nearest entrance. She glanced around several times to confirm that no one was following her.

As she approached the entrance, she caught a glimpse of a familiar vehicle in the lot and paused to take a closer look. At the same instant, she realized that someone in the driver's seat was watching her. Although the car was a considerable distance away, she was fairly sure that the person she saw was Channing. She quickly looked away and hurried into the terminal. She had planned to check her luggage, but there were several people in line at the counter and her suitcase was small enough to carry onto the plane. She darted to the security station, nervously glancing about as she was cleared into the waiting area. Reclaiming her suitcase, she slipped into a restroom.

She looked at her boarding pass and checked her watch. Her flight was due to leave in an hour. Although she could not be sure the person in the parking lot was Channing, the car matched his and the man inside resembled him closely. She was not eager to spend the better part of an hour in the restroom, but she had already put so much effort into avoiding Channing that she decided to stay where it was safe. She paced back and forth, occasionally looking into the mirror to comb her hair whenever other women came in, hoping she wouldn't arouse any interest or suspicion. Knowing Channing, she could imagine him paying a bystander to go into the restroom and look for a woman who matched her description.

Her nerves refused to calm down as she carried her luggage into one of the stalls. With little space to maneuver, she managed to open her suitcase and pull out a change of clothing. Unable to stretch her legs fully, she struggled to slip off her blue jeans and step into a pair of dark slacks. She took off her blouse, replaced it with a plain white T-shirt, and put on her blonde wig. Boarding announcements echoed from a loudspeaker just outside the restroom door, and as soon as her flight was called, she exited the stall, glanced at the mirror, and quickly combed her wig.

She opened the door far enough to see in several directions. She pulled a slip of paper from her pants pocket and looked down at it, pretending to read it as she headed across a large open area toward an escalator. When she reached the upper level, she spotted a line of passengers waiting to board her flight. As she stepped to the back of the line, she looked back and was shocked to see Channing approaching the bottom of the escalator.

Setting the suitcase behind her to claim a spot in line, she moved up beside the next person, using his body to shield her from Channing's view. The man gave her a puzzled look and then smiled in the apparent hope that she would strike up a conversation. He started to speak, but she held a finger up to her lips and whispered, "There's a guy coming up the escalator who's been following me. I'm trying to hide from him. Please don't turn your head or say anything."

The man nodded and mouthed the word "Okay."

She leaned her head back just enough to catch a glimpse of Channing as he reached the bottom of the escalator. The line moved forward a bit as another passenger was cleared to pass the ticket counter. Channing was looking around in several directions, so she guessed that he had not seen her yet, but the line wasn't moving fast enough. Unless he went in another direction when he reached the top, Channing would get to her before she could pass the counter. She picked up her suitcase and moved forward, passing five people in line until she reached the ticket agent. Holding out her boarding pass, she spoke softly. "Excuse me, I'm terribly sorry to break the line like this, but there's a man who's been stalking me, and he's right back there." She motioned with her head and looked in Channing's direction. "Please help me."

The agent glanced back and spotted him at a distance of about thirty yards. Channing saw him look up, just as several people at the front of the line turned around to stare in his direction. He ran forward, heading straight toward Susan.

The ticket agent grabbed Susan's boarding pass and quickly

motioned with his arm. "Go! I'll try to stop him."

Susan dashed through a door and found herself on the tarmac outside the building. A midsized commuter plane was directly ahead of her, about forty yards away. Without looking back, she started to run, gripping the suitcase tightly as it bounced against her leg. Inside the terminal, Channing headed straight for the exit as the ticket agent stepped away from the counter to block the door. Short of breath, Channing stopped just in front of him and spoke quickly. "I have to catch up to that woman. I'm her husband, and it's urgent." He tried to brush past the agent, but he resisted, and a crowd began to form nearby.

"Sir, I can't let you through without a boarding pass. Please step aside."

Channing shook his head. "I understand, but it's an urgent matter. I'll come right back." As he spoke, Channing shoved the agent aside and charged past him. The agent reached out to grab his arm but was too late. Rushing back to the ticket counter, he pressed a red emergency button. As an alarm bell blared, a security officer appeared in an instant from an office that was shielded by one-way glass. Holding the door open, the agent pointed to Channing, who was running on the tarmac, gasping for breath as he chased Susan.

Susan had almost reached the steps that led up to the plane's entry door when she heard the alarm. Turning her head, she saw Channing coming straight toward her. She slipped by a young girl who was about to climb up to the plane, shouting "sorry" as she shoved her aside and leapt onto the steps. The security officer sprinted across the tarmac, dodging a baggage vehicle before catching Channing by the arm, just as he approached the aircraft.

"Hold it right there!" he commanded.

Channing frowned and was prepared to resist, but he was completely out of breath and would have been no match for the officer. Panting like a dog on a summer day, Channing protested. "My wife forgot her medicine. It's an emergency. I'm just trying to catch her and let her know."

The officer gripped Channing's arm as Susan ducked into the plane. She looked back to see that Channing had been stopped and then disappeared, tugging the suitcase behind her.

The officer planted himself between Channing and the plane, addressing him in a stern voice. "Sir, do you have a boarding pass?"

Channing continued to breathe rapidly, leaning forward and

stooping over as he tried to catch his breath. In a few moments he replied. "No, sir, Officer. Like I said, I was just trying to tell my wife she left her medicine."

The officer scowled. "Sir, this is a restricted area. If you need to contact your wife, you have to tell the ticket agent. You can't just run out here. Now, let's go back inside and talk about this."

Releasing Channing's arm and putting his own arm behind Channing's back, the officer firmly guided him back inside the terminal. As the door closed behind them, the officer instructed the ticket agent to contact the tower and keep the plane on the ground.

Turning to the small group of passengers who had assembled nearby, the officer announced that they could continue to board. "There will be a slight delay, but everything is fine. Thanks for your cooperation." He escorted Channing to the security office, locked the door, and instructed him to sit in front of a desk in the middle of the room. "I'm Officer Parker. Gillespie Parker. And you are?" Channing opened his wallet, removed his driver's license and handed it to the officer. "All right Mr. Booker, now what's this all about?"

"Officer, I apologize for any inconvenience. I didn't realize the rules are so strict. My wife forgot some medicine, and I was just trying to catch her to let her know. It was just a misunderstanding. I didn't mean to cause any trouble."

Parker sat at the desk and put the driver's license next to his computer while he typed on the keyboard. "I see. And how did you arrive at the airport today?"

"I drove myself."

"So your car is parked outside?"

"Yes, sir, that's correct."

Parker picked up his phone and summoned another officer, who appeared in an instant. "This is Officer Sydney Broylan. She'll take you to your car to retrieve the medicine."

Channing shifted in his chair and clasped his hands together to keep them from shaking. He coughed several times to give himself time to think. "Pardon me. The pollen in the air has affected my sinuses. Actually, the medication isn't in the car. My wife left it at a hotel, and the manager called me to let me know. I wanted to tell her I would get a new prescription and email it to her. Actually, if you could give me the phone number for the other airport, I could contact them and maybe get a message to her when she lands."

The two officers exchanged glances before Parker responded. "Which airport are you talking about? What is her destination?"

Channing pressed his hands tightly together against his stomach. His shirt was damp with perspiration. He had gotten overheated while running across the hot tarmac, and his throat was getting drier as his story started to unravel. He hoped his voice wouldn't falter and reveal his nervousness. "Uh, well, to be honest I'm not sure. She told me she had to take a connecting flight. I was hoping you could look up her schedule and help me track her down."

"Couldn't you just call her?"

"Well, I think her cell phone battery is dead. Or actually, the hotel may have found it. In all the confusion, I can't remember exactly what they told me. You know, I was in such a hurry to get here, I can't remember all the details."

Officer Parker caught a glimpse of his partner shaking her head. "Mr. Booker, this is a very serious situation. You violated several federal aviation regulations. You may well be telling the truth, but we're going to have to investigate this matter fully. I'm sure you understand that our highest priority is the safety of our passengers and crew."

"Yes, I understand. Again, I apologize for any inconvenience. I don't want to take up too much of your time. I'm sure I can get hold of her on my own. If you don't mind, I'll just check with the airline out front. They should be able to take care of it."

Channing could hear the irritation in Parker's voice as he replied. "Mr. Booker, as I said, we're going to have to investigate this before you can go. I'm requesting that you take everything out of your pockets and place it on this desk, and allow Officer Broylan to search your car. Now, you can refuse to give permission, but we can get a search warrant, and that will delay this whole process."

As a lawyer, Channing's instinctive reaction was to object and fight the matter in court, but he knew there was little to gain by resisting. With just nine days to go before the ticket expired, he had no time for distractions. "Okay, I'll be happy to cooperate. I know you're just doing your job, and I don't have anything to hide. I'd like to accompany the officer during the search, if that's all right with you two."

Officer Broylan nodded and Parker agreed. Channing handed over his keys, emptied his pockets, and left with Broylan. They returned about twenty minutes later, and Channing waited in

Parker's office while the two officers huddled in the next room. In a few minutes, they came in to speak with him again.

Parker did all the talking. "All right, here's the situation. Officer Broylan indicates that she found no contraband in your vehicle. While you were gone, I asked the crew on the plane to talk to your wife. She confirmed that she knows you but says she's not on any medication and doesn't want to talk to you. I don't know what kind of game you're playing here, but we could have you arrested based on the disruption that you've caused today. Now, do you want to tell me what's really going on, or do you want to do this the hard way?"

Channing did his best to sound contrite. "Look, I don't want to make this difficult. The truth is, my wife and I are getting divorced, and we had a meeting with her lawyer this morning. I just wanted to talk to her to see if we could work things out without a bunch of lawyers making it more complicated. There's no restraining order on me or anything like that. We didn't have a chance for just the two of us to talk this morning, so I just wanted to meet with her privately. That's all it was. I admit I went a little overboard, but you can see I don't have any weapons or anything. I didn't threaten anybody. I was planning to talk to her out in the parking lot, but I didn't see her out there so I came inside. She was about to get on the plane before I could get her attention. It was just a dumb mistake. I apologize again."

"I see. Well, your wife confirmed most of that. If this was my call to make, I'd have you arrested. But your wife doesn't want to testify, and my supervisor is willing to let this go if you agree to give a sworn statement and plead guilty to disorderly conduct. We'll let the federal charges go, and you can pay a fine. I recommend that you accept this offer. It's the only one you're going to get."

Channing quickly agreed and was escorted to another office to give a statement and sign some papers. An hour later, he was back in his car and on the phone with Billy, who was still in the parking lot at the Blue Ridge Apartments. "Anything going on there, Billy?"

"Nothing at all. She hasn't left the apartment since we got here."

"Well, whoever she is, she's not Susan. I tricked the cops into confirming that Susan is the woman who got on the plane. I tried to get her ticket to see where she was going, but she got away. All I know is where her flight was headed, but it's probably just a layover."

"How could you let her get away? I thought you were desperate to find her!"

"It's a long story, man. Now I really am desperate. I'm guessing the woman you're watching is a secretary at Lucas's law firm. Stay there and follow her wherever she goes. If she returns to the law office, watch the building and follow her when she leaves."

"Well it's about six now. I doubt she'll be going back there tonight."

"Yeah, I know. You'll have to spend the night there. Sorry, but I'll make it worth your time. Let me know where she goes tomorrow. If she goes to the law office, then we've got two options. We can try to bribe her to get Susan's address, or we can break into the office and try to find it."

"Well, I hope she talks 'cause it's gonna be risky to break into a law office. They've probably got a good security system."

"Yeah, I saw sensors all over the place when I was in there today. Do you think you can get in there?"

Billy hesitated before answering, as he considered the implications of Channing's question. He was being paid well for his work, but not enough money if there was a significant risk of being caught. He had already taken a chance when he broke into Susan's parents' house to bug it, but they had no security alarm. "Chan, I don't know. I haven't seen their system, and I really don't want to go back to jail. Are you sure you want to get into something like this?"

"Billy, I'm desperate. I thought I'd have Susan's location pinned down by now, but I don't see any other way to get it by the time I need it. I'll pay big money if you'll do this."

"Well, we can talk about it if this woman won't give up the information."

"Okay, let's do this. If you see her go to the law office, I'll bring some bribe money and you can make her an offer. I'd like you to do it because if she works for Lucas, she might recognize me. If possible, I don't want Susan to know I'm involved, but if this woman won't help us, then I'll do whatever it takes. I'm thinking you could go to the office and pretend you need a lawyer. You could take a look around and see what kind of security they've got."

"Good idea, but if the woman doesn't take the bribe, then she'll know who I am if I go in there. I could probably get my brother to go take a look around."

"Okay, good idea. Keep in touch."

CHAPTER 29

Susan was in the living room, surrounded by boxes and packing materials, when Sylvia returned from work. Susan had arrived home after midnight and slept until midmorning, hours after Sylvia had gone to the office. Trotter was sprawled on a couch but jumped off to greet his owner when she walked into the room. She patted him on the back and greeted Susan. "Hey there, sorry I faded out before you got back last night."

"No problem. I didn't expect you to stay up."

"So how did it go?"

Susan followed a narrow path between several boxes and books as she walked to the couch and sat down. Sylvia joined her as Trotter parked himself at their feet. "Well, it was okay until I was at the airport on the way back. I don't know how he did it, but Channing followed me there and almost attacked me in broad daylight. I'm lucky I got away. I swear, the man's crazy."

Sylvia touched her arm and gasped. "Oh, no! What happened? Didn't your escape plan work?"

"I thought it worked like a charm until I saw him at the airport. When I left the office with Lucas's secretary we didn't see anybody following us. I slipped through the store like we planned and headed to the airport. The secretary called me when she got home and said she didn't see anybody, so we thought everything was fine, but then when I got to the airport I thought I saw Channing in the parking lot. I changed clothes in a bathroom and was ready to board the plane when he came after me. I ran for the plane, and luckily a cop stopped him before he got to me. They asked me some questions on the plane and then let it take off. I don't know what happened to Channing, but I don't think he could track me here. He knows where the commuter flight went, but I don't think he can find out where my connecting flight went after the layover."

"Wow, I hope you're right. At least you used my credit card to book the flight. I hope he can't figure out a way to access the airline's billing records."

Susan wiped her forehead and shook her head. "I don't know. He's a slick bastard. It looks like I was right to hide from him and avoid using my credit cards all these months. It's not convenient, but it's the safest thing to do."

"Yeah, but it's strange that he tried to attack you. I thought Lucas said he had been hinting at a divorce settlement."

"Well, I can't figure that out. I don't know what he's up to, but his lawyer asked some strange questions at the deposition. He wanted to know if some of the things I took from the house have sentimental value. Lucas said that's irrelevant, so I don't know what Channing's doing, but I don't trust him one bit. It's like he's thinking of trying to get some of my property. And there's more bad news.

"He doesn't have much money left. His list of assets was pretty skimpy. Lucas is going to investigate it, but if the list is for real, then I won't get much money out of Channing." Sylvia patted Susan's arm and tried to comfort her as she continued. "I'm going to sell more stuff to tide me over until I can get a job. I don't know what Channing's trying to do, but if he wants to take my things just to hurt me, then I'd rather sell them to somebody else."

"I thought you were holding off on working so Channing couldn't track you down through Social Security or tax records," Sylvia replied.

"You're right, but at some point, I've got to take a chance. Plus I won't be getting much alimony, at least not the way things look now."

"Well, you can keep helping me around the farm or at the office until you get something more permanent. I could delay paying you until next January so you won't have to file a tax return anytime soon."

Susan's voice wavered as she looked Sylvia in the eyes and responded. "You've been incredibly good to me. I can't tell you how much it means to have such a good friend."

∽✄∽

Channing pulled into his garage and turned off the engine. He dreaded what was coming later that night. Billy would arrive in an hour with whatever equipment he felt was needed, and the two would drive to Culpeper together. The plan was fraught with risk, but Channing had run out of options. In one week the lottery ticket would expire.

Billy had followed the unidentified woman yesterday as she left her apartment. She drove to Lucas Morton's law office and remained there all day, so it was apparent that she was one of the firm's employees. Billy approached her that evening as she returned home, handing her $300 just to listen to his proposal. He explained that he was a private investigator trying to locate a woman who had failed to pay off her car loan and had disappeared with the vehicle. It was an expensive import, and she still owed more than $50,000 to Billy's client. He had seen Susan's name in a newspaper's legal notice when her husband filed for divorce. Checking the court file a few weeks later, he found her responsive pleading, filed by her Culpeper lawyer. If the secretary would provide Susan's address in confidence, Billy would pay her another $1000, and his client could repossess the car. He assured her that it was a routine request, one that had worked well on many occasions in the past. She agreed to think it over, and Billy gave her his phone number.

Earlier today, she had called Billy with unfortunate news. Susan's file did not list her address, which was unusual. A note in the file indicated that her location was confidential and that any communication with her must go through Lucas himself. With next Wednesday's deadline approaching, Channing's only alternative now was to break into the law office and hope that Susan's address was somewhere in Lucas's desk or on his computer.

Billy's brother had consulted briefly with Lucas earlier that afternoon, dropping in without an appointment to ask about representation for a charge of reckless driving. Since he had not brought his traffic summons with him, he made an appointment to return in a few days. He got a quick look at several security alarm sensors that were visible in the offices and reported his observations to Billy, who had spent the afternoon gathering information and tools that might disarm the system. Billy warned that there was no guarantee it would work, and he insisted that as soon as the system was deactivated he would leave the building.

Channing would be on his own while Billy kept a lookout from a safe distance down the street. If he could not disable the alarm within a few minutes of entering the building, Billy would immediately abort the mission. At that point, Channing could stay or go, but Billy would be out of the picture entirely.

Channing left the garage and entered his house through the front door, stopping to pick up the mail on the way. He would eat a quick dinner, change clothes, and then wait for Billy to arrive. He sorted through the mail as he headed to the kitchen, stopping in his tracks when he came to an envelope addressed to Susan. The letter was from his health insurance company and was marked personal and confidential. The envelope did not have the appearance of junk mail, and he opened it and began to read.

> *Dear Ms. Booker:*
> *An independent auditing firm has reviewed our accounts as part of our ongoing effort to ensure that we maintain the highest standards of accounting and good business practices. This review was conducted in a manner that ensures the privacy of our policyholders and confidentiality of all medical records. The audit revealed an open claim for charges associated with treatment that you received at Saint Albert Hospital in Charleston, West Virginia. An initial treatment authorization request was received and granted on an emergency basis. However, no additional information was provided to support the claim.*
> *Your contract requires that all invoices must be received from any health care provider within six months of treatment. Failure to submit invoices and supporting documentation within such time will result in automatic denial of the claim. Attached is a copy of the initial authorization request that was submitted electronically on the date of your admission to the hospital. This form identifies the health care provider(s) and contains pertinent information about your claim. If you intend to pursue your claim, the provider(s) must submit the appropriate information within six months of the initial request date as shown on the attachment. Thank you for your cooperation.*
> *Sincerely,*
> *Robert James, Jr.*
> *Claims Specialist*

The attachment showed that an emergency authorization was requested by the hospital for treatment on December eleventh, the Tuesday after Susan had disappeared from home, soon after she received a parking ticket in Charleston. Channing was convinced that Susan was living in Charleston or somewhere nearby. Billy hadn't been able to trace her when he investigated the parking ticket, but he had no way of knowing she had been hospitalized. There was a chance that the hospital's medical records would have Susan's new address, or contain some clue as to her whereabouts. As Susan's husband and with a forged power of attorney, Channing could easily obtain her treatment records. There was no risk involved in pursuing this lead, unlike the hazards inherent in his plan to break into Lucas's office later that evening. There was just enough time to get the medical records and then, if it was still necessary, to raid the law office later.

When Billy arrived, Channing met him in the driveway before he got out of his car. The back seat was covered with burglary tools and electronic equipment to be used in Culpeper. Billy cut off his engine and got out of the car, and the two men spoke briefly.

"Billy, there's been a change of plans. I'm going to hold off on the Culpeper operation for now. I got lucky with a clue that I need to follow up on. It'll be safer to check it out first, and maybe we won't need to go to Culpeper after all."

"What are you talking about, man? After all this time you got a break? What happened?"

"Just today I got a notice from my insurance company. It turns out that Susan was in a hospital last December in Charleston, West Virginia, around the same time she got that parking ticket. If I get hold of her medical records, I can probably get her address or track her by finding out how she paid her bill. She never confirmed a claim with the insurance company, so she must have paid by check or credit card, or maybe she's still paying it off over time. She must be living somewhere in West Virginia."

"Maybe so. It's worth checking out, and a lot easier than busting into that law firm. There's a good chance you'd get caught if you went through with that."

Channing glanced through the car window at the gear in the back seat and replied, "I don't know. It looks like you've got enough stuff to get me in and out of there. But you're right, it's risky. I don't want to do it unless I have to."

"Okay, so what do you want me to do? Just sit tight until I hear from you?"

"Well, I think we should both go to Charleston. I don't have time to screw around with this, and two of us can work faster. I don't know what we'll have to do out there. Anyway, I'd have to get back here before we could go to Culpeper, so it won't be any faster if you stay here. I doubt I can do anything at the hospital in the middle of the night, so let's leave tomorrow morning. Say around eight. I'll pick you up and we'll go together. If we have to split up in Charleston, I'll get you a car."

Billy nodded and got back in his car. Before closing the door he confirmed the time, and Channing told him to get some sleep. Billy drove away, not noticing a dark green sedan parked across the street with a man inside, crouching down low and pointing an electronic eavesdropping device toward Channing's house.

CHAPTER 30

Billy waited in the hospital cafeteria, eating a late lunch while Channing searched for the billing department. A receptionist at the main desk directed Channing to the bursar's office on the third floor. He stepped off the elevator and consulted a floor directory, then headed down the corridor. He hated the whole idea of walking through a hospital, as it was depressing to see so many patients and visitors with grim expressions. Fortunately two attractive nurses passed by, but he was on a mission and had no time to follow them. He quickly located the office and went inside, where a young secretary was busy typing on a computer keyboard when he walked in.

"Good afternoon, ma'am. I'm Channing Booker. My wife was a patient here last December." As he spoke, he reached in his pocket and pulled out the insurance letter. "I got this letter from our health insurance company, and there seems to be a problem with the billing. Can you help me straighten this out?"

The secretary skimmed through the letter before answering. "Let's see, this was last December. Oh yeah, we had some trouble with our records back then. There was a huge snowstorm and a lot of employees couldn't get in here for several days. It could be that something got lost in the shuffle back then. I'll need to see some identification before I can help you, though."

Channing smiled and handed her his driver's license, as well as a power of attorney, explaining that he was both Susan's husband and her attorney. Exuding a false but convincing charm, he made every effort to impress her with his authority.

Unaware that he was a snake in disguise, the secretary was fooled by his demeanor. Channing's experience in front of juries had taught him that when you can fake sincerity you've got it made.

He requested paper copies of Susan's entire hospitalization records. The secretary typed some information into her computer and replied that there were fifty-eight pages of records. She noted that the hospital charged a copy fee of $2.00 per page, and Channing promptly pulled out his wallet. He found two $100 bills and handed them across the counter, smiling and telling her to keep the change.

She objected at first. "Thanks, but I'm not supposed to accept tips."

"I understand, but you deserve it for being so helpful. With these records, I'll be able to collect a lot of insurance money, so I'm happy to reward you for your time. I don't need a receipt."

"Well, I guess it'll be okay just this once," she replied.

"Absolutely. It's just between you and me. You know, my wife told me the staff treated her extremely well here, and I can see why she was so pleased. You all do a wonderful job here," Channing gushed.

"Well thank you very much. I don't like to brag, but last year our hospital was ranked number one in a patient quality survey. We came out ahead of all the other hospitals in Charleston," she beamed.

"That's remarkable," Channing exclaimed. "But I'm not surprised. You folks are great!"

The secretary smiled broadly and then excused herself to retrieve the records from a printer that churned them out nearby. She returned with a stack of paper and gently set the pile in front of Channing. "Do you need a folder or a metal clip to bind them?" she offered.

Channing held the papers upright in his hand and lightly tapped the bottoms of the pages against the counter to keep them neatly together. "I think I'll be fine just like this," he answered. Before turning away, he snapped his fingers and set the records back on the counter. "Oh, I almost forgot. My wife wanted me to get the name of the patient she shared her room with. She said they got to know each other well, but she forgot to get her name so she could check back to see how she's doing. A few days after my wife was discharged, she came back to visit her roommate, but she couldn't find her. Things were kind of hectic at the time, so she didn't follow up with anyone. If you could just look her up, my wife would really appreciate it."

The secretary hesitated before answering, weighing her options. "Gee, I'd like to help out, but I'm not supposed to give out patients' names except to next of kin. You know, it's to keep things confidential and private and all that."

Channing nodded as if in agreement, but pressed on. "Yeah, I know, things have gotten so official nowadays. Everything's by the book. There's so much red tape to deal with. Really all I need is the patient's name, though. I wouldn't want any private details on her medical condition or anything like that. You know, my wife just wants to follow up with her to see how she's doing, and thank her for being so kind when she was here. I promise I won't get you in trouble. I'd be glad to pay you for your trouble," he added, placing another $100 bill on the counter.

She thought for a moment and then glanced around the office to be sure no one was watching them. Tucking the money in her pocket, she leaned forward and spoke in a soft voice. "Well, I guess if all you want is her name, that's probably okay. I'll do it as a favor, but remember to keep it confidential, please."

Channing nodded, and she consulted her computer screen for a few moments before jotting a name on a sheet of scrap paper and sliding it across the counter. Channing thanked her and quickly left in search of Billy, carrying the pile of records under his arm. In the cafeteria, Billy was eyeing his dessert when Channing dropped the records on the table. Warning Billy not to spill anything on the documents, Channing searched through the pile for clues.

He scanned some of the pages quickly, ignoring rows of numbers and test results. He spent more time on other ones, straining to read handwritten notes scrawled by doctors and nurses. Near the middle of the stack he found a page that piqued his interest. He cursed when he saw that Susan had given her parents' address as her home, but a moment later he slapped the palm of his hand against the table, looked at Billy and smiled. "I think I've got something here." A note was scribbled under "intake remarks." "How about this? 'Patient brought to ER by unidentified motorists. Patient involved in MVA near mile marker thirty on I-64.'" Channing folded the edge of the page to mark it, and then flipped through the rest of the records. When he reached the bottom of the stack he turned back to the intake notes and jotted the information down on a napkin.

Channing motioned that it was time to go, and Billy shoved the last bit of cake into his mouth. The two exited the building and retraced their steps to the parking lot, where they got into the car. Channing turned on the engine and cranked up the air conditioner before describing his plan. "I wish we had two cars, but I think we can get by with one for now. I'm gonna work on finding Susan's car. I searched for its repair records on the Internet several times but couldn't find anything recent, so maybe the car was totaled. I'll try to find out if it's in a junk yard around here. I'll check with the police to see if there was an accident report. If there was, it might have her address or the names of passengers or witnesses who could lead me to her."

"Sounds good. What should I be doing?"

Channing handed him a sheet of paper. "Let's go to the police station first, and after that I'll start calling junk yards. You can try to track down this woman. I checked the phone book, and she's listed in there. That's one break I've gotten, at least."

Billy looked at the piece of paper and read the name. "Let's see, Annie Louise. Who's she?"

"She was a patient in the same room with Susan. Maybe Susan told her something useful. If we're lucky, maybe she knows where Susan went. It's not likely, but who knows?"

"What if she won't talk?"

"Make her talk. Whatever it takes."

Billy nodded. "Okay, I'll try, but she might not know anything. Your wife planned a damn good escape, so I doubt if she told this woman anything. I mean, she even paid her bill in cash. Nobody does that."

"Yeah, I know. If we don't get anywhere, I'll check with her doctor, but if she told him to keep quiet, it'll be tough to get anything out of him. He probably won't even remember her—it's been almost six months. Anyway, we'll try this first. Keep your phone handy and I'll check back with you."

Channing slipped behind the car, which was backed up close to the wall, and lifted a pair of blue jeans, two old shirts, work gloves and some hiking boots from the trunk. He waited for a car to pass by and then ducked down to change clothes. He slipped a pair of work gloves into his pants pocket and got into the car. Handing Billy a pair of gloves and a dark blue shirt, he pointed to a white oval patch above the shirt pocket. In the center of the patch the name Eddie was embroidered in red script letters. "That's your name today."

At the police station, Channing went inside to check accident reports while Billy waited outside. Billy put on the blue shirt and left the air conditioner running as he leaned his head back against the seat. He was asleep when Channing returned a half hour later, but the sound of the car door opening woke him up. "Whew. I guess I conked out there. It's been a long day."

"Yeah, tell me about it. There's no accident report on Susan's car. Maybe she ran off the road and hit a tree or a guardrail and there wasn't much damage to the car, so the cops didn't write up an official report. Maybe her car was parked on the side of the road for a few days until she got out of the hospital and came back to get it. I don't think that's likely because the medical records show she was in bad shape when those two guys brought her to the hospital. I wish to hell they had given their names so I could ask them what happened to the car." Channing pulled out into the street and followed the directions he was given to find a library. "I'll check some old newspapers in there. Maybe there was an article about a car wreck around the time Susan went to the ER. Meet me back here as soon as possible."

After Channing got out, Billy searched until he saw a faded wooden sign next to a long row of mailboxes, identifying the entrance to Rudy's Trailer Court. A few dozen mobile homes were jammed onto the lot. Most of the trailers were connected to large above-ground propane tanks that were partially concealed by tall weeds. Window air conditioners jutted out here and there, humming and rattling and dripping water that soaked into the ground below. Several large, rusty barrels were stuffed with garbage, while others were empty except for a deep layer of ashes that remained after trash had been burned inside them. Trailer trash was literally all around the neighborhood.

Two old vehicles with missing tires rested on cinder blocks in the back of the lot. Their paint had faded years ago into patches of dull brown and rust. Several children's bicycles lay flat on the ground, along with scattered toys, around a few trailers. The main difference between this neighborhood and a junk yard was the fact that people lived here.

Billy spotted an old bearded man sitting on a plastic lawn chair halfway down a gravel road that ran through the middle of the lot. He was barefoot, and his legs stretched out in front of him as he held a beer bottle in one hand and a cigarette in the other. Several empty bottles lay on the ground beside his chair.

Billy parked in front of his trailer, leaving the engine running. He put on sunglasses and got out of the car, making sure that the gun in his front right pocket was not visible. He approached the trailer, hoping to get information without leaving any clues as to his identity or the purpose of his visit. Fortunately the man was completely apathetic and asked no questions. Billy got straight to the point. "Hey, man. I'm looking for Annie Louise. She lives around here, right?"

The man turned his head slightly to the right and pointed the top of his beer bottle in the same direction. Cigarette smoke escaped from his mouth as he replied, "Third trailer down from here. She just got off work."

Billy answered with a simple "thanks" and drove down the street, stopping in front of Annie's trailer. With his sunglasses still on, he walked to her door and stepped up on a concrete platform. A screen door with an aluminum frame was closed, but the inner door was open. Billy could hear the sound of a TV inside the trailer as he knocked on the screen door. A female voice answered. "Yeah, who is it?"

"Hello, ma'am. I'm sorry to bother you today. I was hoping you can help me locate someone who was a patient at St. Albert Hospital last December. The folks at the hospital said you might be able to help me." There was no immediate response, and Billy listened for sounds of movement inside. He heard a creaking noise and then footsteps before a woman appeared. She wore a waitress's uniform and had a beer in her right hand. Her left hand was hidden behind the inner door, gripping its handle.

She left the screen door closed as she spoke. "I didn't catch your name there."

"Yes, ma'am, I'm Eddie Roberts. You must be Annie. I'm just trying to find a patient named Susan. The doctor down at the hospital said you might be able to help me find her."

Annie squinted as the sunlight made it difficult to see his face. His eyes were invisible behind sunglasses. She hadn't thought about Susan in months, but she began to recall some of their conversations at the hospital. She remembered that Susan's husband was a sorry jerk, and she was trying to hide from him. "I'd like to help you, but I don't remember nothing about the hospital. I was real sick and it was a long time ago. That other lady didn't hardly talk much."

Billy watched the door closely, ready to move quickly if it began to close. "Yeah, I know how it is. But that doc said she talked a whole lot while he was with her, so I figured you might remember something. All's I need to know is if she told you where she lived or where she was going. You know, she done had a wreck before she came in. The problem is she was driving my car when it happened, and I can't get my insurance to pay on it unless they can talk to her. She took off after she got out of the hospital, and my insurance man needs to get a statement from her. It's just some stupid paperwork thing, but you know, I need to collect that insurance money. You know how it is."

"Yeah. Well, sorry, but I just can't remember nothing. I bet the hospital could help you find her address, especially if she ain't paid 'em yet." She began to close the door, but Billy stepped forward and seized the screen door handle.

He pulled the screen door open and jammed his leg against the inner door, pushing it back. Annie dropped her beer bottle and cursed as the door shoved her backward. Billy jumped inside and slammed the door behind him before she could yell for help. He grabbed one of her arms, squeezing tightly until the pain convinced her not to struggle. He told her to stay quiet as he glanced around to get oriented.

They were in a small entryway area, with a tiny kitchen to the right and a living room to the left. He pushed her toward the living room and made her sit on a couch. She glared at him but remained silent. He spotted a telephone beside the couch—a land line—and hurled it against a wall, smashing it into pieces. Seeing a remote control on a coffee table, he nodded toward it and ordered her to turn off the TV. After she complied, he stood up and put on his gloves, then stepped back to draw the curtains across a window that faced the street.

Annie's eyes widened when he pulled a gun from his pocket. Her lips quivered as she pressed against the back of the couch.

Billy spoke in a calm but firm voice. "Now, Annie, here's the deal. It doesn't matter who I am or why I want to find Susan. What matters is that you're lying, and we both know it. You're gonna tell me what she told you, and you're gonna tell me where she lives. If you tell me what I need to know, you'll be okay. You give me the information and I'll leave. You don't want to know what happens if you don't talk."

Annie's hands shook. Her first instinct was to rip into him with every cuss word she knew, but she was terrified. On the other hand, if this man with a gun in her face was going to kill her anyway, she might decide to go down swinging. She clenched her jaw and asked a question. "How do I know you'll leave me alone if I talk?"

"You don't, but you might as well trust me 'cause that's your only chance. I got nothing personal against you, so if you don't give me any trouble, there's no reason for me to hurt you. You can't identify me, so I don't need to get rid of you."

She thought about it and decided to cooperate. She sympathized with Susan, but not enough to risk her own neck for a stranger. She blurted out everything she could remember. Susan was from somewhere in Virginia and was running away from her husband because he drank, snorted coke, gambled, and cheated on her. She was heading out west somewhere to stay with a friend.

Billy listened closely and let her rattle on until she stopped. "Okay, that's pretty good, but I need to know where she went. And remember, I know where you live. If you lie to me, I can come back here and find you."

Annie tried to think as carefully as her nerves would allow. She couldn't remember exactly where Susan was going, but if she could give him a clue, he might let her live, at least until he had time to check it out. To make sure he got the message, she pointed out the advantage of letting her live. "Look, I swear I'll tell you all I can remember, but I can't think too good while you're holding a gun on me. It's been a long time since I was in that hospital, see, and there wasn't no reason for me to try to remember everything we talked about. I didn't care where she was going to 'cause it didn't make no difference to me. So I'll tell you all I know and if you can't find her, you can come back here. If I can think on it for a while, maybe I'll remember something else. If you kill me now, I can't remember nothing more."

Billy took a moment to consider the logic in her proposal and then agreed. He lowered the gun but kept a finger on the trigger. "Okay, so tell me everything you remember."

Annie took a deep breath, exhaled, and then began to speak. She rocked back and forth as she talked. "Okay, let me think now. I know it was somewhere out west. Something like Abilene. I remember it sounded like some kind of cow, like maybe Angus or Aberdeen or something like that. I think it was in North or South Dakota. Yeah, I'm sure of that. It was either North or South Dakota, definitely one of them two. I swear that's all I can remember. I don't hardly know that woman, so there ain't no reason for me to protect her. Maybe you ain't even trying to hurt her anyway. Maybe all you want is to get some insurance money on your car, like you said. Hell, I don't know and it don't make no difference to me. It ain't none of my business."

Billy saw a magazine on the floor and ripped off its cover. "Okay, that's good. I need you to get me a pen and I'll write this down, and then I'm leaving."

She found a pen and repeated the names while he jotted them down. Shoving the paper in his pocket, he ordered her back onto the couch. "Okay, I'm leaving now, but you sit right there for ten minutes. If I see you look out any window or open the door, you're dead."

When he left the trailer, he closed both doors behind him and wiped the screen door handle with his shirttail, then walked quickly to the car. He glanced up the street and saw two young boys throwing a football, but they ignored him. The man who was drinking in front of his trailer was still there, apparently paying little attention to anything. Billy hopped in the car and sped away.

ɛɔɛɔ

The telephone line was inside a narrow metal tube that shielded it from the weather and secured it to the side of Channing's house. The intruder sliced through the tube with heavy duty cutting pliers and exposed the wires inside. Repositioning the pliers, he cut through the line. It was possible that the alarm signal would be transmitted wirelessly, but he would have to take that chance because there was no more time for delay. He didn't know how long Channing would stay in West Virginia, and in five days the ticket would expire. There was no guarantee that it was inside the house, but it was a logical possibility.

There were several points of entry, but the door that opened into the back yard was the most secluded. A privacy wall surrounded the yard, protecting it from the neighbors' view. He stayed close to the side of the house as he approached the door, watching for security cameras. He kicked the door several times, but it was solid and didn't budge. It had both regular and deadbolt locks, so he knew the job would be difficult. Opening his toolbox, he sorted through it in search of the right implements. In fifteen minutes, he was ready to push on the door, expecting an alarm to sound as soon as he cracked it open. He would have to find the master alarm panel and either disarm it or destroy it to stop the noise. He hoped the neighbors were away or would think it was a false alarm. If he was lucky, the system would be hardwired to the phone line that he cut, and no signal would go out to the monitoring station.

Holding his breath, he shoved on the door. The alarm sounded, and he raced through the house to the front door. As he had predicted, the control panel was on the wall beside the door. Instead of taking time to figure out how to open the panel, he simply smashed it with a hammer. The house quieted instantly, and he quickly went to work.

CHAPTER 31

Channing opened his eyes and turned his head until he could see the bedside clock. It was almost seven a.m. on Sunday, and the ticket would expire next Wednesday. He was tired and dispirited, but a sense of urgency motivated him to get up. In the next bed, Billy was still asleep and snoring lightly. They had compared notes last night and come up with a plan of action.

Channing would go by the hospital and try to talk with Susan's doctors. It was unlikely they would reveal any useful information, either out of loyalty to their patient or because they had no reason to remember anything other than medical details of her treatment. Billy had reported that the trailer park woman probably knew very little and was telling the truth. Abilene and Aberdeen were general clues, but not much to go on. They already knew that Susan intended to disappear without a trace, and it was likely that she had kept quiet at the hospital.

After Billy returned from the trailer park, he and Channing had spent the rest of the afternoon visiting junk yards and body shops in the area. None of the junk dealers had received a Volkswagen Passat around the time of Susan's accident, and the employees at various body shops either refused to talk or had no record of repairing her car. No accident reports or newspaper accounts matched the time and location of her wreck.

Yesterday afternoon had turned to dusk when they drove past the mile marker that was noted in Susan's hospital record. Along the way they saw several spots where guardrails were damaged. Apparently they weren't repaired very often.

Channing was convinced that Susan's car was somewhere on one of the slopes below the highway. If it had remained on the road for several days while Susan was in the hospital, there should have been a record of it being impounded or reported to the police.

He left Billy sleeping and grabbed a quick breakfast before heading to the hospital. The names of six different doctors appeared in Susan's hospital records, but only Drs. Bogert and Nokes had spent much time in direct contact with her. Dr. Bogert was off duty and away from the hospital, but Channing convinced his secretary to call him. After a quick conversation, it was apparent that he could barely remember Susan. Channing wandered the halls in the trauma wing until he found Dr. Nokes. The doctor was in a hurry but agreed to see Channing for a few minutes. He remembered some details about Susan's condition and asked if any scars were still visible.

Channing pressed him for any information she may have shared about her accident or where she was going when it happened. Nokes remembered nothing, except that Susan had a large sum of cash when she was brought into the emergency room. Channing had already seen a reference to the money in the records. Nokes recalled that Susan had come in during a large snowstorm, and explained that he was overwhelmed with patients at the time. "There was no time to get to know Susan on a personal basis," he said.

Not surprised that he had learned nothing new, Channing excused himself and hurried back to the hotel.

Billy was finishing a ham and cheese omelet from room service when Channing arrived. "Well, did you find out anything at the hospital?"

"Not a damn thing, but I had to check. I'm gonna put on some old clothes and then we'll head out to look for the car."

Billy washed the rest of his breakfast down with a beer, and they left the hotel. Channing found mile marker thirty on the highway and pulled his car over on the shoulder. They felt the midday heat as soon as they got out and stood on the hot pavement. Channing instructed Billy to start walking along the guardrail toward mile marker thirty, while he would head in the opposite direction. "Stay on the shoulder until you get to the next mile marker. Look for skid marks or damage to the guardrail. If you don't see her car, climb down the hill about twenty yards and start back this way. Call me if you see anything. Watch out for snakes."

Billy frowned and shook his head. "Well, this'll be fun," he grunted.

Channing began to perspire as soon as he started to walk. He spent most of his days in air-conditioned offices, and his body was not accustomed to heat. The sun's rays baked the asphalt under his feet. After walking about 300 yards he noticed faint skid marks in the road. They ran about twenty yards before angling to the left and then back to the right. They continued for a few more yards before disappearing near the edge of the shoulder. Not far ahead, the guardrail was twisted and streaked with gouge marks. He approached the guardrail, resting his hands on it as he leaned forward to peer into the trees and brush on the slope below. Beads of sweat dripped from his forehead as he strained to see any signs of a vehicle.

He noticed that the trunks of several small pine trees had been snapped off just beyond the guardrail, and several pieces of glass were visible nearby. If Susan's car was somewhere below, there was at least a slim possibility that the Dickens novel with his lottery ticket might be inside it. He decided to explore further before calling Billy. There was no reason to reveal the real purpose of the search unless it became absolutely necessary.

He climbed over the guardrail and stepped gingerly on the hillside, shifting his weight uphill as he crept sideways down the slope. Holding onto scraggly bushes and saplings to maintain his balance, he noticed faint tracks on the ground. It appeared that someone had crawled up or down the slope, leaving behind small trenches where shoes had slipped. A patch of briars scratched Channing's clothes and arms as he continued down the hill. Soon he spotted a metal object about ten yards ahead. He pressed forward slowly, panting and red in the face as he struggled in the sticky heat. The object was a side-view mirror. Its metal housing was scratched and faded, but it was blue—the same color as Susan's Volkswagen. He was nearly exhausted, but he pushed ahead, realizing that Susan's car might be nearby.

He continued down the hill, occasionally slipping and losing his balance, which brought forth a flurry of obscenities each time. He collapsed against the side of the hill several times and lay on the ground as he tried to catch his breath. His clothes were soaked with sweat and smeared with dirt, but he kept searching. Finally he saw it. The car was on its side, pressed against a tree. Several windows were shattered, and bits of glass were scattered inside and around the car. Weeds had grown up around it, and a disgusting moldy smell hung in the air. All four tires were flat.

He brushed the weeds aside and peered through a gaping hole in one of the windows. The interior was a mess. Clothes were strewn about in musty piles, along with leaves and dirt. The dry, tattered remains of a dead animal—apparently a squirrel—rested on top of a shirt in the back seat. The scene before him and the odor emanating from the car made Channing feel faint. He turned away to catch his breath before pulling on the door handle. He was surprised when the latch worked and the door began to open. His weak arm muscles were no match for the downward pull of gravity, and he could not hold the door open very long. Several minutes of searching produced a suitable stick to prop it open. Other than glass, clothes, and a few faded papers, he could see nothing of interest inside the vehicle.

Leaning in, he extended an arm toward the glove compartment. It was stuck, but after struggling with it for a few minutes he was able to pry it open. He removed the contents carefully, placing each item on the ground. In addition to an owner's manual, a registration card, and some makeup materials, he found Susan's cell phone and a road map. He stuffed the phone and map into his pants pocket and stepped away from the car to breathe clean air for a few minutes. He found another stick and returned to the car, intending to poke through the clothes and look for more clues. As he leaned inside, his shoulder brushed against the stick that held the door open, knocking it out of place. The door pushed against him as it began to close, squeezing his body against the door frame and causing him to lose his grip on the stick. As it fell into the car, he heard an ominous buzzing sound.

The stick had disturbed a colony of wasps in a nest underneath the front seat. Dozens of them flew out of the car and attacked him as he leapt back in horror. He slipped and fell as they began to sting him. Waving his arms wildly about, he staggered to his feet and crashed through the underbrush on his way downhill. The wasps were relentless, stinging him multiple times as he stumbled forward and screamed. He finally outran them and then collapsed, rolling on the ground and groaning in pain.

Exhausted and feeling miserable, he lay in the dirt until the rush of adrenalin began to fade and his heart rate returned to normal. Red welts appeared on his face and arms. He slowly crawled toward a tree and grabbed a low branch, pulling himself to his feet. Reaching for his cell phone, he discovered that it was crushed. Susan's phone had sustained some damage when he fell, but its battery was dead so he couldn't test it. Though his body ached and he had little energy left, he began a gradual ascent up to the highway. He passed Susan's car at a safe distance, but stopped to remove his shirt and tie it to a tree branch nearby. He hoped it would be visible from above.

It took him about thirty minutes to climb up the hill. When he reached the guardrail he sat down and leaned against it, waiting for Billy. He could see his car parked in the distance but was too tired to walk to it. Over the next hour several passing motorists slowed down to look at him, but none of them stopped to offer assistance. By late afternoon he heard the sound of someone tramping through the underbrush below, and he called Billy's name.

A short time later, Billy appeared. His clothes were soaked in sweat and dirt, and his shirt was torn in several places. Wiping a sleeve across his face, he called to Channing. "Man, I'm beat. Where were you? I tried to call. I crawled all over this hill and didn't find anything except a bunch of bottles and trash."

Channing waited until Billy climbed over the guardrail before answering. "It's a long story, man."

Billy was shocked at Channing's appearance. "What the hell happened? You look awful."

Channing nodded. "Yeah. You look pretty good yourself." As they walked back to the car, Channing brought Billy up to speed on what he had found. They sat in the car, running the air conditioner at full blast. Channing guzzled the contents of a water bottle and then pulled the map from his pocket, managing to smile as he showed it to Billy. He pointed to a red ink mark near Aberdeen, South Dakota. Next to it was a handwritten notation with the name Sylvia and a phone number. "I think we found her."

Billy grinned. "Good work. I didn't think we'd ever do it. When do you wanna go out there and get her?"

"I'd like to fly out today, but it's late and I feel horrible. I need some sleep and some food. I have to buy a charger that fits her phone to see if it works. If I'm lucky, I can check her contacts and see who she called before she wrecked the car. I also want to get a better look at the car. We'll get a tow truck out here tomorrow and pull it up. I want to check the trunk and all around inside and make sure I haven't missed anything. This is the best lead I've had, and I need to get everything I can out of it. I'll reserve a flight and we can head out tomorrow. Right now I want to soak in a bathtub and drink some beer."

CHAPTER 32

Lee opened the door at the main entrance to The Cook's Treat and stepped inside. The restaurant was on the outskirts of Aberdeen, not far from his hotel. As usual during the hours when brunch was being served, a large crowd filled the main dining area. There were several smaller rooms on each side of the central part of the establishment. Although he had found several photos of Susan during his investigation and would recognize her on sight, he had asked her what she would be wearing. He gave her no hint that he knew anything about her background.

She told him on the phone that she would be in blue jeans and a light green blouse, with a yellow scarf around her neck. She would reserve one of the tables in a side room under the name Finley. He said he would arrive at eleven-thirty, wearing khakis and a dark blue polo shirt.

A young waiter in a casual uniform greeted him, consulted a reservation list, and then escorted him to one of the smaller dining rooms. Lee saw her at the far end of the room as he entered. She was alone at a table near the corner. At the table to her right, a woman sat by herself, facing away from Susan and reading a newspaper.

Lee introduced himself, shook hands, and sat down. He had hoped to get right down to business, but he found himself distracted by Susan's beautiful face and figure. Lustrous black hair cascaded down to her shoulders in sweeping curls, framing her evenly tanned cheeks and forehead. She had crystal blue eyes and delicate eyebrows, and circular gold earrings dangled amidst her curls. Her lips were full and inviting as she smiled, and he saw that she wore no wedding ring. Even with only light makeup on, she was alluring, and her expression radiated warmth. He was immediately attracted to her. They exchanged a few pleasantries until the waiter returned to take their orders. Lee knew that time was running out, and he had to force himself to concentrate on the matter at hand. After the waiter departed, Lee made a few gentle attempts to steer the conversation to Susan's book collection, but she seemed in no hurry to discuss business.

She asked him about his background and career. Lee had no way of knowing whether she had done any research to investigate his credentials. In his email he had told her of his interest in collecting rare books, particularly novels by Charles Dickens. He knew there was nothing on the Internet or in any public records that would identify him as a collector or literary authority. In recent days he had given himself a crash course in the life and works of Dickens, cramming as if to prepare for an oral exam. He had to be careful not to make claims that could be easily disproved, and the one thing he absolutely could not reveal was his true interest in acquiring Susan's collection of books.

As they continued to talk, Lee found it increasingly difficult to lie to Susan. He felt an emotional connection with her, and she seemed to be a truly decent person. He made an effort to be as honest as possible, within limits. When he told her about his wife's murder, he could tell that her concern was genuine. "I'm so sorry, Lee," she said, reaching out to touch his hand. "I can't even imagine how hard that must have been."

When he felt her hand touching his, Lee was briefly overcome with emotion. A wave of sorrow washed over him as he recalled his last moments with Andrea. At the same time, he sensed the faint possibility of a romantic attraction in Susan's eyes. He was at a loss for words. Gently holding her hand, he thanked her for her sympathy. He relaxed his grip, but Susan continued to hold his hand for several seconds before giving it a gentle pat.

Lee forgot his agenda for a moment as he looked into Susan's eyes. He had not expected to feel any remorse from taking advantage of her. He had come to Aberdeen on a business mission, but he sensed that his visit might develop into something else. He reached for his glass, sipping some water as he struggled to gather his thoughts.

He could abandon his search for the ticket, but it would serve no purpose to let it expire. If the ticket still existed, someone should cash it in, but he began to question whether he should be the one to claim it. He assumed that Susan was its rightful owner.

The waiter returned and set their dishes on the table with a flourish. Lee explained to Susan that his wife had enjoyed reading old novels before she died. He began to share her love of Dickens's works a couple of years ago. He had received a large life insurance payment and decided to invest some of the money in rare books. The books that Susan had already sold to him on eBay were great additions to his collection. He mentioned that he was acquiring books for his own enjoyment, not for resale. He was gradually filling the shelves in his library, but had not yet joined any book clubs or national organizations. Susan listened intently, not revealing that her Internet searches had failed to link him to any book-related groups.

As their conversation continued over toast and scrambled eggs, Susan occasionally volunteered some details of her personal life. She was surprised that Lee seemed interested in her background. She mentioned the difficulties in her marriage and her escape from Charlottesville. Lee was sympathetic. "I'm sorry you had to go through all that," he said. "I know what it's like to lose someone. Not the same way, but even if he was a jerk, it has to be hard to see your marriage fall apart."

"You're right," Susan agreed. "I was basically alone for the last two or three years of my marriage, and I'm so tired of that." She looked directly into Lee's eyes as she spoke. Her gaze was hypnotic, commanding Lee not to turn away. For a long moment he was lost in her blue eyes.

"I know how you feel," he replied. "But you're still young. You've got plenty of time. I'm sure the right person will come along." He hesitated, wondering if he should continue. "At least that's what I keep telling myself," he added. Susan smiled and looked away. The woman at the next table caught her glance, shook her head, and rolled her eyes, struggling not to laugh.

The two continued to talk until the waiter returned. "Could I interest you in some dessert?" he inquired.

Lee smiled and answered before Susan could respond. "I guess we better have some. We've barely had time to talk any business. I don't know where the time went."

The waiter handed them menus and cleared their dishes, promising to return in a few minutes.

Lee pulled a sheet of paper from his pocket and placed it on the table. "Ms. Finley—" he began.

"Oh, there's no need to be so formal. Please call me Susan."

Lee was happy to comply. "Thanks, Susan. I really enjoyed meeting you. I guess we got a bit sidetracked and forgot to talk very much about your books."

Susan smiled. "I guess we did, Lee. But this was fun, and there's no rush. We could get together again if you want more time to discuss details."

Lee definitely wanted to see Susan again, but he knew she was mistaken about there being no rush. Wherever it was, the lottery ticket would expire in two days. "Well, I'd love to see you again, but I'm prepared to go ahead and make an offer, assuming that the books are in good condition. I have to get back to Charleston to take care of some business this week, so I'll put an offer on the table." He chuckled as he slid a sheet of paper across to Susan. "Literally."

Lee watched intently as Susan read the paper. She nodded her head before looking up at him. "This seems like a fair offer. Can you give me just a little time to think it over?"

"Certainly, although I'd like to make a deal very soon if you're interested in my offer. If possible, maybe I could take a look at the books while you consider it. If you need more time after that, we could get in touch after I finish up in Charleston. I just have a couple of things to wrap up there. If it's convenient for you, I could look at the books today or tomorrow morning and then confirm my offer. I'm sure they'll be fine, but just to be safe I'd like to see them before the offer is firm. We can always work out the details later."

"Fair enough. I'll call you later today or tomorrow."

Lee nodded and pulled a pen from his shirt pocket. "I'll jot down my cell number on the sheet I gave you. I'm staying at a hotel in Aberdeen. You can reach me anytime." Susan handed the paper back to him, and he wrote his name and number on it. As he passed it back he mentioned his most recent eBay purchase. "Oh, I almost forgot to ask you. Did you happen to bring the two books that I won in your last auction?"

Susan shook her head and replied in an apologetic tone. "I'm sorry, there was a mix-up with the friend who I live with. I had it packed and ready for mailing before I got your email. When I heard you were coming and wanted me to hold onto it, I left it by the front door and was going to bring it today. Unfortunately, my friend thought I wanted it to go out, and she mailed it on her way to work yesterday. I'm really sorry. But it should be there as soon as you arrive back home, and I packed it carefully. I'm sure it won't get damaged."

Lee had hoped to check the two books before going to the trouble of searching through Susan's entire collection. If one of them contained the ticket he could cut his visit short and forget about South Dakota, at least for the moment. Now he had no choice. "Well, that's okay. No problem. I'll get it when I'm back in Charleston."

The waiter appeared again, and they ordered ice cream. With the business out of the way, their conversation drifted to other topics. As if they were on a first date, they talked about their hobbies, movies they enjoyed, and life in general. The waiter loitered at the opposite end of the room, eager to finish his shift. The restaurant was nearly empty when Lee and Susan were ready to leave. Lee paid the bill, leaving a generous tip to impress Susan, and they strolled to the front entrance. Outside, he extended his hand and thanked Susan for meeting with him.

She gently clasped his forearm with her left hand as they shook hands. "It was great talking with you. I think we're close to a deal. I'll be in touch soon. I'm just going to slip back inside and use the restroom before I leave. I'll call you soon."

She watched him walk to his car and waved as he drove out of the parking lot. As soon as he disappeared from view, she hurried back inside. Sylvia was still at the next table, having folded up her newspaper and claimed her check from the waiter. She left some cash on the table and followed Susan back to the main entrance. Sylvia laughed as soon as they got into her vehicle. "Girl, you are such a flirt! I can't believe you! What the hell were you doing in there?"

Susan's face turned a shade of pink as she laughed with her friend. "I really don't know, but it sure was fun."

"Yeah, so I heard. I started to lean over and tell you two to get a room."

"Well, maybe you should have," Susan chuckled.

"So what are you going to do?"

"You tell me. I want your advice before I do anything, but his offer looks great. I went down to Lilian's shop and got an estimate from her. He's offering more than what she recommended. Not to mention that I'd like to see him again."

Sylvia nodded in agreement. "He did seem like a nice guy. Looks like you didn't need me to keep an eye on you after all."

"Yeah, but it was a good idea anyway. You were right that we should meet at a public place away from the farm. Thanks for being there. It didn't sound like he was somebody working for Channing, did it?"

"No, I think you're safe. He sounded legit. I didn't hear anything suspicious. Well, except that it sounds like he'd like to hop in the sack with you."

Susan laughed again. "Good. I'm going to call him."

CHAPTER 33

Channing's forefinger gently adjusted the focus on his binoculars as he scanned the distant landscape. He had parked the car several hundred yards down the road, well off the shoulder and behind a tree so it was not visible from the farm's entrance. His knees ached from squatting down in the tall grass, and it was difficult to hold the binoculars steady while staying low enough to remain hidden. He and Billy were too far from the main house to hear any voices, but they could see any activity that occurred outside. Although it was still early, the Tuesday morning sun had already covered them with a stifling blanket of hot air.

Billy shifted his weight several times, hoping to find a comfortable position as he waited for Channing to decide how to proceed. Periodically he let out an audible sigh and commented on the heat. At about nine, a woman opened the front door of the main house and walked across the yard to a pickup truck that was parked under the shade of a large tree. Channing could not identify her, but he could see her well enough to know that she wasn't Susan. He guessed that the woman was Sylvia Ricketts, whose name appeared in the online real estate records as the property owner. He kept his binoculars focused on the truck, following it down the long driveway to the road that led to Aberdeen.

As it disappeared in the distance, Billy speculated that Susan might be alone in the house. "The place looks pretty quiet, man. Do you wanna go on in there? We could probably walk around through one of the fields and surprise her before she sees us coming. I doubt she would have time to call the cops before we could grab her."

Channing kept the field glasses trained on the yard and considered his options before answering. "I'm not ready to move in yet. Maybe Susan has a job in the city and will be leaving soon."

Billy turned toward Channing with a puzzled look on his face. "I thought you wanted to find her. Why would you let her get away, after all the crap we've been through to get here?"

Channing kept his gaze on the farm. "I'll grab her if I have to, but I'd rather look around the place without her knowing we're here. I told you before—she took something of mine and I want it back. If possible, I want to get it and take off without being spotted."

Billy reached for a stalk of tall grass, broke it off and clamped it between his teeth, hoping to keep some moisture in his mouth. "Well, I guess we could sit here on our asses all day, but what if she doesn't leave? How long do you want to sit out here in the middle of nowhere?"

Channing set his binoculars down, wiped sweat from his face and looked directly into Billy's eyes. "Not too long, actually. I need to take care of this pretty damn soon, one way or the other, or it's not going to matter anymore. If she hangs around much longer, we're going in. Here's how I want it to work. You'll go in with your gun and tell her it's a robbery. Tell her if she keeps her mouth shut, she won't get hurt. Find a room and put her in there. Stay nearby and keep an eye on her, and then call me. Once she's out of the way, I'll come in and search the place. If I can't find what I want, we'll have to ask her some questions. I might have to talk to her myself, but we'll see how it goes."

Billy nodded his head and thought for a moment, weighing the risks involved if the situation escalated. "So, how far are you planning to go with this, if things don't go real smooth in there?"

Channing answered immediately, patting his hand against the pistol that was tucked in his belt. "Whatever it takes."

Billy glanced at Channing's hand and then looked back at his face. "You know I'm in, buddy, but I'm gonna need some serious coin if this gets out of hand." He paused before continuing. "And don't you want to tell me what you're looking for? Maybe I can help you find it."

"We'll play that by ear. Just keep your phone with you and stay in touch. And don't worry about getting paid. If this works out, I swear I'll pay you good money."

The two remained in position as the sun gradually rose in the sky. There was no breeze to stir the sweltering, stagnant air around them. Perspiration trickled down Channing's forehead and around his eyes, moistening the eyepieces of his binoculars. Occasionally he rubbed them dry with his shirt and then resumed his gaze, waiting for any sign of movement at the house. As Billy checked his watch, a light brown sedan approached the farm entrance and slowed to a crawl. They ducked lower in the grass and watched as it turned into the driveway and continued toward the house, raising a cloud of dust in its wake. As the car reached the end of the drive, Channing followed its brake lights through the thick dust that hung in the air. It was difficult to get a clear view of the driver, who stepped out and crossed the yard with his back to Channing and Billy.

The man knocked several times on the door as Channing adjusted his binoculars to keep him in sharp focus while the dust dissipated. As the door opened, Channing caught a brief glimpse of a woman and instantly recognized Susan. He saw her flash a broad smile, and the man went inside. He scanned the field glasses back and forth across the front of the house, but most of its windows were covered by shades or curtains to repel the sun's scorching heat. Billy chewed on a stalk of grass as he waited for a decision.

Channing noted the time and kept his glasses trained on the house. Periodically he waved a hand quickly about his head to ward off an obnoxious swarm of gnats that had discovered the men about a half hour earlier. He cursed each time he swatted at them, as he and Billy tugged on their shirt collars to protect their necks from the airborne pests. About twenty-five minutes later, Channing saw the front door open. The man emerged first, followed closely by Susan. The man's cap cast a shadow on his face, and Channing strained to get a look at his features, hoping to identify him. The man walked with a slight, almost imperceptible limp as Susan accompanied him to a small gate that opened into a large pasture.

They appeared to be having a lively conversation as they began to cross the field, wending their way through knee-high grass in the direction of a long, low barn that stood about halfway between the house and an adjoining field of tall, thick corn. Some of the leaves on the corn stalks had begun to turn a shade of pale brown under the duress of dry weather.

Channing was unable to identify the man before the two arrived at the barn and went inside. In a few minutes, Susan reappeared and slowly walked alone through the field, retracing her steps to the house. She sat for a while in a wooden chair on the front porch before going back inside.

They watched the house and barn for another ten minutes but saw no sign of movement. Channing checked his watch several times as they waited, and finally announced that it was time to make their move. "Okay, I think we have to fish or cut bait. I'm not going to sit out here and burn up all day. It looks like Susan's not going anywhere for a while." They slowly got to their feet, stretching their legs as they slapped their hands against their pants to brush the dirt off.

Their legs were sore from prolonged squatting, and they walked stiffly to the car as Channing gave Billy further instructions. "All right, don't forget your gun and your phone."

Billy checked his phone. "I hate to break it to you, but I'm not getting any signal here."

Channing looked at his own phone and confirmed the bad news. "Well, we're in the middle of nowhere," he muttered. "We'll have to do the best we can."

They reached the car, and Channing pointed to the driver's seat, motioning for Billy to get behind the wheel.

Once inside, Channing turned on the air conditioner and continued to lay out his plan. "I'll get in the back seat and stay down low so nobody can see me until we get to the house. If we're lucky, Susan might not see us coming until you're inside. I hope she hasn't locked the door. I'm guessing she left it unlocked so the guy in the barn can come back in, but if you have to break in just do it as fast as possible. I don't want her to have time to call the cops if she's got a land line in there."

"Well, if there's no cell service out here, you can bet there's a land line. If I see one going into the house, I'll cut it."

"Okay. Just get in as fast as you can. Keep her out of the way and tied up in case I need you. I'll wait a few minutes and then come in behind you. I need to search the house, and that'll take some time. I'll be as quick as I can. Just keep Susan out of sight. I don't want her to see or hear me unless it's absolutely necessary."

"What about the masks? Why don't we just wear those so we're safe?"

Channing shook his head and replied quickly. "No, I need her to think there's only one of us, and she has to know it's not me."

"Well, she'll know it's not your voice when I talk to her, even if I wear the mask, right?"

Billy was right, but Channing was out of time and in no mood to negotiate. "Look, Billy, there's no way she'll know who you are. We'll leave her tied up when we go. I'll take care of the guy in the barn if he gives us any trouble."

Billy put the car in gear and guided it down the driveway. His eyes darted back and forth between the barn and the house as he parked and got out. Clutching a small duffel bag, he pulled his cap down over his forehead. As he moved toward the front porch he glanced along the side of the house, looking for an incoming phone line. Seeing no evidence of one, he considered circling the house to check the side and back walls, but decided against it. If Susan happened to see him sneaking around the yard, she might have time to call for help before he could locate and cut the line. He walked quickly across the lawn and climbed the porch steps two at a time. He pressed an ear against the front door as he gripped the knob with his right hand. As quietly as possible, he squeezed the handle and applied gentle pressure to see if it would turn. He heard no sound from within, and the door began to open after the knob yielded to his touch.

He pushed the door slightly, peeking through the crack for a moment before opening it wide enough to slip silently inside. Ignoring Channing's instructions, he removed his cap quickly and pulled a ski mask over his head. Easing the door shut behind him, he pulled the gun from his belt before advancing. He listened for any sound as he crossed the front room. Reaching the hallway entrance, he heard the muffled noise of a TV or radio somewhere in the house. The sound seemed to come from behind a closed door at the end of the hall. He crept forward, clutching the bag in his left hand and pointing the gun ahead.

In the kitchen, Susan sliced a large tomato on a cutting board and glanced at the oven timer. Her salad was almost complete, and the casserole would be ready in forty minutes. Lee had eagerly accepted her invitation for lunch, anticipating that it could take several hours to search through all of the books that were stored in the barn. Susan had explained that the boxes were strewn about in no particular order, and that it would take some time to sort through them. She warned him that the lighting was poor inside some of the stalls and that he might need to carry some of the books outside to get a good look at their condition. She gave him a flashlight and utility knife to help with the task.

She had offered to help him and was disappointed when he

declined any help. She knew it was impractical to hope for a romantic relationship with Lee, as he lived halfway across the country and would be leaving as soon as he bought her books. Nevertheless, she felt an attraction to him and allowed her imagination to consider any fantasy that might bring them together again. Sensing that Lee might be interested in more than a business relationship with her, she had suggested lunch to prolong his visit. Setting the salad bowl on the table, she sat down and began to daydream.

Suddenly the kitchen door flew open without warning. Susan whirled around in her chair, twisting her back as she stared at the intruder a few feet away. She instinctively raised her arms and pushed back in her chair as he approached her. The table shook as she pressed against it, knocking several pieces of silverware onto the floor. She shrieked when he grabbed one of her arms. Pointing the gun directly at her face, he ordered her to be quiet. Her body shook with terror as she clenched her teeth and complied.

Billy's voice had an ominous tone that belied his effort to calm her down. "Keep quiet and do exactly as I say and you won't get hurt. I'm only here to take your money and jewelry. If you cooperate, you'll be okay."

"Please don't hurt me," she pleaded. "You can take whatever you want."

He gripped her arm and made her stand up. Her muscles were tense, but she offered no resistance. He turned toward the door and began walking back to the hallway, bringing her along beside him. As they reached the hall, he stopped and relaxed his grip. He motioned toward the bag that he had left on the floor. "Now, I'm gonna let go of your arm so I can pick up my bag. Just stay put." Waving the gun in front of her, he added that "I don't want to have to use this, so don't do anything stupid." She nodded, and he picked up the bag. "Now, show me where the nearest bathroom is."

Her lips trembled as she responded. "What do you want? Please, I can show you where the valuables are. You can take everything and go. I haven't seen your face. I can't identify you. You don't need to hurt me."

"Just do what I tell you and don't worry. Now, let's go." He followed a few feet behind her as she walked to the end of the hall and stopped in front of the bathroom door. "Okay, step inside and sit on the floor with your back to me." Susan complied but started to beg for her life as soon as she was on the floor. Billy replied in an irritated voice. "Look, I'm tired of telling you. Shut up and you won't get hurt. I'm gonna tie your hands and feet so you can't get away until after I'm gone. If I wanted to hurt you, I would've done it already. Don't piss me off or I might change my mind."

Susan nodded and held her hands behind her back, fighting to hold back tears as he removed a rope from his bag and wrapped it around her wrists. When the knot was secure, he turned her around and tied her ankles together. She kept her head down and avoided looking at him while he worked. He finished quickly and then tested the knots. "Now, I'm gonna go through the house and get a few things. I haven't gagged your mouth, but if I hear any noise from you, you're gonna piss me off big time. Just keep quiet and I'll be gone as soon as I'm done. You got that?" Susan nodded and shut her eyes, praying that he would let her live.

Outside, Channing raised his head just enough to peek through the car window, nervously waiting for some indication that Billy had secured the house. He remained in place until the front door opened and Billy motioned for him to come inside. He walked quickly across the yard, glancing back over his shoulder to confirm that the stranger was still out of sight in the barn. He entered the house and asked Billy for an update.

"I've got your wife tied up in a bathroom down at the end of this hall," Billy said, pointing toward the corridor at the opposite end of the front room.

"You sure she can't get loose?"

"Yeah, I tied the ropes tight, and I can tell she's too scared to run for it."

"All right, that's good. Stay here and make sure everything's clear outside. That guy's still out in the barn, and the other woman might come back anytime. I'll go through the house as quick as I can."

Billy sat on the edge of a couch next to one of the front windows, resting the gun on his lap. Seeing no books in the room, Channing climbed the staircase to the second floor and began his search. He made a quick check of each room to see if any books were in sight, pausing to look inside all of the closets as well. A few books were scattered here and there, but none of them appeared to be old. He leafed through each one anyway, rapidly flipping the pages and checking the covers to see if the lottery ticket was inside. Within ten minutes, he had completed his first pass through the upstairs rooms, finding nothing but a couple of bookmarks. He hurried downstairs and began checking each room on the first floor. Billy offered to help, but he waved him off, continuing to search until he was sure he had checked everywhere except the bathroom. He looked at his watch and then returned to the front room. "Okay, I need to look some more, but first tell me about the bathroom. What's in there?"

"What do you mean? It's just a bathroom, with a toilet and a sink and maybe a closet. I didn't really take a close look at it."

"Okay. Did you see any books in there?"

"What the hell, Channing? Tell me we didn't come here just to steal some books!"

"Well, maybe. She took some rare books from our house when she moved out. They could be worth a lot of money. I want 'em back."

"Man, you gotta be kidding! I can't believe we went through all this for some books! What the hell are we doing?"

Channing held up his right hand, extending its palm up in Billy's face, like a policeman stopping traffic. "Look, I don't have time to go into it now. The books are damn valuable, okay? A couple of them are worth several hundred thousand dollars. Maybe more, for all I know. I'm gonna double-check the rooms again and then come back down. If I don't find the books, I want you to go ask Susan where they are, and make her talk. I was hoping I could find them and just leave, but we may have to talk to her. Just wait here and keep a lookout."

Billy shrugged his shoulders. "Whatever, man."

Channing retraced his steps and searched each room again. He checked his watch often, worried that someone would discover them in the house if he took too much time. He rummaged through drawers and closets, throwing objects aside and muttering obscenities as he became more frustrated and desperate. He looked under mattresses and furniture, furious that the ticket was so small and easy to hide. Out of breath and sweating, he ended his search and broke the news to Billy. "Okay, go ask her where the rare books are. Don't tell her anything. Just find out where they are. Do whatever it takes to make her talk, except don't kill her or knock her out unless you check with me first."

Channing glanced through the window and then flopped down on the couch as Billy disappeared down the hall. Slipping the mask out of his pocket, Billy pulled it over his head and stepped into the bathroom. Susan raised her head as he closed the door behind him. Her face was ashen and her body quivered as adrenalin raced through her veins. Billy had the gun in his hand, and she was sure he had come back to kill her. Before he spoke, she began to cry, begging for her life. He stooped down in front of her and placed a hand over her mouth as she pressed her back firmly against the wall.

He leaned forward and looked into her eyes. "I need to ask you a question. I don't have time to play games. You tell me the truth and you won't get hurt, but if you lie to me, it's the last thing you'll ever do. Understand?"

Susan grunted, unable to speak with a hand over her mouth. Her nostrils flared as she breathed rapidly through her nose, straining to get enough oxygen. Billy held his hand firmly against her mouth as he asked her the question. "I'm looking for some rare books, and I know you have them. Where are they?"

As he removed his hand, Susan took several gulps of air. She thought of Lee out in the barn, an unsuspecting victim who might be killed if she answered the question. She said nothing for several seconds as her thoughts spun wildly out of control.

Billy pressed the gun against her forehead. "Woman, I'm not going to ask you again," he snarled.

Fearing for her life, and unable to think of any alternative, Susan capitulated. "There's a barn outside in the middle of a field. The books are in boxes in the barn. Please, just take them and don't hurt anybody."

Billy shoved the gun in his belt and stood up. Susan began to sob uncontrollably as he left the room.

CHAPTER 34

Lee sliced through the packing tape that ran along the seam at the top of the box and then slipped the box cutter into his pocket. As far as he could tell, there were no other boxes left to check. He peeled back one of the cardboard flaps and shined the flashlight inside. Pushing his hand into a layer of white foam packing peanuts, he touched several objects, none of which felt like a book. He pulled one of the items out and held it in his hand. Completely disgusted, he tossed the candlestick back and stood up slowly, conscious of the ache in his back from a morning of stooping over to sort through Susan's possessions. The task had taken less time than Susan had predicted, as she had expected him to examine each of her books carefully to evaluate its age and condition. Under any other circumstances, he would have enjoyed her company in the barn, but he could not reveal the real purpose of his visit. He had quickly flipped through the pages of her books and checked their covers, setting each volume aside as soon as he confirmed that nothing was inside.

He had discovered several Dickens books in one box and checked each one thoroughly, then emptied the box completely to see if the ticket had fallen out during shipping. He recognized their leather jackets and titles printed in gold lettering, checking his photo to confirm they were the same books. Setting them aside, he had continued looking until it was clear that the ticket was gone. Unless it was in one of the books that Susan's friend had mailed to him, his search had ended in failure.

He leaned against the wooden frame at the stall's entrance, wiping a hand across his face to clear some of the sweat away. Barring a miracle, his hours of investigative work would produce only a crushing disappointment. As he reflected on the events that brought him to an isolated farm more than 1,300 miles from home, his disappointment was coupled with an odd sense of relief. In pursuing Channing's lottery ticket, he had lied, committed several felonies, and otherwise compromised his principles. The series of criminal acts and ethical lapses weighed on his conscience and self-esteem. If his search was at an end, at least he could begin to repair his integrity. He could find some comfort in knowing that no one had been permanently hurt by his actions. He had not actually stolen anything of real value.

With the life insurance money from his wife's death, he could afford to honor his offer to Susan and buy at least some of her books. He could recoup most of the money by selling them later. Something positive might even develop out of what he had done. Perhaps there was a chance of romantic involvement with Susan, in spite of the geographic distance between them. Stranger things had happened before.

Shaking dust off his shirt, he turned to leave the barn. Midway down the central hall he stooped to pick up the two Dickens novels he had set aside, and then continued toward the exit. As he turned a corner, he saw a figure ahead. The man was a silhouette framed by the bright sunlight that drenched the field outside the barn. Both men froze in place and waited for their eyes to adjust to the lighting.

In a few moments Lee began to discern the features of the man who was facing him. Having seen photographs of Channing on the Internet, Lee had the advantage of recognizing his adversary. His presence was surprising and alarming, but Lee reacted quickly and feigned friendliness. "Hello, there. I was just on my way out, but I'll leave the light on for you. You sure picked a hot day to be in this barn." Lee began to walk toward the door, but Channing held up his hand, signaling for him to stop.

"Hold on," Channing commanded. "What've you got there?" he asked, pointing to the books in Lee's hands.

Lee stopped before answering. "Oh, just a couple of books. There's several boxes of 'em back there. I'm a collector, and I think I might buy these two." Lee shrugged his shoulders and forced himself to laugh. "My wife keeps telling me to stop cluttering up the house, but I love old books. It's been a hobby of mine for a long time." He began to step forward as he continued talking. "Well, anyway, I don't want to hold you up. It looks like you're busy." He tilted his head to his left and added, "Those are some good-looking horses down that way. Looks like you're taking good care of them."

Channing stepped sideways, blocking Lee's path, and held up his hand again. "Not so fast there. Which books do you have?"

Lee remained outwardly calm, but he could feel his heart rate increasing as the tension mounted between the two men. He assumed that Channing knew the lottery ticket was stashed inside a Dickens novel, as those were the only books pictured in the photo that Lee discovered months ago—the one that was now folded in his wallet. The ticket was not in either of the volumes he was carrying, but Channing already seemed suspicious and might recognize the titles from seeing the photo. Struggling to hide a growing concern for his safety, Lee held the books up to his face and replied in a voice as cheerful as he could muster. "Well, let's see now. This one is called *A Christmas Carol*, and the other one is, uh, well, it's a little hard to read in here. Oh, yeah, it's *The Battle of Life*. They're by Charles Dickens."

"Yeah, I know, and they're very rare, too. I need to take a look at 'em."

Lee's mind began to race. It was apparent that Channing knew the ticket was hidden in a Dickens novel, so he must have placed it there. His insistence on examining the books suggested that the ticket was still inside whatever book Channing had chosen. Channing had to know that the ticket would expire tomorrow, so he was obviously desperate. There was no way to tell whether Channing could remember exactly which book the ticket was in.

Lee silently berated himself for leaving his pistol in the car. He had recovered considerably from his gunshot wound, but there was no guarantee that he could overpower Channing or outrun him, especially if Channing were armed. Praying for luck, Lee extended his right arm, offering the books to Channing.

"I need to look through these," Channing growled, as he stepped backward toward the door. He kept his eyes on Lee until he reached the doorway and then set one book on a bale of hay as he flipped through the pages of the other one. He checked both books carefully and peeled back their covers, looking up frequently to watch Lee. Setting the books down, Channing glared at Lee. "I don't know what Susan told you, but it so happens that all of the Dickens books belong to me. I left a special bookmark in one of them, and I want it back. You know what I'm talking about. If you hand it over now, you can have these books for free." He stood in the middle of the doorway, directly in front of Lee, and waited.

Lee considered trying to run past Channing and escape into the field, but the doorway was narrow enough that Channing would undoubtedly be able to grab him. There was another door at one end of the barn, but it had been closed all morning, and Lee hadn't checked to see if it was locked. He was about to turn and run back into the barn when Channing whipped a gun from under his shirt and pointed it at Lee's stomach. "It's not a request," he said coldly. "Empty your pockets."

Lee raised his arms slightly, with his palms open and facing Channing, as he desperately considered his options. There was no lottery ticket in his pockets, but the photo of the winning ticket was tucked inside his wallet. There was no way to predict what might happen when Channing opened the wallet, but Lee could not take the risk. He decided there was no alternative but to fight. Unable to disguise the fear in his voice, he replied, "Okay, take it easy, man. I got nothing to hide. Take all the money I've got. I'm just gonna pull my wallet out of my back pocket and hand it over, okay?"

"Do it nice and slow."

"Okay, no problem. Just take it easy."

With his right hand, Lee slowly reached behind his back and eased the wallet out of his rear pocket. He brought it forward and transferred it to his left hand, then put his right hand in his side pocket as he partially extended his left hand. He felt the utility knife in his pocket and pressed its handle, sliding it forward to extend the blade. As Channing stepped up and reached for the wallet, Lee lunged forward and swatted Channing's right hand away. At the same instant, Lee jerked the knife from his pocket and shoved its blade into Channing's abdomen.

Lee tackled Channing and knocked him backward as a bullet roared out of the gun barrel. The shattering noise of the gunshot partially drowned out Channing's scream as he collapsed backward with Lee on top of him. Lee rolled to his left, pressing Channing's right arm against the ground as he waved his left hand wildly about in an effort to grab the gun. He felt Channing's right wrist and gripped it tightly, pushing it away as he twisted his head around to locate the gun before Channing could get off another shot. Channing shouted and groaned as they struggled on the ground. Lee got a fleeting glimpse of Channing's right hand and was surprised to see that the gun had disappeared. As he turned back toward Channing's body he felt a searing pain in his right shoulder. His head jerked to the right in time to see a knife in Channing's left hand.

Lee shrieked as he instinctively shoved his arms forward to push away from Channing. He staggered backward, wincing in pain as his eyes darted about, searching for the missing gun. Channing's shirt was soaked with blood and his chest was heaving, but he held on tightly to the knife as he struggled to get to his feet. Lee pressed his left hand against the wound on his right arm, feeling warm blood that oozed out and ran down to his elbow. Lee glanced rapidly in every direction, but the gun had been swallowed up by a thick stand of tall weeds along the side of the barn. About six feet away, Channing was on his knees, gripping the knife and fighting to maintain his balance.

Lee frantically weighed his options. He could try to disarm Channing, or he could try to find the gun before Channing attacked him with the knife. The second option quickly evaporated, as Channing was almost on his feet. Lee could either fight or run. At that instant a bullet smacked into the side of the barn behind him, and a split second later Lee heard the blast of Billy's pistol as the sound caught up with the bullet. He ducked and whirled around in time to see Billy at the edge of the yard, running toward the gate that opened into the field. Lee caught his balance and began to sprint toward the barn, racing to pass Channing before he could catch him. Channing lurched forward, but he was slowed by the intense pain of his wound. He waved the knife toward Lee but missed by several feet as Lee rushed past him, heading to the far end of the barn. Channing shouted to Billy, who was sprinting across the field.

Unable to aim accurately while he ran, and afraid that he might hit Channing, Billy held his fire as Lee disappeared around the corner of the barn. Lee raced toward a corn field about 100 yards in the distance, just past a barbed wire fence that separated the two fields. He could hear shouting behind him, but the words were muffled by the barn that stood between the men. Gasping for breath, he reached the fence just as Billy and Channing appeared from behind the barn. Lee clawed his way over the fence, cutting his hands on the wire and ripping his pants in the process. As he fell to the ground on the other side, a shot rang out. The bullet missed him and whizzed over his head on its way into the corn field. He scrambled to his feet, looking back only once before he crashed into a wall of corn stalks and pushed forward into the field. He heard a loud pop as another bullet slammed into a fence post behind him, penetrating and cracking the wood.

Lee plunged ahead, blinded by a thicket of stalks and leaves that whipped his face as he ran through the corn rows. Reaching skyward, the stalks were about two feet taller than Lee. He heard swishing sounds as bullets raced through the corn crop around him, slicing cleanly through vegetation in search of flesh. He kept his head low, looking down to shield his eyes from the leaves that constantly slapped his body as he staggered headlong into the field. As exhaustion overcame him, he collapsed onto the ground. In the distance, he could hear the sound of someone thrashing about in the corn, punctuated by an occasional gunshot. With his face close to the ground, below the lowest leaves on the stalks, Lee could see open lanes about eighteen inches wide that separated each row of corn. He crawled along a lane, moving in the opposite direction from the sound of his pursuers. He tried to avoid shaking the stalks, hoping to conceal his location and movement.

He paused occasionally and listened for sounds to estimate how much distance separated him from the others. He could still hear movement somewhere in the field, but the sounds were fading and there were periods of silence. Presumably his pursuers were listening for sounds that would give away his position. He pulled his cell phone from his pocket and held it in front of his face. Seeing that no service was available, he tossed it aside and continued down the row.

About a hundred yards away, Billy and Channing separated and pushed forward through the thick maze of corn stalks. They held their fire as they spread out, afraid of shooting each other. They agreed that if one of them heard or saw Lee, he would fire a single shot in the air as a signal to the other. Blood continued to seep from Channing's wound, soaking his clothes and sapping his strength as he fought his way deeper into the field. He staggered forward, losing his balance several times and sprawling onto the dirt. Each time, his arms flailed about as he tried to grab corn stalks to break his fall. Lying on the ground, he swore he would kill the man who had fled into the field, as well as Susan. Weakened and short of breath, he decided to rest before continuing the pursuit. *I can't believe it has come to this*, he thought.

As the afternoon wore on, Lee's shoulder wound began to ache and his pain increased. The blood on his shoulder and arm had dried and clotted, stopping the bleeding but leaving him weak from the loss of blood. He forced himself to press on, knowing that he could be discovered at any minute. He lost track of time, as his watch band had broken and fallen away sometime during his escape. Smeared with dust and blood, he finally reached the edge of the corn field. He crept forward, nervously approaching the last row of stalks. Staying close to the ground, he inched along until he could see what lay beyond. A few feet away was a barbed wire fence, with an open hay field on the other side. The last row of corn extended for at least a quarter of a mile to his right, and about 200 yards on the left.

Judging by the position of the sun and the direction in which the corn stalks' shadows were pointing, he guessed that Susan's house was somewhere to his left. Hugging the edge of the last corn row, he limped toward the corner of the field, keeping a constant lookout. Reaching the end of the row, he peered out at the landscape to get his bearings. In the distance to his left, he could see the barn, with the house and outbuildings farther to the right. Just in front of him, the barbed wire fence ended at the edge of another field, which was encircled by a dark board fence. A few trees grew at intervals along the board fence, with several horses clustered in the shade under some of them. He could see his parked car jutting out behind a tree near the house. There was no sign of any human activity.

Hoping that Channing and his henchman were still lost in the corn field, he decided to sneak along the board fence and try to get close to the house. The fence, trees and horses would provide limited cover, and if he reached the back yard he could make a run for his car. Crouching down, he moved forward, pausing behind each tree to look out across the fields. The horses watched him as he passed by, but otherwise ignored him. He quietly opened a gate that led into the back yard and staggered toward a large storage shed, where he stopped to catch his breath. Continuing, he came to the end of the shed and peeked around the corner. A tree blocked his view of the barn, but he saw no one in the field.

As he stepped around the corner, a dog that had been sleeping at the far edge of the yard raised his head and leaped to his feet. Barking loudly, Trotter ran toward Lee and jumped up and down in front of him in a playful manner. Lee dodged him and began running toward his car. The dog chased after him, leaping against his right leg as he ran. As he attempted to sidestep around the animal, Lee lost his footing and tumbled onto the ground. Trotter pressed his nose against Lee's face, lapping at his cheeks with his wet tongue. As Lee got to his feet, he glanced toward the barn in time to see a figure emerge from the corn field and begin climbing over the barbed wire fence. Lee shouted at the dog and shoved it aside, then began running to his car. Trotter yelped and followed him as Lee crossed the yard, slowing down as exhaustion overcame him. Gasping for breath, Lee opened the door and fell into the front seat. He opened the glove compartment and grabbed his gun. Raising his head, he looked through the passenger window in the direction of the barn. His pursuer was now halfway across the field, racing toward him with a pistol in hand.

Lee reached into his right pocket and was horrified to discover that the key to his rental car was missing. Recalling that he had left it in the house, he backed out of the car and headed for the nearest tree. A car window shattered behind him as two shots rang out. He dove behind the tree and crouched down. Leaning forward just enough, he saw the man crawling under the fence at the edge of the yard. Standing up quickly, Lee extended his hand beyond the tree trunk, aimed the pistol, and squeezed the trigger. The shot was wide of its mark, but its sound stunned the man at the fence, who had not expected Lee to be armed. The man struggled to pull his legs through the gap as he tried to aim his gun in Lee's direction. Lee fired again and again as the man began shooting back without having time to aim. Lee's ears were ringing as he sent a wave of bullets across the yard.

The man's body dropped against the grass and his arms went limp. Lee fired three more shots and then stopped. The man lay motionless at the edge of the yard. Lee waited about a minute, alternating his gaze between the body and the field beyond the yard. Seeing no movement anywhere, he held the gun out and ran to the house.

He burst through the front door and collapsed onto the floor. In pain and completely out of breath, he lay there for several minutes, clutching the gun on top of his chest as he watched the door.

When he regained some strength, he sat up and continued to aim the gun at the front door. He glanced over his shoulder several times, unsure whether someone else might still be in the house. As soon as he could stand, he hurried across the room to the hallway entrance. Pointing the gun ahead, he crept forward, listening carefully for any sound.

He opened the door to each room, aimed the gun inside as he looked around, and then moved on. At the end of the hall he opened the door to his left, and his eyes met Susan's.

"Thank God!" she gasped, as he rushed forward to comfort her. "I heard all the shots and thought you were dead!"

"Me, too, for a while," he replied, as he struggled to untie the ropes around her legs and arms. "Is there anyone else in the house?" he asked.

"I don't know. It was quiet for a long time, and then I heard all those shots near the house. I don't know how long I've been in here. I've been scared out of my mind."

"That makes two of us." As Lee got the last knot untied, Susan leaned forward and wrapped her arms around him. She cried softly as they held each other. Lee cupped his hand behind her head and gently stroked her hair. They hugged each other in silence, and then he helped her to her feet. "We need to call nine-one-one," he said.

She held his hand and followed him to the kitchen. He called the police, and then Susan called Sylvia. Lee locked the doors that led to the hall and out into the side yard, then pulled the curtains across the kitchen windows.

As they waited, Susan got a wet rag and helped Lee take off his shirt. He sat on a chair in the middle of the room with the gun in his hand, looking back and forth between the two doors, worried that a gunman might force his way into the kitchen at any moment. Susan began to clean the gash on his shoulder, gently washing off dirt and dried blood. His shoulder and both arms ached, and the skin on his elbows was raw and bloody from crawling through the corn field. His hands were covered with deep scratches from the barbed wire fence. His ragged pants were smeared with blood and dirt. His whole body was sore and worn out.

Lee's eyes searched the kitchen until he spotted a clock on the face of an oven. It was three-twenty-five p.m. in Aberdeen and one hour later on the East Coast. Wherever the lottery ticket was, it would expire in just over twenty-four hours. Although he was exhausted, hungry, and in pain, he was not yet resigned to writing off a $241 million jackpot. It was now obvious that Channing had put the ticket inside a Dickens novel. It was also clear that Susan either didn't have the ticket or didn't know she had it. The last place that Lee could think to look for it was inside the books that Sylvia mailed to him by mistake a few days earlier. He checked the clock repeatedly, knowing that his last chance to find the ticket was slipping away as each minute passed.

He had booked two flights out of Aberdeen. One was destined for Richmond, Virginia, where he would have flown if he had the ticket in hand. Since the winning ticket had been purchased in Virginia, the rules required that it be presented only at lottery headquarters in Richmond. In about twenty-five minutes that flight would take off without him. The more pressing concern was the other flight, which was bound for Charleston. It was an overnight flight with two transfers, landing tomorrow morning in Charleston. It was scheduled to depart in ninety minutes.

When Lee told the nine-one-one dispatcher that at least one gunman was still at large, she instructed him to stay with Susan inside the house until police arrived. He could follow her directions and risk missing his flight, or he could head for his car and hope that the other attacker was too far away to stop him before he reached the highway. Complicating his decision was the prospect of leaving Susan in the house, alone and unarmed. His head began to throb as he struggled to keep his emotions in check, unable to decide whether to leave or stay.

They both froze for a moment when Trotter began barking somewhere near the front of the house. Lee stood up and motioned for Susan to get behind him. He pointed the gun at one door and then the other as they waited in silence. Seconds later the sound of multiple sirens could be heard over the barking, becoming louder as three vehicles raced down the driveway toward the house. "Let's go," Lee whispered, and they crept over to the door by the hallway. Lee opened it and looked in both directions before taking Susan's hand and leading her toward the front of the house. "Stay low," he said, as they approached a window that looked out across the front porch. He raised his head enough to peek out at the front yard, just as the cars skidded to a halt in the parking lot.

Six men jumped out of the cars, some carrying shotguns as they fanned out into the yard to surround the house. Lee could see an ambulance with flashing lights approaching farther down the driveway, partly obscured by thick dust that was kicked up in the road. He set the gun down on the floor and told Susan to stay in place as he opened the front door, raised his arms above his head, and stepped out onto the porch.

A voice boomed out from behind a tree and ordered him to step forward slowly. He kept his arms up and walked to the top of the stairs, waiting as an officer rushed forward with his shotgun pointed directly at Lee. A second officer approached from Lee's left side and stopped about ten feet from the base of the stairs, holding a pistol in both hands and training it on Lee.

The first officer barked out an order. "Lie down on your stomach and put your hands behind you!" he commanded.

Lee spoke slowly as he complied. "It's all right, gentlemen. I'm the man who called nine-one-one. I'm Lee Barnett—a friend of the lady who lives here. She's just inside the front door. I'm a retired police detective from Charleston, South Carolina. I left my pistol on the floor in there."

One of the officers patted Lee down, snapped handcuffs on his wrists, and then they both helped him to his feet. "We'll talk about it in the car over there," one of them replied, as they guided him away from the house.

Two other uniformed men moved forward, guns drawn, and climbed the porch stairs. Lee looked to his left and watched as one of the officers dragged the barking dog toward its pen, gripping the collar tightly to prevent him from biting an arm. Another officer was crouched over the body near the fence at the edge of the yard, checking for a pulse, as paramedics rushed across the lawn to assist.

An officer opened the rear door of the police vehicle and directed Lee inside. Leaning his head back against the seat, Lee felt the air conditioner blowing against his legs. His clothes were still sticky with sweat and dirt. One of the officers sat in the front seat, watching him through a metal grate that separated them.

Lee spoke first, not waiting for the questioning to begin. "Look, Officer, I don't want to cause any trouble, but I have to get to the airport to catch a plane. As I told you, I'm a retired detective. My name's Lee Barnett. I'll be glad to give you a statement, and then I really do have to go."

"I'm Lieutenant Rush Cortland. Do you have any identification?"

"Not with me at the moment. One of the men who attacked me took it. It's probably over near that barn," Lee added, nodding his head in its direction. "Are these handcuffs really necessary?"

"Just until we can figure out what happened here, and how you fit in."

"Okay, here's how it went down. I was in that barn looking through some old books that were being stored out there. Some guy came up and pulled a gun on me. I knocked it out of his hand and took off. Another guy ran out of the house, and they both chased me into that corn field. They shot at me, but I got away and looped back around to the house. They had tied up the woman who lives here. I was going to buy some of her books. I untied her and called nine-one-one. That's all I know. You can ask her. She'll confirm it all."

"We're interviewing her right now. What about the body in the yard?"

"I didn't get a close look at him. He was shooting at me, so I returned fire and took him out. It's self-defense all the way."

"I see," Cortland replied, as he scribbled in a small black notebook. "Anything else you want to tell me?"

"That's all I can think of right now, but if my wallet turns up, I'll give you my card. You're welcome to contact me if you have any other questions."

The officer opened his door and hopped out before leaning his head back inside. "Wait here. I'll be right back." He hurried over to another squad car and spoke briefly with an officer inside, who immediately began speaking into a microphone. Cortland signaled to several other officers, and they huddled together before four of them spread out into the field and headed toward the barn. With a grim expression on his face, Cortland returned to the car and got in. "One of my men's gonna look for the wallet by the barn. I'll have to hold you until we can sort this out. I'm sorry."

Lee shook his head. "Look, Officer," he replied in a loud voice. "I know my rights. If I'm not under arrest, I want to leave." Cortland rubbed his chin and looked at Lee without responding. "So, am I under arrest or not?"

"Not at the moment, but if there's an armed man out there, and I can't confirm your identity, I'm gonna hold you as a material witness until I can investigate further. I'm sure you can understand that."

Lee slumped backward in disgust. He watched as the paramedics draped a white sheet over the dead man's body and lifted it onto a gurney. Another police vehicle rolled into the parking lot and screeched to a halt. Several bloodhounds leaped out of the rear compartment, yelping as they were led toward the barn. A detective examined bullet holes in the fence at the edge of the yard as two others moved slowly about the lawn, carefully searching the ground for evidence. Lee waited impatiently as he watched the investigation unfold around him. Looking back at Cortland, he asked what time it was.

"It's ten after four."

Lee shook his head. "I'm screwed," he muttered.

Twenty minutes later an officer approached the car and signaled to Cortland, who got out and closed the door behind him. Lee strained to hear their conversation over the blowing air conditioner. When they finished talking, Cortland opened Lee's door and leaned inside the car. "Okay, let me help you out of there," he said, gripping Lee's upper arm to help him out of the vehicle. His body ached as he straightened his legs and back.

Cortland removed the handcuffs and handed Lee his wallet. "We found this in the weeds over by the barn, with your driver's license inside. We ran a check on it and talked with the Charleston Police Department. Your record's clean and your story checks out with them and with Ms. Finley." Cortland nodded in the direction of his partner and continued. "This is Detective John Caminski. He'll take you inside so you can give a formal statement, and then you're free to go."

Knowing it was already too late to catch his flight, Lee accompanied the detective to the house. He rubbed the red marks on his wrists where the handcuffs had pressed against his skin. As they stepped inside, Susan hugged Lee and patted him on the back. "Thank God, we're safe. If you hadn't been here, I don't know what would've happened to me. I can't thank you enough, Lee."

Lee smiled and gently wiped several tears from her cheeks. "I'm just glad we're both still alive. We were lucky." He took her arm and guided her to the couch by the front door, where they sat together while Caminski stood at the front door. Lee held her hand as they talked quietly for a few minutes, and then he stood up. "I have to give a statement to the detective, and then I'll be back."

"Okay. You're welcome to use the kitchen or anywhere else. I'll wait here. My friend Sylvia should be home soon. The police stopped her at a roadblock and told her to wait while they searched the farm. They said you saw another man out there."

Lee decided not to mention Channing's name. "That's right, there were two of them. One's dead, and they took his body away."

"Yeah, I watched through the window. It's terrible. I'm still scared to death. The cops said they'd stay on guard here tonight if they don't find the other man."

"That's good. I'm sure you'll be safe now."

"Thanks, Lee. What about you? Do you still have to get back to Charleston right away?"

"Yes. I'm so sorry to leave you while all this is going on. Unfortunately, I missed my flight, but I have to get back as soon as possible. Listen, I hate to ask you for a favor, but I've got some urgent business in Charleston tomorrow. While I'm talking with Detective Caminski, would you be able to find out when another flight leaves?"

"Sure, no problem at all. I think I'll actually feel better if I do something instead of just sitting here thinking about what happened."

Lee nodded and followed Caminski down the hall to the kitchen as Susan searched for flights on her computer. When Lee returned she handed him a sheet of paper with her notes. "I hate to tell you, but you've missed the last flight out of Aberdeen today. You could leave from Aberdeen tomorrow, but the quickest way back to Charleston is to fly out of Fargo. You'll have to drive to the airport in the middle of the night to get there on time, unless you leave pretty soon." Lee studied her notes as she continued. "You're welcome to stay here tonight if you want to. We've got a guest room right down the hall there. If you leave by two in the morning, you'll have time to get to Fargo."

"Hmm, I don't know. What time is it now?"

"It's around five-twenty." Susan touched Lee's arm and smiled. "Lee, you look exhausted. I'd hate to think of you driving right now. You'll feel better if you wait a while before you get on the road. You can take a shower, and I'll fix you some dinner. I'll have a neighbor bring you some clean clothes. You can get a few hours of sleep and then it'll be safer to drive. You won't be so tired."

By sundown the police had called off their search at the farm, planning to resume at dawn. Roadblocks were in position several miles up and down the road, and vehicles would be stopped and checked throughout the night.

After Sylvia returned and went to bed, Lee and Susan adjourned to the living room, talking into the night. They were exhausted and drained by the day's events, but their lingering emotional trauma kept both of them awake past midnight.

By one a.m., Susan drifted off to sleep, leaning her head against Lee's shoulder on the couch. He held his arm around her and closed his eyes, briefly allowing his feelings for her to crowd out the plans that were becoming more urgent by the minute.

Realizing that he might doze off, he forced himself to focus on his original agenda. With his free hand he gently caressed Susan's face and then whispered her name until she woke up.

She opened her eyes and rubbed them before sitting up straight. "Sorry, I must have conked out. What time is it?"

"It's about one-fifteen. I'd love to stay here with you, but I've got to get on the road."

She patted his leg and smiled. "I wish you could stay, too. I hope we'll meet again, and under better circumstances."

"You can count on it."

They stood up and walked together out onto the porch. There was enough moonlight to illuminate the way to Lee's car, and they crossed the yard in silence. They walked quickly, fearing that the second gunman might lunge out of the darkness at any moment. A police officer was slouched in the front seat of a squad car, watching the house. Lee nodded as they passed by him, and then paused before getting into his rental car. He turned to Susan and looked into her eyes. "I'm so glad I met you. I'll call you in a few days."

She leaned forward and kissed him softly on the lips before pulling back to say goodbye. "Thank you for saving my life, Lee. I hope I'll see you again."

"I guarantee you will."

Fargo was about three and a half hours away. He started the car and headed up the driveway. *I'm not sure I can get there on time*, he thought.

CHAPTER 35

The plane touched down at Charleston International Airport at eleven-thirteen a.m. Lee had not bothered to check any luggage, as he knew there would be no time to retrieve it from the baggage carousel inside the terminal. With a quick phone call to his hotel in Aberdeen he had extended his checkout for several days, and his belongings could stay there until he had time to think. One way or the other, his search for the ticket would end in less than three hours. After that there would not be enough time to get to Richmond.

As the plane taxied toward the terminal, Lee gripped his armrest and prepared to jump up and establish a position in the aisle. In the rows ahead of him, virtually everyone else was playing the same game. Except for a few elderly couples, all of the passengers were jockeying for position, certain that their agendas and schedules deserved top priority. At the first opportunity Lee sprang to his feet, preparing to push forward to the front of the plane. Standing in the aisle, he felt a sharp pain in his lower back, just where his doctors had predicted he would feel it. When they had abandoned attempts to remove the bullet fragment near his spine, they warned him that unusual exertion might cause it to press against the bundle of sensitive motor nerves that lay beside it.

He had felt twinges of pain the day before as he clawed his way through the corn field, but a rush of adrenalin and the distraction of being shot at had masked its effects. Overnight his muscles had become stiff and inflamed, and the swollen tissue was pressing the bullet fragment against his spinal nerves. His body ached from the abuse it had taken the day before, and he could no longer ignore the pain.

He forced himself to continue, feeling a burning sensation in his back as he walked through the airport. Outside the terminal, he found a taxi and got in before handing the driver a $100 bill. "I have two more if you get me somewhere fast." He gave the address, and the driver sped away. As they reached the airport exit, Lee pointed to the clock on the dashboard. "Is that accurate?"

"It's about three minutes fast, sir," the cabbie replied.

Lee adjusted the wrist watch that he had picked up at the Fargo airport and tapped his fingers against the door handle. He read billboards and other signs along the way, trying to distract himself from the pain that ran from his lower back down into his left leg. Less than twenty-five minutes later, he arrived at his house, handed two bills to the cab driver, and limped toward his front porch. Instead of a package by the door, he spotted a delivery notice taped to the door jamb. The courier would attempt another delivery tomorrow, or he could pick up the item at the local warehouse. He checked the address and glanced at his watch. In minutes he was in his car, heading west.

The warehouse was a long, one-story metal structure with a row of loading docks along the side. At twelve-twenty, Lee pulled into a parking space beside a sign that identified the office entrance. A man with a small brown package in his hands slipped past him as he opened the door. Fortunately no other customers were waiting at the counter. Lee thrust the delivery notice in front of the clerk, a large man with a bold tattoo on one arm, who looked as if he could eat a side of beef at one sitting. "I'll need to see some ID there, partner," he drawled.

Lee fumbled through his wallet and handed over his driver's license. "I'm sure you hear this all the time, but I really am in a big hurry. Can you help me, man?"

The clerk laughed and slapped his hand on the counter. "You got that right, buddy. I hear it all day long. Well, it's almost my lunch break, but I'll see what I can do for ya."

Lee slid a $100 bill across the counter. "Maybe this'll help speed things up."

The clerk's eyes widened as he picked up the bill. "My man! It sure will." With the notice in one hand he disappeared through a doorway. Several minutes later he emerged from the back area and set a cardboard box down in front of Lee. Seeing Aberdeen on the mailing label, Lee grabbed the package and headed for the exit.

"Wait! You gotta sign for that, buddy!" the clerk yelled.

Lee looked over his shoulder and raised his left hand as he continued toward the door. "Sorry, man, I'm out of time."

Sweating profusely as he got into the car, he turned on the air conditioning and locked the doors. The package was wrapped tightly in layers of thick tape, and he was unable to pry it open with his hands. He pulled the house key from his pocket and dug it underneath the tape, ripping it apart as he tore open the box. He tossed aside wads of crumpled newspaper until he found the two books inside, neatly covered in plastic wrapping material. The first one was *The Haunted Man and the Ghost's Bargain*. He opened it and quickly flipped through its pages, but found nothing inside. The second book was another Dickens novel, *The Cricket on the Hearth*. He repeated the process as beads of sweat dropped from his face onto the book. When he reached the last page without finding anything, he grabbed his key and pushed it between the back binding and the leather flap that secured the book's cover. He held the book up and shook it. A thin piece of paper fluttered out and landed on his lap.

Holding his breath, he quickly wiped his right hand on his pants and picked up the paper by its corner. He had memorized the winning numbers and recognized them as he read the third row: *2, 6, 9, 17, 55,* and *12*. He gasped and took several deep breaths, laughing uncontrollably for a few moments. But there was no time to celebrate. His watch indicated the time was twelve-twenty-eight.

His shirt was damp, so to protect the ticket he slipped it inside his wallet and pushed it deep into his front pocket. He backed the car out of the parking space and sped out of the lot. At the first red light he pulled out the new phone he had bought in Fargo and called the Charleston airport. There were no direct flights to Richmond, and the fastest one-stop trip would take about two hours and forty minutes. He resisted the urge to drive much over the speed limit, unable to afford the delay that would ensue if a cop pulled him over. The next flight was at one-forty-five, but it was full.

With luck, he could make it to the airport in thirty minutes, so there was time for one quick stop. He pulled into the nearest branch of his bank and hustled inside, wincing in pain as he walked from his car to its entrance.

Six minutes later he returned to the car. Its tires squealed as he shot out into the street and headed for the airport. He put his windows down, hoping the rushing air would dry out his shirt.

He ran through two red lights and drove straight to the terminal, parking illegally in the closest available spot. As he got out, a uniformed guard approached and demanded that he move the car. Lee pressed his car keys and a wad of $100 bills into the officer's hands. "Take the car. It's all yours. My lawyer can do the paperwork." He darted inside and searched for the right airline. As he passed several people who were standing in line, he handed out $100 bills to each one and explained that it was an emergency.

Before the ticket agent had a chance to speak, Lee stepped up to the counter and shoved a wad of cash forward. "There's a flight leaving for Richmond, Virginia at one-forty-five with a connection in Charlotte. It's booked up, but I'll give you $5,000 in cash if you get me on it. It's truly urgent."

The agent stared at the pile of bills and thought for a moment. "Do you have any bags to check?" he asked in a low voice. Lee shook his head and waited. The agent nodded toward a security camera and pushed the cash back to Lee. He leaned forward and whispered, "I can't do this right here. Go over to the newsstand behind you and wait. I'll bring you a ticket in a few minutes."

Lee ducked into a small store across from the ticket counter and bought a pack of envelopes while he waited. Standing with his back against a wall full of paperback books and magazines, he waited until no customers were within ten feet of him, and then transferred the ticket from his wallet to one of the envelopes. He folded it and shoved it into his front pocket, where it would stay when his wallet, shoes and belt rolled through the x-ray machine at the security checkpoint. The ticket agent appeared a few minutes later with a boarding pass in hand. Glancing around nervously, the agent quickly stuffed his pockets with cash and then hurried away.

Lee rushed through security and boarded the plane a few minutes later. According to the flight attendant, the airport was about eleven miles from downtown Richmond. She quietly accepted a bribe and carried a wad of cash to the front of the plane to negotiate on Lee's behalf. Accompanied by a businessman in a blue suit, she returned a short time later and directed Lee to a seat in row A. He checked his watch every few minutes until the pilot announced the final approach to Richmond International Airport. The aircraft landed at four-twenty-four, a minute later than the official arrival time.

Intense pain shot through the nerves in Lee's back and left leg as he ran through the terminal, weaving and gasping for air like a wounded animal fleeing a predator. He burst through an exit door and collapsed into the nearest cab, dumping a pile of crumpled $100 bills onto the front seat. "Just go!" he barked. The taxi lurched forward, barely missing a cargo van as its driver slammed on his brakes to avoid a collision. Lee struggled to catch his breath and then called out an address on East Main Street. The engine roared as the cab sped through the exit lanes and screeched onto a highway ramp.

"What's going on?" the driver shouted, as he accelerated to pass a pickup truck.

Lee pulled more bills from his pockets and tossed them on the seat. "Just get me there before five. I'll pay whatever it takes. There's probably three or four thousand dollars there," he said, as he continued to dig more cash out of his pockets. He felt the envelope with the lottery ticket and pulled it out, gripping it tightly in his right hand. With his other hand he pulled the last bills from his left pocket.

"Okay, man, I'll do my best. It's rush hour, so it'll be tight. I can't promise we'll make it."

Lee checked his watch and nodded. The driver's eyes darted back and forth between the road ahead and the rearview mirror as he zipped through traffic. Tall office buildings loomed ahead as they approached the downtown area. Noticing a backup several blocks ahead, the driver glanced at his dashboard clock. "It's four-fifty-two. We're not gonna make it if I try to go straight ahead. I can come in on a side street and get you within one block, but you'll have to run from there."

"How much time will I have?"

"I'll get you there in three minutes. Hold on tight." He raced through a red light and swerved around a minivan before careening into a one-way alley. Three blocks ahead, traffic had stopped at a red light. The cab raced forward until it was thirty feet behind the nearest car, and then the driver slammed on the brakes. Lee threw his door open and rushed down the street, fighting the searing pain that jolted him each time his feet hit the sidewalk. Knocking a pedestrian aside, he bulled his way through double glass doors at the building's entrance. Having done his homework weeks ago, he knew that the lottery office was on the second floor. There was no time to wait for the elevator, so he rushed to the stairwell.

Exhausted and close to fainting, he arrived at the next landing and staggered forward, yanked open a door, and collapsed on the floor.

CHAPTER 36

Wally Pennington was stocking cigarette packs on the shelves behind the checkout counter when the customer walked in. Dressed in khaki slacks and a polo shirt, the man spotted Wally and smiled broadly. He stepped forward and extended his hand across the counter. "Remember me?" he asked.

Wally studied his face for several seconds before recognizing him. "Oh, yeah. It's Lee, right? What's it been, a couple of months now?"

"Something like that. It's been a while since I've been in town. How's everything in Charlottesville?"

"Oh, pretty much the same, I guess." Wally looked down and shook his head before continuing. "Well, except for some strange news. There's a local lawyer who used to come in here a lot. I heard that he attacked his ex-wife out in South Dakota, of all places. Somebody told me the cops found him dead in a cornfield with a knife wound in his gut. And a guy who ran a pawn shop here in town was killed out there. Nobody can figure out what they were doing out in the middle of nowhere. And there's been some kind of scandal at the lawyer's office. I heard rumors that a senior partner got fired for harassing a junior associate, and the associate got promoted. The whole thing is very strange."

"It really is." Lee stepped back to allow a customer to check out, and then continued the conversation. "Look, Wally, I know you're busy, but I wanted to stop by and see you before something else hits the papers. I'd like to make a deal with you."

Intrigued and curious, Wally stepped from behind the counter and stood next to Lee. "Really? What's on your mind there, buddy?"

Lee pointed to the plastic DVD case that still rested beside a boom box on the counter. "I'd like to buy the DVD you've got there. I don't know if you remember it, but I came in here a few months ago, and we talked about it. In a couple of days they're going to announce the winner of that lottery jackpot, and I know who it is."

Wally stared in disbelief as his mind worked to sort out the implications of Lee's offer. Suddenly he grinned and slapped his hand against the counter before extending it to shake Lee's hand. "Well, I'll be damned! That's incredible! Congratulations, man. That's really awesome! I never would've guessed it. How could you keep quiet so long?"

Lee laughed as they shook hands. "Well, I had to make some arrangements and take care of a few details first. I didn't want to rush it."

"Man, that's really something. I just can't believe it!" Wally stepped back and pulled two beers from a refrigerated display case. He handed one to Lee as he opened the other one and took a sip. "Sorry, I don't have any champagne." Picking up the DVD, he held it in one hand and watched as Lee began to write a check.

"It's Walter Pennington, right?" Lee asked as he scribbled on the check. "How does twenty grand sound?"

Wally set his beer on the counter and watched Lee's expression to see if he was joking. "For real?"

"You bet," Lee replied, as he wrote the check. He folded it and slipped it into Wally's shirt pocket.

Wally shook his hand again. "Thanks, man. You're a real winner. I really appreciate it. Hey, do you want to watch the DVD back in the office?"

Knowing that the disc was blank, Lee put it in his pocket and shook his head. "Thanks, but I need to get going. Maybe I'll stop in when football season starts. You take it easy now."

He slipped out of the store, happy that Wally had not looked at the check. He wanted to disappear before Wally learned his last name and connected it to news accounts of the events in South Dakota. He hopped into his car and arrived at the University grounds ten minutes later.

He parked in front of the main library and walked to a stately brick building that housed the school's religion department. Professor Wynfield Strubeck was waiting in his office when he knocked on the door. The two had stayed in touch after Lee was a student in one of his ethics classes years before. Strubeck had delivered the eulogy at Andrea's funeral and helped Lee cope with his grief in the months that followed.

Strubeck greeted him with a hug and offered a glass of iced tea before they sat down on a couch under a portrait of Thomas Jefferson. Several large oak trees cast shadows through a window behind Strubeck's desk. The professor listened intently as Lee began a long, rambling recitation of recent events. He described his search for the lottery ticket, his feelings for Susan, and the shootout at the farm near Aberdeen. He withheld some of the specific details of his investigation, but confessed that he had crossed a series of ethical and legal boundaries. "I broke into Channing's house, lied to several people, and misled some others," Lee explained. "I shot one man and stabbed another one. It was self-defense, but I still feel bad about it. And I've got millions of dollars that probably should belong to someone else."

When Lee finally finished, Strubeck set down his glass of tea and leaned forward. "So it sounds like the ticket might have been lost forever if you hadn't found it, right?"

"Well, I think that's probably true. Susan didn't know about it, and she still doesn't. The lottery office said they'd delay the announcement for a few more days. She probably would have sold the book with the ticket to someone else before her husband found her. Whoever bought it wouldn't have known there was a ticket tucked inside the cover. Most likely the ticket would have expired before anyone ever found it."

"And this couple had no children, right?"

"That's right, Wyn."

Strubeck stroked his chin as he pondered the ethics of Lee's situation. "So the ticket would have expired, or else her husband would have stolen it?"

"I guess that's how it would have worked out."

"Why do you think this guy Channing didn't tell his wife about the ticket and offer to split the money?"

"Good question. I really don't know. Maybe that was going to be his final option, and he never got to that point. It's only a guess, but I think he was just too greedy to do that."

Strubeck leaned back on the couch and said nothing, considering the matter further before offering advice. "Well, Lee, only you can decide what to do. You could give some or all of the money to

Susan. You could give it to charity. You could tell Susan the whole
story and see what she thinks. You could do a lot of things. I'm not
sure what would be best. Have you asked anyone else for advice?"

"Just Reverend Leavell back home."

"And what did he recommend?"

"He said it was my decision, but if I give all the money to Susan,
my conscience will never bother me again."

Strubeck smiled. "I see. So what did you think of his advice?"

"Well, I decided to get a second opinion."

Strubeck laughed and swallowed the rest of his tea. "I can tell that
you love Susan. She sounds like a wonderful woman. But, you
know, if you really want to find out how she feels about you, now's
the time. After they announce the lottery results, it'll be harder to tell
if she loves you for yourself or for your money." Lee nodded but
said nothing. Looking at his watch, Strubeck continued. "Why don't
you come by the house and we can discuss this over dinner? Cynthia
took the kids to see her parents, so we could talk about it without any
distractions."

Lee checked the time and shook his head. "Thanks, Wyn. I'd love
to come over, but I'll have to take a rain check. I need to get to the
airport. My flight leaves in ninety minutes."

"Are you heading back home tonight?"

"Not tonight. I'm on my way out west. I think my future is
waiting for me in Aberdeen."

CPSIA information can be obtained
at www.ICGtesting.com
Printed in the USA
LVHW092356180619
621683LV00001B/6/P